STRENGTH OF THE RISING SUN

THE BORDERS WAR #5

S.A. MCAULEY

Trademarks Acknowledgement

The author acknowledges the trademarked status and trademark owners of the following wordmarks mentioned in this work of fiction:

Olympics: United States Olympic Committee Corporation

ABOUT STRENGTH OF THE RISING SUN

Book five in The Borders War series

Merq's always known there's only one way Armise and he can end.

The Opposition is losing—both the war and the fight for citizen support—and the Revolution's victory appears certain. Despite that success, Merq knows his leaders won't let two of their greatest assets simply walk away. But with Armise fighting for his life, getting out becomes Merq's primary objective.

Almost two decades of selfishness can't be alleviated with one right decision, and Merq is faced with the reality of how deeply he has wounded Armise in ways that cannot be seen from the outside. Merq's world has been upended more times than he can count and he's always survived, but life without Armise is no longer an option. He just has to prove that to Armise.

Merq believes there are few who are strong enough to challenge them when they stand together. But when the secret Armise has been protecting Merq from is revealed, the truth has consequences neither of them can prepare for.

Reading Order

To C. For giving me Priyessa, Tiam, Torga, Dakra, Lucien, Tallitia,
and the Thunders.
You inspire me every day.
(take 2)

1

September 2560
Merq Grayson's 37th year
The People's Republic of Singapore

ARMISE WAS DYING and there was nothing I could do but wait.

I'd been in enough battlefield situations to know that the urgency with which the wounded were treated said more about their chances for survival than their outward injuries. In Armise's case, both indicators were bad. I could understand enough of the Singaporean dialect the people around me spoke to glean answers to some of my questions about his status. Enough to know there was nothing I could do to help Armise live.

A knife, I told them when asked what had taken off his arm.

A man, I answered when someone asked who had done it. Even though Dr. Blanc had mentioned his son at the door and that was what had gained us entrance, I didn't think anyone else needed to know Armise was Ahriman's victim.

Because of his association with me, Armise was now a victim. Guilt slashed inside me, responsibility cutting at me every time I glimpsed his marred body.

How the fuck had I allowed that to be done to him?

They tied him down with rope and long strips of cloth when he tried to roll off the bed and to his feet after they stuck a syringe of something into his veins. His blood had to have been heavy with the weight of intravenous nanos. Dr. Blanc pushed aside certain solutions in favor of others and I hoped that he knew enough about what Ahriman had been feeding us that he could avoid a toxic combination of competing nano-laced cocktails. Armise didn't wake and yet his body reacted.

That gave me hope and it shouldn't have.

I looked at the stump where his arm had been and my stomach rolled, threatened to purge what little was in there. His arm was gone and there was nothing I could do to fix him, to change this, to make a different decision and never leave that first camp in the steppe. We should have forced Ahriman to us and killed him on sight. I should have felled everyone in my path and emptied the land around us so no one would dare to come close.

I should have protected Armise.

There was so much I'd misjudged—so many incorrect decisions and outcomes I'd drawn—that I didn't know where to start cataloging my errors and offenses. I had brought harm to the one person I didn't want to live without. The only person I valued more than myself.

And there was a chance Armise wouldn't live for me to tell him that.

The color was draining from Armise's face and he was fever hot, sweat rolling off him. There was no part of him that was consciously aware. He was deep into the pain, lost to it. I couldn't lose him like this.

I can't lose him. I just can't. That thought repeated in my head as I watched over him, crowding all other thought out and ramping up the anxiety building in my veins.

I couldn't....

I—

'*Not everything is about you, Merq,*' I remembered Ahriman saying, the memory of his accusation slamming into me. I didn't want to admit that anything Ahriman had ever said made sense, let alone that I believed it and took it to heart. But this critique was pointed at the correct target. What Armise was enduring right now wasn't about me.

Armise didn't deserve to die like this.

"He's getting worse," I barked at Dr. Calum Blanc, Ahriman's father, who was at Armise's side checking his vitals with a scanner.

Dr. Blanc finished what he was doing then turned to face me. "We know. Now get out." He went back to work over Armise and I took a step away from the bed, stumbling as I lost my equilibrium.

"Don't fucking touch that!" I heard Dr. Blanc yell at a man who stood by Armise's head and my vision started to white out as I realized that someone had tried to touch the chip implanted at the base of Armise's neck.

"Get out of here, Merq," he chastised me again.

I staggered from the room, deeper into the house, into a glass-encased space where the ceiling soared high above. The sky outside was swaths of gray, undulating clouds. When I looked down again my neck cracked from the movement and I clenched my hands only to find that they were sticky, tacky from being drenched in Armise's blood. I sucked in a breath and peered down at my clothes, realizing just how much blood I was covered in.

My stomach rolled again, surged, and I was swallowing

down an acidic bite of bile. I had no way to reach out to the people I knew could help. Shit, I had no idea if any of them were still alive since it had been four months....

I didn't know if I wanted to reach out to anyone in the States who was part of the Revolution. Armise didn't deserve to lose his life to a cause that wasn't his own.

To a cause that wasn't mine anymore.

When he woke up, and we could find our way out of Singapore, I was done. I'd given enough of myself to a movement that had never given me anything back, when I had a man at my side who'd willingly given me everything.

* * *

It was hours before Dr. Blanc came to find me, and the only reason I knew that was because of the darkness settling in above the atrium ceiling.

"He may not live," was the first thing he said to me.

I choked on a dark laugh. Hours later and Armise's prognosis hadn't changed, but my view of my world had irreparably shifted.

"He will or you won't."

Dr. Blanc turned on his heel and plopped down next to me, resting his head on the wall and closing his eyes. "You're not the worst threat I face by treating him."

Ahriman. The unknowns from Anubis. War. Strife. There were so many threats I couldn't maintain a count or catalog of their severity anymore. Dr. Blanc was right though, I wasn't on that list.

"Then why are you doing it?"

He pulled off a pair of gloves, chucking them into a waste bin, and swiped his bare hands on his pants. "I believe medicine can still do good."

I huffed and took to my feet. I couldn't sit. As I paced back and forth in front of the door leading to Armise's room, I ached to get inside there and evaluate every inch of him. I needed to see some indication that Armise was fighting this, or that his genetmods were.

"Do you have the stitch mod? Did you try it?"

Dr. Blanc faced me. "Since he's the son of a shaman, you may want to retrieve his beads."

I stopped pacing in favor of staring at him slack-jawed. "What?"

He scrunched his brows together. "Which part?"

"All of it."

"His mother was a shaman—a spiritual leader. The bracelets he wears are a northern nomadic tribal tradition. One set for the left and one for the right, for balance. He's obviously missing the set for the right. I don't know if they work or not but if he believes enough to wear them...." Dr. Blanc shrugged.

I hadn't thought of Armise's bracelets—why the fuck would I when whether or not he continued to breathe was the most important thing to me? But those bracelets, they meant something to him. I should have thought of that first. I furrowed my brow.

"How do you know that?"

Dr. Blanc stood. "I know too much about both of you. Yet I still want him to live."

Unease grabbed hold of me, as if my skin were tightening, making me claustrophobic in my own body.

"We can't be here," I said and made a move to get past Dr. Blanc and into Armise's room.

Dr. Blanc put his hand up. He was a thin man, weak, who had relied on me to face Ahriman when he couldn't do it. But I stopped regardless, because maybe I was being too rash. I couldn't afford to make the wrong decision when it came to Armise's life.

"You have nowhere else to go, Merq. You leave here, he will die. With me he has a chance since I'm the one who gave him most of his genetmods. You may want to let me work."

"You're the one who did this to him?"

Fuck being rash, at that moment I wanted to rip Dr. Blanc apart for having any hand in what Armise had become. Without those modifications, without this war and Anubis, Armise likely would have lived a traditional nomadic life.

"Fuck no, you're not touching him anymore."

Dr. Blanc put his palm on my stomach and tried to push me away from the door. The only thing keeping me from ripping his fingers off was that there was a sane part of me, barely at the surface, that recognized Armise needed those fingers to work.

"You listen to me. Armise has the right mods to give him a fighting chance. Anyone else would have been dead just from the shock and blood loss. But his modifications did what they were supposed to, slowing his heart rate, cooling his body—"

"He was fucking burning up!"

"So let me work," he said as he jabbed a finger into my chest. "And don't bother threatening me. I'm already a dead man."

"You're not," I insisted. "If Ahriman hasn't killed you by now he's not going to."

"My son is an arrogant, sadistic piece of shit who has a major god complex, but he's not the one I'm worried about."

I gaped. "You're telling me there's someone worse out there? Who scares you more? Your son just removed Armise's arm for fun!"

He shook his head emphatically. "He did that to mess with you."

I scoffed. "And you're telling me Ahriman isn't the person I should be worried about?"

6

"You should be worried about Armise surviving. The last few years of my life has been dedicated to trying to subvert Anubis. I was the one who restarted it and I will finish it. Genetic modification of human beings has to end. Despite that belief I'm doing everything I can for Armise to survive. So you.... You should back the fuck off me and let me do my job."

I held up my hands and took a step away from him. "Got it."

With my anger subsiding and exhaustion taking over, the fight in me was waning. I stalked away from Dr. Blanc but kept an eye on him, watching as he interacted with the medical staff who walked in and out of Armise's room. Physically, he had a passing familiarity to Ahriman, enough to note that they were related, but there was a light to his eyes that Ahriman had never exhibited.

When we were alone again I asked, "You gave Armise all his mods?"

Dr. Blanc deflated. I didn't have the brainpower to figure why my question affected him that way. Instead of answering my question, he beckoned me. "Come in and see him."

He pushed the door open and let me enter first. I'd expected to be met with the scene I'd left—Armise writhing in unconscious pain, sweat dripping off him from fever and the bloody stump of his arm exposed to the polluted air. I gritted my teeth, expecting to lose it again when I saw him. It didn't matter how much I tried to prepare myself, that's exactly what I did. My vision whitewashed and I fumbled for the wall. The only thing different in front of me was that Armise's shoulder was wrapped. The rest of his condition was the same. His skin was gray, sweat-soaked, and he was tied down to keep his writhing body from falling off the bed.

All of it made me sick.

"Were you there the entire four months?" Dr. Blanc asked as he approached the bed and checked the bandages on Armise's shoulder. I didn't know if he meant to distract me from what I was seeing in front of me, but his question worked. I ripped my eyes away from Armise.

I cleared my throat and leaned against the wall, trying to find my strength. I'd seen worse before. Much worse. I had to keep it together for Armise.

"As far as I know," I answered in a voice that was strangled. Off. Everything about this scene was just...wrong. "You weren't?"

Dr. Blanc shuddered, a visible shake that traveled up his spine and down his arms, leaving his hands unsteady to the point that he had to stop working on Armise's shoulder. "No."

He went quiet and I remembered Manny saying that things had changed with the war in the last four months. At the time I'd been more caught on the idea that we'd been held for so long, but now I had time—if not the mental capacity—to consider the world outside this medical room.

"I want access to a newsfeed," I told him, making sure he understood that was not a request.

"I'll arrange it." He looked at the bandage and frowned as he started to leave.

I grabbed his arm as he walked by and brought him to a stop. "You were the reason I was able to break through the injections Ahriman forced on me."

Dr. Blanc nodded. "I started injecting smaller and smaller doses of the Sleepsense so that you were more aware. That last shot was nothing but saline. Armise barely got any of the Sleepsense. I mixed the dosages so that he would be out but not paralyzed. With you...I couldn't do that. I'm sorry I couldn't do more."

I hated Dr. Blanc for his part in this, but he was the reason Armise was alive right now. "You've done enough. You think I can go back to where Ahriman was holding us to get Armise's bracelets? That Ahriman won't be waiting?"

"He won't return there," Dr. Blanc verified. "Once Armise is stable I'll make sure you're outfitted with the gear you'll need to protect yourself so you can get them. Maybe there will be something else there you can find that would be helpful."

I wanted to ask him why he was helping us at all, but I had to assume there was much more complexity to his answer than I wanted to hear let alone try to parse out.

"I'll be back with someone to replace his bandages," he continued. "I need to take a look at what other medicine they have available. Maybe make a trade for what we need."

I dragged a chair across the room to Armise. I set my hand on his belly. It moved with the erratic up and down of his breath, harsh in and out drags. He wheezed with effort. His skin was slick and waxy, the bold thick lines of his tattoos standing out against his ashen pallor.

"Shit," I muttered and sat down next to him before my knees could give out.

I dragged my hand off his stomach, down the line of his left arm and over the flame tattoos, fingertips skimming over the scars underneath. I fought to breathe as I turned over his left hand, unable to touch the dimpled flesh from where I'd taken his finger. I'd nearly lost *my* arm and life in the DCR but Armise had ensured I made it out alive and in one piece.

I lifted his hand and settled mine under his, grasping his wrist and holding on. He wouldn't be able to hear me, but I had to give voice to everything swirling in my head.

"Ahriman thinks that putting that encryption chip inside you will motivate me to risk your life. That I'll choose a fucking chip over you. He doesn't understand—" My throat started to tighten. There was so much that Ahriman would never have the capability to understand, and what Armise and I were to each other was of a scope I could barely comprehend. "Fuck the encryption chip. If all that comes of it is the memory of how to do more like this to humanity—to hurt and maim and kill.... Maybe it is better if we let the old knowledge die."

Armise's nails dug into my wrist as he shuddered and arched off the bed, his features pulled into a grimace. I held my breath and waited for the waves of agony to pass through him. He didn't open his eyes as he settled onto the bed again.

"I'm done with the Revolution, Armise," I confessed when he was quiet. Too quiet. I would tell him all of this when he woke up, but for now I had to get it out. I had to make my decision real by giving it voice—by telling him. His opinion was the only one that mattered to me. "I'm done fighting. I'm tired of not having control of my life."

I kept my left hand circled around his wrist, my fingers intertwining with the beads there. His mother had been a spiritual leader. How did I not know simple things like that after fifteen years with him?

"You asked me once if there was a death I regretted...." I thought of Vachir, of Armise's older brother whose life I'd ended, but could only guess which he was in a long line of too many dead people. I ran my pointer finger over the scars at his wrist. "I would regret your death."

I didn't want to look at him anymore, but I owed him this. "I'm sorry. And I'm not quite sure what I'm sorry for, just that this all feels so wrong and I know I play a big part in...." All of it. All of it was my responsibility. "I'll find a way to make this better."

If Armise wanted a synth, his best bet was with the States' doctors—the same ones who'd given Simion his new leg. But that would mean returning, putting me back in a position where Simion would try to convince me to go into active duty. I wanted to get Armise and run, to never look back so I could never be dragged back in, but that wasn't fair.

I had to hear what he wanted first.

And despite how close to death he still was, I couldn't see any other outcome besides me hearing his voice again.

"I don't want to go back there, ever, Armise. But you wake up...you tell me that's what you want and I'll go back with you. For you."

2

I was in an underground tunnel with my chest pressed against Armise's back. Above our heads the residuals of sonicbullets whizzed through tubes that disappeared into an unknown location deep below the stadium floor. Armise's heartbeat slowed, yet I could still feel it—a rhythmic thump just below skin and muscle, a heart protected by bone and his strength of will.

I wanted him. Needed him.

I didn't know how to disengage myself from him.

I loved him.

Armise pulled a gun and put the barrel to my head.

This man would be the death of me.

My eyes slammed open and I had my hand around Dr. Blanc's wrist, wrenching it to a painful angle, before I was fully awake.

The doctor's face was just as calm, just as in control as when he'd left me. I didn't remember falling asleep but there was a fresh bandage on Armise's shoulder and his beard and hair were trimmed close. My body ached from the awkward position I'd slept in.

"He's past the worst of it, we think. His blood count is good and the nanos seem to be holding off infection—"

"He'll live."

Dr. Blanc gave a pointed look at the spot where I held on to his wrist. When I let him go he continued speaking. "For now. If he has any complications we can't treat him here. You may want to get him closer to somewhere that knows how to prepare him for a synth. We were able to get our hands on a comm with security capabilities. You have someone you want to talk to?"

Only him, I thought as I surveyed Armise. He was still asleep. But I nodded my assent to Dr. Blanc anyway.

"I'll have it brought in and give you privacy."

Moments later an old comm device was wheeled into the room on a table and dropped off. My first call was to Manny's comm.

"How is he?" Manny asked immediately, his lips drawn into a frown when his face appeared on the screen.

"Alive for now. They're working on him. How about Chen?"

Manny nodded. "She's good. I've got her in the village. Can't reach the guy she says is her caretaker."

"Neveed."

"Yeah, that's the name. You know him?"

"That's the former General Neveed Niaz. I'm guessing you probably studied him in Dark Ops training too. I'm also guessing he's dead."

"Shit."

"Let's hope it's just that he isn't answering any comms right now."

"Not likely."

"I know." I wanted to figure out how Ahriman had gotten to Chen without Jegs knowing. I wondered if Neveed was still alive and what kind of shape he was in knowing Chen had been missing for four months...or if he even knew she was gone. But there was a bigger part of me that didn't want to know at all if he was dead. There was nothing I could do for him if he was.

My entire focus had to become Armise. I scratched at my chin and realized just how tangled and unkempt my beard was. All of it would have to be shaved off soon. "Best bet may be to take her to his house. Even if Neveed's not there it's probably safer than the village. Then you'll also have access to all of her equipment. If I need her assistance at least I'll know where to find you and her."

"I'll handle it. You need anything right now?"

I looked away from Manny and to Armise. "For him to wake up and walk out of here. You got any hybrid secret that could help him out?"

"None that I know of. I've got Chen, you take care of Darcan."

When I signed off the aircomm, I readjusted my chair so I was next to the bed, but none of Armise's body could be seen on the video feed. I hoped it would be Simion answering his own comm, but had no guarantee the President of the Continental States and the leader of the Revolution wouldn't be otherwise engaged.

"Holy shit, you're alive," Simion answered, a wide smirk growing as the picture jumped around with his movement.

"Where the hell are you?" His hair had grown out again, marking the months I'd missed, an errant blond lock falling onto his forehead.

"Fuck you, man. Where the hell are you?"

I sucked in a breath and tried to keep up with his light mood. Simion didn't know what had happened and may never hear about it if I didn't tell him. If Armise wanted to disappear instead of returning to the States for care, then this may be the last time I spoke to Simion.

"Alive," I evaded.

He frowned. He knew me too well. "What's going on?" He moved in closer to his BC5 screen, as if he was trying to get a better look at me. "I'm on the move in the DCR, about to meet with Kariabba. Can't see much, Mig, but what I do see doesn't look good."

I didn't have to draw this call out any longer than I needed to.

I kept my eyes locked to his. "I'm done, Pres. What do I have to do to buy my freedom?"

I caught movement next to me but wasn't willing to let Simion see anything about Armise's condition quite yet. I set my hand on Armise's chest and held it there, trying to tele-graph that he needed to be quiet and still. Then I felt the familiar chill of Armise's skin as his left hand settled over mine. He was cold, so cold, and that had to mean he was better. I lost my string of thought and Simion peered at me as I tried to appear unflustered at the pieces of myself that stitched back together when I could feel Armise's eyes on me again.

"You sure you're okay, Mig?"

I held back the pull on my chest, the absolute need I had to meet Armise's eyes. "I was built to make it through the worst, right?"

Simion didn't reply for a moment, then, "When you coming home? We can talk about...whatever you need. Just talk."

"I have something I need to figure out first. I'll call back if I can."

"Good to hear your voice, Merq. Don't make it another four months."

"Yes, sir," I responded, knowing it could be a lie.

I shut off the aircomm and turned to Armise. He was just as gray, but his eyes were clear. Focused. "Good morning."

"Is it morning?" he rumbled in a low, scratchy voice. The

15

unease inside me settled with the utterance of that simple question.

"I don't know."

Armise swallowed, his throat moving with the effort to speak. "It is really gone."

His eyes hadn't been anywhere else besides on me since they'd opened and I realized that was his survival instinct kicking in. I couldn't keep my gaze from darting to his bandages though. "Wish it had been part of Ahriman's fucked-up mental manipulation, but it wasn't. You're okay."

"I do not know if I would say that." He let go of me and fixed his gaze on the ceiling, the clarity I'd just seen traded for emptiness that was mirrored in his voice.

I took my hand off him. The chill of his skin left a trail that settled into my bones in an uncomfortable way. All of this was wrong. "I know."

"Who were you talking to?"

"Simion...." I didn't know when I should be bringing up what came next, but Armise had always been one to cut right through the bullshit. "You should be a good candidate for a synth. We can get you back to the proper medical facilities and see what they can do. But there's something else. Ahriman put the encryption chip back inside you with an explosive shield around it. Probably something like what they have around the hybrids' kill switches. Apparently you can breathe and move and live while it's in there, but no one can touch it and you can't transport or it goes off."

"We know whether that's true?"

I shook my head. "I don't care if it is or not."

It wasn't coming out. No one was going to risk Armise's life for that chip.

He furrowed his brow and winced.

I began to stand. "Let me get Dr. Blanc. He was seeking out better meds—"

Armise's attention snapped to me. "Calum Blanc?"

"He's the reason you're alive now," I reassured him. "He hasn't tried to hurt you."

Armise closed his eyes. He shivered, bumps rising on his skin.

"Tell me—" I started to say, *tell me not to trust him and I won't.* But Armise was already out again.

I didn't have to go in search of Dr. Blanc because he was entering the room before I could get up to find him.

"Did I hear Armise?" he asked as he came to the bedside.

"He woke, but only for a moment."

I watched Dr. Blanc evaluate Armise's condition and tried to see between his actions to any hidden, ulterior motives. While his participation with Ahriman's sick games were part of the reason we were here, I couldn't see how he'd had any other choice than to do what Ahriman had demanded of him. He'd been a prisoner as much as we had. But I had to be smarter, more paranoid, when it came to protecting Armise right now.

"If you weren't in the same facility as us for the four months, why didn't you try to get away from Ahriman when you could?"

Dr. Blanc stepped away from the bed. "Ahriman told me he was luring you in. He's never been as bright as he thought he was. When he didn't show up for a few days I wanted to press my advantage and try to escape again. But I knew if anyone would get away from Ahriman alive it would be Armise. So I stuck close. I stuck with you."

"Why? Armise told me he was the one who would bring you back when you got away from Ahriman."

Dr. Blanc shifted on his feet. "That's true. Despite that, I want Armise to live. If I have any kind of legacy I'd rather it be him than my son."

* * *

Across the room a biocomp screen was lit up with a feed from the international press corps. The shrouded figures on the screen spoke of citizen uprisings across the globe, their metallic voices and genderless garb setting me just as off-kilter as they had for years. I hoped I could trust what I was seeing.

They spoke of an Opposition that was fractured since the destruction of the hybrid camps. Of a populace that was outraged that the camps had existed at all. I watched President Ricor Simion visit the jacquerie in the States and the DCR, the sorrow in his features unhidden when he spoke to mothers and fathers who had lost children. I caught sight of Jegs in the background of more than one place where Simion was.

I smiled when I saw Exley's face on the day he was named Simion's vice president. That same day he announced an education initiative that would start with the most vulnerable children in Revolution-protected land. The world was burning, but not in the way Ahriman had planned for. It was a fire licking through the veins of citizens grasping onto their power and turning their back on him. I puffed up with pride and celebrated the success with them, even though I would never be part of it again.

I went through all four months of feeds, flipping through images and reports to catch up on what had happened since Armise and I had gone off-grid....

Off-grid. Right.

Fuck. This was a disconnect from my previous life that made it feel like the first thirty-six—or was it thirty-seven?—years had been lived by someone else.

The weapons circling around my waist, on my back and attached to my forearms weighed more than their physical load. I didn't know how I'd gone so many years without grasping the heaviness I carried in my soul, always being prepared for a fight.

As I lingered at the end of Armise's bed and watched him, I set my hand to the pistol at my side and wanted to be free of the burden that came with it. I was about to leave Armise alone— more fucking vulnerable than I'd ever seen him—with people I didn't know. I was headed out on a mission for Armise, but that didn't alleviate my worry.

"I won't be long," I said to Armise, even though he was still asleep, and I tore myself away from his side.

He hadn't woken up since that first time and I was agitated by his lack of progress. There was no other way around it. I would do anything I had to, to give him a fighting chance, and I had no qualms about putting my own safety on the line to retrieve something that could make a difference in his recovery.

I had to force myself to walk through the door of the safe house without turning back to check on him again. I didn't remember the way we'd taken to this building, but Dr. Blanc had drawn a map for me that I carried in my pocket. I had the directions memorized, but I wasn't going to risk lingering in the city longer than I needed to. Dr. Blanc told me there was no chance Ahriman would be anywhere near the building where he'd held us, but after Armise's reaction to Dr. Blanc treating him I knew I had to be on guard.

It was nighttime when I exited the safe house, a heavy blanket of darkness greeting me. I had to wait for my eyes to shift to the lack of light. Armise's room hadn't been bright, but this...this was darkness that normally didn't exist in a city. There were no Singaporean citizens on the streets so I made sure to keep to the shadows to avoid any roaming Opposition soldiers. While the fake identity chip still implanted in my wrist wouldn't raise any flags—Av Garratty wasn't a death-dealer or Revolution soldier—the sheer amount of weapons I had on my person would.

I made it to the building Dr. Blanc had identified without

running into anyone, and in a city this size, with the distance I had to travel, that shouldn't have been possible. I wasn't going to discount any luck that decided to shine down on me at this point. The door wasn't locked or barred in any way and the edges were smeared with a substance that had to be dried blood. Armise's blood.

The inside of the building was just as dark as the outside, but with the door shut tight and no windows visible, I activated the light attached to my uniform even if it might draw attention. Dr. Blanc must have known there would be no power here to outfit me with that addition. I was met with a maze of hallways that branched off from the main entry.

"Fuck," I muttered into the dark. I hadn't thought to ask Dr. Blanc where to go once I got into the building. My training was slipping.

I took a methodical approach, clearing the building piece by piece as I kept my pistol at the ready. I couldn't remember going down any stairs when we left, but when the first floor was empty and I couldn't recognize any of the rooms—and they appeared as if they hadn't been occupied in years—I took the stairs to the second floor. The dust on the stairs was disrupted in a way that suggested someone had been through here not too long ago. It was a tell I wouldn't have noticed prior to Armise's tracking lessons on the steppe. I would have expected the marks of multiple feet since it had been Armise, Dr. Blanc, and me leaving the building, but there was only the subtle mark of one set.

I couldn't hear anything as I took to the landing for the second floor, but the quality of the silence gave me pause. It was unlikely Ahriman was here, his style didn't conform to the definition of subtlety. The building could be occupied by squatters or nomads, it wasn't as if the rest of the city housed luxurious accommodations— Luxurious. The word hit me. It was one I only knew because of Armise.

Focus. I had to focus to stay alive and get back to him.

I swept to the right, making sure the hallway was empty, then turned to the left. Something about the configuration of the doors was familiar. I crept forward inch by inch, trying not to give away my presence or my location just in case there was anyone in the building or on this floor.

The first door to my right was cracked open and the room across from it had no door at all. This I remembered. Much too clearly. Before I could stall or freeze, I placed my fingertips on the entry to the room where Armise had been held—where he had been brutalized—and pushed inside. I was met with the fetid smell of rotting flesh and the bitterness of copper and I couldn't hold back my physical reaction. I dropped my pistol and retched on the floor, emptying my stomach and effectively announcing exactly where I was if there was anyone around me. But I couldn't control my reaction.

Armise's arm was in the corner of the room where Ahriman had thrown it, that angry red swipe of his blood still slathered down the wall. A couple of days in the heat, pollution, and humidity of this Singaporean sinkhole was all it had taken for the appendage to begin to disintegrate. Armise's bracelets were still around the wrist, as was his watch.

I was going to have to slide the bracelets off—I couldn't cut them off if I wanted to preserve them. I swiped the back of my hand across my mouth and prepared to spend concentrated minutes working to get those bracelets free.

But before I could steel myself for the job I had to do, I felt breath on my back, whipped a knife out of the sheath on my forearm and spun on my heel to strike out. My knife was knocked away and the man in front of me kicked my pistol to the side even as he held up his hands, palm facing me.

The swirling tattoos on his arms were unmistakable, as was his size and his infuriating speed.

"Going to kill me this time?" I asked Dakra.

He shook his head then spoke as well. "No."

I laughed. What other reaction could I have? All of this was wrong and I didn't know how to break free from my new reality. Worse, I knew I couldn't and I was having trouble holding on to my usual tethers to sanity. I tipped my head toward the corner of the room. "You want to help me get those bracelets off and back to their owner then? You know, since you had a part in them being abandoned here."

"Okay," he agreed without hesitation.

I had no idea how to interpret all of this. I leaned down to pick up my pistol and watched him crouch next to Armise's arm, lift it without thinking twice, and begin to remove the wood and stone circles with discreet care.

I slumped to the floor with my back to the torture chair and watched him. Dakra was part of me and part of Armise. He was supposed to be uncontrollable and unstable, but both Armise and I suffered from moments of instability as well. I realized with a start that we had moments of care just like this, too.

"Were you waiting for me?" I asked, my interest piqued.

He slipped the first bracelet off and set it to the side as he answered. "Yes. I told Calum I wanted you to return."

Dakra had been in touch with Dr. Blanc and Ahriman's father had neglected to fill me in on that fact. He'd sent me here when he knew the hybrid would be waiting for me? I wanted to be furious, but maybe...maybe Dr. Blanc knew I wouldn't have agreed otherwise.

"Why?"

He dusted off the beads and started to loosen the strap of Armise's watch. "I was told you're the only one who can kill me."

"I don't want to kill anyone else," I protested. I was so damn tired of death. "And even if I did, I get the feeling that you're way too impregnable for me to ever find a way. Not by myself."

Dakra completed his job, looped the bracelets and watch over his fingers and offered them to me. "When you discover how to do it, I'll find you."

I took Armise's beads and watch and slid them into my pocket. Then Dakra disappeared in the flash of a transport burst.

3

The door to the safe house opened before I could knock. A different woman from the one who had let us in the first day was there, eyes wide and hands clenching and unclenching as she cowered.

"Calm him," she begged in heavily accented Continental English. "Please."

Calm? Why had Dr. Blanc allowed Armise to get agitated at all? He should have been using whatever meds he had to keep that nervous itch of a downed fighter from taking over Armise when he needed to rest and heal.

"Where is the doctor?" I tried to ask her with the little Singaporean I knew. I brushed past her when she started speaking to me and I couldn't keep up an accurate translation in my head.

"Gone, gone, gone," she repeated behind me, and that word I knew.

Dr. Blanc had abandoned us.

I pushed into Armise's room and was met with a scene that both terrified me and made me want to rage. Armise had two feet on the floor, but he was barely standing, his hip leaned against the bed for support. There were three men in the room with him, all of them with guns drawn and pointing at Armise. A crimson stain wept through his bandage and droplets of his blood fell to the floor, pooling around where he stood. How long had they been in this standoff?

Armise grimaced when he saw me and tried to stand all the way on his own, but slumped into the bed when his balance was thrown off by the movement.

"Tell them to put the guns down, Armise," I said to him in Mongol.

His head snapped up, fury contorting his features. "You think I didn't try that already?"

I kept my eyes locked to his and approached him slowly. "I can't speak Singaporean, Armise. I can barely understand it—"

Armise coughed and his entire body tensed then was wracked with waves of pain. "Where the fuck were you? Getting prepared to leave?"

I motioned to the men to start moving away from the bed and toward the doors as Armise's anger came full force at me. I reached into my pocket and pulled out the bracelets and his watch, tossing them onto the bed next to him. Any color he'd gained during his rage drained away at the sight of those beads.

"Where's Dr. Blanc?" he asked.

The armed men had fled, the room empty except for us, but Armise wasn't calmed by my presence. "He's gone. I don't know anything else, just that he's not here anymore."

"So where the fuck did you get those?"

"From where Ahriman held us."

His jaw ticked as he glared at me. "You did not go back there."

"I'm here," I fired back. He knew I was capable and he'd told me he trusted me. "I'm fine."

"Goddammit, Merq. You went into a dangerous situation without backup again. I have lost fucking count—" His chest heaved with the effort to breathe. "If you don't care about when you die...?"

"I'll choose the way I die." There was heat in my reply that he didn't deserve right now, but my ability to go out on my own, to be capable enough to protect myself, was an old fight. One we should have been long past by now.

"Of course you will," Armise bit out.

My anger kicked up without thought at the iciness in his reply. "What the fuck does that mean?"

He clenched his jaw and pushed off the bed, losing only a step to uncertain footing as he came at me. "Fuck you and your questions."

"Fuck me?" I said in disbelief.

He got in my face, close enough that I could smell his blood and take in the chill radiating off him. "I may be down a hand, but an injury like this would have killed you. I can still pound your ass into the ground."

I barked out a laugh. "Now you're all bravado? I fucking carried you here, had to endure days of waiting, watching you writhe in pain, knowing—"

"You?" he scoffed, all derision and venom. "It is always fucking about you."

I ignored him and the echo of Ahriman's voice in my head and plowed forward, needing for him to hear how things had changed for me.

"Knowing"—I emphasized to get his attention—"that I was the one responsible for you having to fight for your life. I'm the reason you lost your arm! So yeah, that's on me. And I won't do it again. I told Simion I was done with fighting. I'm done with the Revolution."

Armise was still in front of me, a deathly calm settling over him that I had witnessed before, but only when he was at his most fatal.

"No, you told him you wanted to buy your freedom. I was awake enough to hear that pathetic cry for mercy. They do not own you, Merq. You want to walk? Then do it. No one is stopping you. Not even me."

"I'm not leaving your side."

"How fucking courteous of you," he said, a sneer contorting his face.

"That's the same thing you promised me, you asshole!" I yelled at him.

He didn't flinch, didn't back off.

"I also told you I love you. You going to mimic that one back to me?"

Now he was taunting me. "I'm not going to repeat something I don't believe in just to appease you."

He leaned in, jabbed a thick finger into my chest, and I took a reflexive step away from him. "You are the most frightened man I know. You are still that five-year-old child unable to walk after his house was bombed out and his parents abandoned him."

I bristled. "You don't know me."

"If only that was fucking true," he said, and I felt the truth of that accusation like a knife in my chest. He pushed away from me and stumbled toward the bed, his steps leaving drag marks of blood on the floor. "I am going back to the States, getting this fucking chip out of me and getting fitted with a synth. I am not done fighting until Ahriman is dead. You do whatever the fuck you please."

His tirade ended there, but I could hear what he didn't say at the end.... '*As usual. You do as you please, just as you always do.*'

I stalked out of the room before I took off his other arm.

* * *

S.A. MCAULEY

October 2560
Merq Grayson's 37th year
Somewhere in the Indian Ocean

SILENCE AND COLD were two things I would always associate with Armise. But Armise had been different since we'd been smuggled from Singapore by a guide and put on a boat to the DCR, making our way to where Simion and the Revolution had temporary headquarters. Armise's quiet was like the charge in the air before an electrical storm. It was the unheard rumble of a quake, buried deep inside the earth, just before it fractures the ground around you.

And the bitter iciness of his skin.... I knew all too well what that meant by now.

That Armise was on his feet at all should have been impossible. It *would've* been impossible for anyone who didn't have the genetic modifications he did. I waited for him to fall apart, but he didn't.

We shared a cabin on the boat, we shared a bed, and it wasn't that he stopped talking to me. It was how he spoke to me. It was the breath between the words he said to me that held the most weight.

He would fall asleep with his back to me. His bandaged shoulder, the surge-healed spot where the encryption chip sat at the base of his neck, and his years' worth of scars and tattoos exposed to me. Every night. Those marks were a barrier, a wall he put between us by how he positioned himself, and I couldn't find the strength to try to reach out to him and break through.

I spent sleepless nights running over our fight in the safe house, picking apart the motivations for his anger, for him lashing out at me. It was what he hadn't said that ate at me.

28

As usual.

Whether the intention had been there or not on his part, whether or not that was really what he believed, I heard those words just as certainly as if they'd been uttered out loud. I held on to them, taking them inside and testing the truth of them against my memories. What I found cut me to the core.

I couldn't fault him if he did see me as a selfish prick. I couldn't find error in that assessment. Me doing whatever the fuck I wanted—regardless of his or anyone else's emotions—was how I'd lived my life.

I chose to believe his mood was transitory. A warranted recalibration. And that when he was ready he'd be able to see the shift in me just as clearly as he'd been able to see through me before.

Instead of waiting for him to fall apart, I altered my perceptions again and decided it was my turn to wait him out.

I WATCHED Armise stomp his foot into the boot positioned just right—with the laces opened, loose, and the tongue peeled forward to allow easy entry—then repeat the same thing with the other foot. His jaw clenched as he stared at his boots then looked to me, eyes never really meeting mine.

There were two times of the day Armise didn't have the choice of ignoring my presence. In the mornings when he needed help getting dressed, and in the evenings when we repeated the routine in reverse. Those were the only times I was allowed any type of contact with him. Even then it was like this —me tightening and tying his bootlaces. Me helping him get his shirt on because he couldn't seem to master the angle needed to get his head through if his arm was already in there. He went to the med bay for bandage changes and everything else he was

learning how to do himself. I didn't know if he preferred struggling to asking me for help or if he was sick at the thought of me
touching him more than that. I didn't want to know the answer.

I knelt in front of him and threaded the laces between my
fingers, working as quickly and quietly as possible so Armise
could do.... Well, whatever the fuck it was when he disappeared
for hours during the day.

Job completed, I stood and Armise brushed past me, making
a point to swerve around me so none of him would have to come
in contact with me, and out of the door.

"I'll see you tonight, asshole," I mumbled as the door
slammed shut. I flipped him off and tried to hold on to that flash
of anger, but I couldn't.

Instead I logged in to the BC5 on the desk in our cabin and
made the call I'd been putting off since we'd gotten on the boat.

Simion answered my request for an aircomm within
seconds, his lax persona—all smirk and body slung back in his
office chair—filling the screen.

"How much longer before you make it to the DCR?"

"Two weeks. Maybe more."

"Anything more you want to tell me this time around?"

I hadn't told Simion much in the few calls we'd had between
that first one in the safe house and this one. He knew Armise
was coming with me. He knew we needed to come in for assessment and possible treatment. He didn't know about Ahriman or
the details of what had happened during those four months, Dr.
Calum Blanc's role in our escape, or the encryption chip. He
didn't know about Chen. Or that Armise had lost an arm. I was
still deciding how much I wanted him to know.

I'd hesitated too long to answer him, because Simion sat
forward and slipped into presidential mode. "There's a whole
hell of a lot you're hiding from me, Colonel. I can see it on your
face. And I need to know if I'm taking too great a risk allowing

you and Armise to come where a whole host of Revolution troops are located."

The bunker. He was worried about what had happened at Kersch's bunker, and rightly so.

"Neither Armise nor I is a threat as far as we know. But that's part of the reason why we need to be there. We need professionals to tell us what's going on. We need specialized staff and not another safe house with questionable motives."

"Just how bad off are you?"

I held my breath then blew it out in one long exhale. "Bad."

"Be honest with me on the level of risk I'm taking. Really fucking honest, Colonel."

"It was Ahriman that had us for the last four months."

"Fuck Ahriman Blanc," he scoffed. "Let him try to get in here and make it out alive. He's not a risk or a threat. Just keep your sanity in those waves. I'll do whatever I can to help the two of you out when you get here."

"Thanks, Sims."

"Never needed. Me, your country, and this movement owe you more than we can ever repay. See you in two weeks."

THE BOAT SWAYED, pitched, as it was hit by another wave. I scrambled to hold on to the bar anchored to the wall, running the length of the corridor that led to the galley. I'd been woken by voices and laughter that thundered through the hull, drowning out even the wheeze of wind through the porthole and the crash of storm-tossed water. Armise hadn't been with me when I woke. My stomach flipped from the movement of the boat and swished with a dread I'd been carrying with me for the month we'd been on the sea.

The raucous laughter kicked up again as I drew closer. The

sound rocketing to a riotous, joyful level as I unlatched the door and pushed it aside. The cramped room—of four short tables and chairs bolted to the floor—was packed with more people than what had to be advisable. Shouldn't there have been more crew dedicated to keeping this fucking boat deck-up in a storm?

I frowned but forced my way inside and latched the door shut again before it could come slamming back on me with a rogue wave. The room was hot and ripe with the sweat of human movement. I searched for Armise at the tables and found his back to me...as fucking usual. He tipped his head back as he downed a golden liquid from the glass in front of him.

The wound on his shoulder was long healed by now, but as of this morning he'd still been wearing a bandage around it. He wasn't now. The man sitting next to him was shoulder to shoulder with him, pressed against the dimpled flesh in a way that felt too fucking intimate because even I hadn't touched him there yet.

I rocked back on my heels, more from the sight in front of me—from the unguarded rumble of Armise's laugh I could hear from the other side of the room as the man next to him filled his glass again—than the waves that threatened to capsize us.

I pushed through the fray, everyone around me too drunk or surge-hyped to do more than afford me a cursory glance as I headed for Armise. It took me minutes to cross the small space, my ears ringing from the tinny echo of voices that crashed around me. I stepped up to the table and settled my hand on Armise's back, fingers landing on his spine and between his shoulder blades, where he tensed with the touch.

"You going to fill one for me?" I said. I forced an easy smile and picked up Armise's glass and swallowed all of it. The liquor burned down my throat and intensified the sloshing in my stomach. Armise had gone quiet—so still—and everyone around us was too fucked-up to notice.

"There's always more," the man across from Armise offered and refilled the glass.

I tipped that down my throat too, silently begging for the liquor to burn away the ache that had filled me for too long.

The man motioned for another glass down the table and filled one that Armise drank back. He hadn't looked at me or reacted in any way to my presence next to him since the first unexpected touch. He jumped into a conversation with the people at the table. A man across from him got up and I pushed away, taking my hand off Armise and going for the empty chair. When I sat down, my glass was filled by someone else and I tried to listen to what was being said around me, but all I could focus on was Armise.

His eyes were bluer than I'd seen them since he'd last worn a Singaporean uniform. There was a light to them—no, a light-ness—that I didn't know if I'd ever seen. He was riveted to the man at the end of the table who had hands flailing and liquor wetting the front of his shirt as he talked. The alcohol churned inside me, making me sick, heating my skin and making me sweat. There were too many bodies, too many hands too eager to keep my glass full. There were too many eyes glancing my way, and none of them were Armise's.

The man at Armise's shoulder butted up against him and said something low I couldn't hear. Armise ducked his head, chuckled. When the man stood, Armise followed. I froze, watching them go, waiting for Armise to turn and acknowledge me. When the galley door slammed shut behind them I snapped.

I tipped my glass over as I rushed to my feet to go after them. My vision whited out, my only focus getting out that door. I was unsteady on my feet, my thoughts were disconnected, jumbled, as I struggled to get the door unlatched. Someone reached around me to free the lock. The air in the corridor was degrees cooler and that familiar chill that brought bumps to my skin was enough to clear some of the fog from my brain. There was no one within sight, no way for me to know where they'd gone.

I lurched away from the door and toward my cabin—our cabin. Armise's and mine. I didn't want to believe that Armise would take anyone else there, that we were so broken that he would fuck someone else just to spite me. But that was just it—we were broken. And I couldn't know what to expect from him anymore.

The boat listed—or I listed, I couldn't quite tell which—as I stumbled for our quarters. When I got to the door I paused, listened for voices, and felt the pull of gravity as if it could suck me through the floor and drag me to the bottom of the sea. I didn't want to see what could be happening behind that door, but I had to know.

I clicked the latch, stepped over the threshold and a muscled forearm wrapped around my neck, choking me. I reared back, kicked out my legs, seeking purchase, and gasped for breath. The forearm tightened and I felt lips at my ear.

"You could not give me one night."

Armise didn't release his grip on me. He tightened it when I didn't respond. I scrambled to lock my hands around his forearm to try to yank him away, but he'd always been stronger and he still was. He didn't loosen his hold until I saw spots dancing across my vision. Of course he would know exactly how long to apply pressure before I would start to black out.

"A month," I rasped. "I've given you a month."

"You do not fucking get it," he accused. He relinquished his hold on me, pushing me away.

I rubbed at the tenderness where his arm had squeezed and glared at him. "I don't, Armise. Clearly."

The beard I'd grown while Ahriman held us prisoner had been clipped down, but I'd left enough there that I had to look different. I was different. I needed Armise to see that I was trying —for him. And I didn't know what I had to do for him to see that.

I took the two-step distance that separated us, reaching out for him until he flinched back, as if I wasn't allowed to be that close to him without violence between us.

"I just want your eyes on me again."

Armise gripped my chin, fingers digging into my jaw, and I hoped that maybe this would be the point where we broke through all of the shit from the last month, because it had been too long since he'd had his lips on mine. Too long since he'd spoken to me with a gruffness that conveyed frustrated need instead of anger. Then he sneered and scratched his nails down my jaw as he let go.

"You have had my attention for the last fifteen years. And look where that left me."

He turned his back on me, flopped onto the bed and closed his eyes, falling into sleep with an ease I envied as I tried to piece together what he was telling me.

I didn't know if I'd ever sleep again.

4

November 2560
Merq Grayson's 37th year
Dark Continental Republic—Somalia

THE BOAT we were on would have beached itself in the shallow waters that surrounded Galcaio if we tried to come into port, so Simion sent a heli to pick Armise and me up from the deck. Armise carried all of his gear in a bag that crossed his back in a diagonal fit. He lifted himself into the belly of the Thunder with his one arm, his non-dominant hand gripping the bar above his head and swinging his body inside. It was a move most soldiers couldn't pull off at all, let alone one-armed and with power, grace, and deceptive ease.

We were outfitted with ear coverings to mask the thump of the blades, but neither housed comm capability. The flight to Revolution headquarters—inland and in the desert—was a fifteen-minute ride of silence. Silence I was now accustomed to.

The Thunder landed in a whip of sand that we waited to

settle before exiting. I jumped out first, stalking for the front door. Armise pulled me to a stop from behind. It was the first time he'd touched me since he'd nearly choked me to unconsciousness two weeks ago.

"How much does Simion know?" Armise asked. His eyes narrowed either in reaction to having to speak to me or the sand that whipped around us. I had a feeling which one it really was.

"How much do you want him to know?"

Shit. That was a question instead of a direct answer, and I'd been steadfastly forgoing anything that I knew brought Armise frustration for the last weeks of our trip.

Armise glanced away, to the front door, where Revolution soldiers had started to come out to meet us. His eyebrows were stitched together, as if he was deep in thought. "I will follow your lead."

It was the first time Armise had shown any trust in me for almost two months now. I gave him a clipped nod as he laid a calm, focused gaze on me. There was no heat of passion in his assessment, but there wasn't the usual simmering inferno of anger when he surveyed me either. I'd take what it looked like I was going to get.

"Okay," I agreed. I turned to face the guards that were approaching us.

Simion broke through the line, a wide grin on his face that was wiped clear the second he laid eyes on Armise.

"You didn't tell me, you fucking prick," he shot out at me. He turned to Armise and tipped his chin up. "Fucking sucks, right? You getting the phantom pains?"

Armise clenched his jaw. "Yes."

Simion clapped him on the back and pulled him forward until only Armise and I would be able to hear him. "Talk to my doctors. We can get you set up with a synth in a day or two."

"Thank you. I will."

Simion pointed a finger at me as he backed away. "You. You are seriously a fucking prick. Warn me the next time."

I readjusted the pack on my shoulder. "I'm counting on there not being a next time, sir."

Simion's face fell. "Let's hope. Come on inside. I'll get you set up with a room and we can talk in my office later."

* * *

THE REVOLUTION HEADQUARTERS on this coast of the DCR were the most advanced, the most comfortable, I'd ever been in. That they weren't underground may have influenced my ranking as well. Simion excused himself, but not before leaving us with a graying sergeant major who he assured us would take care of anything we needed.

"One room or two?" the man asked over his shoulder as we walked through the halls.

Armise looked to me for an answer and I did a double take before I realized why.

He was following my lead. Right.

"One," I replied. I got no reaction from Armise either way.

The hallways we passed through were free of damage and everything I'd seen of the broad white building from the air made it appear as if they'd never been attacked. I couldn't believe that could be possible.

"It looks like you've never been bombed out."

"We haven't," he confirmed.

Even Armise looked confused at that possibility. "Shields?"

"We don't need them. The citizens around us—for at least a hundred miles in every direction—keep anything and every-thing away from us."

"Why?"

The sergeant major stopped and faced us. "They want us to use our resources where they're needed. They want us to win."

This was the future Wensen Kersch had spoken of. The future he'd hoped to one day see, where the citizens were active participants in their lives and in the levels of freedom they sought out and tested in their daily work.

I breathed out. "Holy shit."

"We're an anomaly, don't get me wrong," the sergeant major clarified as he started moving again. "But that safety net is why President Simion is here. He's showing faith in them as much as they're showing faith in him."

"He deserves that loyalty," Armise said with conviction.

I peered over my shoulder at him as we walked. I agreed with his assessment, shared it in fact. I had been there for all of the times Armise and Simion had ever interacted—as far as I knew—and I could sift through those memories to pinpoint when and how Simion had gained Armise's respect.

Simion was my polar opposite.

While Armise struggled to view me with anything besides disdain lately, the reverse held true for Ricor Simion. Sims and I weren't the same in style or approach, of anything, and that meant I could learn from what Simion was tuned into that I wasn't.

The sergeant major led us to quarters that were significantly larger than our accommodations on the boat, and that had a window that took up the breadth of the room from wall to wall. On the other side of the glass the desert stretched off to the horizon.

"You'll find a hardwired BC5 at the desk. Use the system to call for me if you need anything before meeting with President Simion. Welcome home, gentlemen."

I offered him a muffled thank you as he departed, sucked

into my own thoughts because until he'd welcomed us home I'd forgotten that Armise and I would be recognized here.

I dropped my pack onto the floor next to the closet but didn't make a move to empty it. Not yet. Despite how safe this place seemed, the bunker had been the same. I didn't trust any structure remaining in a particular state for any length of time anymore. I would leave everything packed until we decided how long we would be here, and even then I would have something at the ready to flee if I needed.

Armise unpacked.

Why couldn't I stop running? I wanted to stop, ached for it, and yet here I was—back inside a Revolution stronghold at the risk of being pulled into active duty—because I ached for Armise even more.

I restrained a sigh and pulled my shirt over my head so I could clean up before we met with Sims. I untied and kicked off my boots and began to unbutton my pants.

"Merq?" Armise said from where he stood by the windows.

My head snapped up and my fingers froze on the buttons. "Yeah?"

He ran his fingers through his hair—so much silver woven through the black in the last two months—and met my eyes. "If Simion asks you to fight again, how will you answer him?"

"If you want Ahriman dead, then I'll fight. But I won't go into active duty for Simion."

Armise crossed the room to me. He ran his fingertips down my chest, making my overly sensitive skin flush with the need for more. He tipped his head up and locked me in with a gaze that held hints of the predator inside him.

"Then go clean yourself up, Colonel."

I TOOK my time in the shower, resting my head against the wall and letting the spray beat down on my neck, shoulders, and back. I wanted to believe that the way Armise had interacted with me today had to mean he was opening up to me again. But I'd made too many assumptions for too long, left too much of our relationship up to him—been passive for way too long—for me to be sure what he wanted me to do.

He wanted me to continue fighting until Ahriman was dead, that much I knew. It was a selfish request on his part, and one that I wouldn't deny him. It wasn't as if I'd been selfless for any length of time in the years we'd been together.

I scrubbed up, shedding the crusting layers from the salt-water that I'd been unable to fully wash off while we were at sea, and heard the door to the en suite open. Armise entered and set his kit down, extracting items one by one and not sparing me a glance. I finished cleaning, opened the door to the shower and whipped a towel off a stack on the shelf. As I dried off I didn't bother to hide that I was studying him.

He'd become much steadier with the use of his left hand and I watched as he clipped his beard down to a respectable length. Not having his eyes on me at all times was hard, even after so many years together. To be crass, his eyes on me had always *made* me hard.

Fuck, I missed his touch.

I missed him.

"Something on your mind, Merq?" he said to me. His focus was trained on his reflection and the unerring swish of the scissors as the silver and black of his hair fell into the sink below.

"Always," I replied as I dried off. "You," I clarified. I needed to see how he would react, if at all, to that.

Armise grunted in reply, that rumbling huff of frustration I hadn't heard in months.

I leaned against the countertop and threw my towel over the

shower door. I wanted to touch him, to have him want to touch me again. I couldn't be passive anymore.

"Honestly? Thinking about how much I miss your teeth digging into my bottom lip, pulling on my lip piercing."

He scoffed. "Should have known your thoughts would be straying to sex."

The unease and hurt of the last two months churned inside me, and I hadn't been able to place why his distance affected me so much, but now I knew.

"Not sex. You. I didn't realize how much of my connection to you was physical—your lips, fingers and body against mine, not just sex—until it wasn't there anymore."

"Was," he mused, letting me know what he considered most important of what I'd said.

"We're not the same as we were before Ahriman, Armise, and you know it. That I find it infinitely less confusing and frustrating to show you what I think of you rather than tell you hasn't changed though."

I curled my fingers around the edge of the counter to keep myself from reaching out to him. "I don't know how to be us without you touching me."

He set the utility scissors down and looked at me. "That's what you want."

"It is...."

He quirked an eyebrow when I didn't finish my thought.

"It's what you want too," I dared to say when I wasn't sure at all. "You've always been the one to come find me. To seek me out when you were trying to prove there was more than attraction between us. So if I'm right, then find me when you're ready—"

"Merq," he growled out, and I saw the anger rising inside him.

"I fully realize I'm asking the same thing of you that we've always done. But this time you don't have to guess whether or not I'm with you on this. You don't have to manipulate me or back me into a corner to get your answer. You come and I'll be there. Anywhere you want me to be."

* * *

SIMION RECLINED IN HIS CHAIR, his legs crossed over the top of his desk as he glared at Armise and me. "I never should have let you go off-grid like that."

"It wasn't your call."

I wasn't trying to assuage his guilt. Simion would carry that responsibility no matter what reassurances I gave him. It was part of what made him a great leader.

"Fucking four months with Ahriman. I don't know how you survived."

Neither Armise nor I spoke to that. The how was of a deeper consequence than Armise and I had yet to acknowledge to each other, let alone talk about with someone else.

"You think whatever he did to you—the mental tripwire as you keep calling it—you think it wasn't real? That it was more about the meds his fuckhead father was shooting you up with?"

"There is no way to know for sure," Armise answered.

Simion nodded. "Maybe Priyessa can pinpoint what it is now that we know more."

"Maybe," Armise replied calmly. He didn't appear as opposed to the idea as I thought he might have been, since we were talking about a PsychHAg poking around in both of our brains.

"How are things with Neveed?" I tested. Armise and I hadn't been in contact with Manny since leaving Singapore and we had no way to know what had come of his ambition to get Chen back to Neveed safely. Neveed's possible death, Manny's involvement with Armise and me, and Chen's transformation, were repercussions Simion didn't need to carry with him either. He had too much else that he needed to focus on.

"He's maintained comm silence since Chen's death," Simion said, giving me at least a partial answer. "If you called he may pick up."

"I doubt that."

I sat forward in my chair and scrubbed my hands over my face. I didn't know what our next play was and Armise wasn't giving me any clues. Following my lead could have been his own perverse version of revenge, because I was too used to hearing his thoughts on everything and relying on his ability to maneuver through layers of deception and tactical moves. Just as his silence gave me no indications of what decision I needed to make, his body language didn't either.

Fuck it. He'd given me one thing he wanted to see from me and I wouldn't go back on that. "I'm ready for active duty, Pres. Where do you want me?"

Simion gaped and looked to Armise, who sat stock-still and quiet, then turned his attention to me again when he realized I wasn't bullshitting him and Armise wasn't going to fight this.

"We're launching an op against the last remaining hybrid camp. We think it's where Ahriman is holed up. One of the analysts figured out a way to block anyone from transporting out and we're currently in a standoff—no one going out and no one coming in. We need that camp to fall."

"If—" I started to say then cut myself off. If Armise can't fight.... Armise would be out of commission for weeks, possibly months, while he learned how to operate a new synth. Since Armise couldn't be the one to take out Ahriman, I would take on that mission as my own. "If I agree to come back then I want to be the one who drags Ahriman's corpse out of there."

"I wouldn't expect anything else," Simion said obligingly.

"I've already spoken to the team that oversees neuro-synthetic implantation. They can operate on you today, Armise."

"Thank you," was the only response Armise gave audibly, but I saw his attention go to Simion's leg.

I wasn't the only one who noticed. Simion knocked a closed fist against the metal of his leg. "They can do the whole deal here—regenerated tissue, reconnecting severed nerves.... Synths can look as natural or as fabricated as you choose." He smirked and settled his legs on the floor, leaning forward on his desk. "I chose the exposed alloy structure for the intimidation factor."

That got a low chuckle from Armise.

"How much risk are we talking here with the operation?" I had to ask. This was Armise's choice and I wouldn't sway him from it. But I was the one who asked endless questions, not him. At the very least he could go into this fully informed.

Simion shrugged and his synth pinged against the legs of the chair as he adjusted his position. "The actual procedure's not as bad as they make you think it's going to be, but the rehab is a bitch."

"How long did it take you before you were comfortable again?" It was a personal question, but one I knew Sims wouldn't answer if he didn't want to.

"A couple months, maybe more. I wasn't all there mentally when I was on the meds for the phantom pain. Losing my leg fucked me up in ways I couldn't have anticipated. I don't know what it will be like for you, Armise. Just know—from one stubborn-ass soldier to another—that I'll do whatever I can to help. Knowing you, this whole thing will be a fucking breeze for you. So we a go for this?"

Armise nodded.

Simion stood and raised his BC5. "Still can't fucking figure out how to do the whole comm thing in-house instead of long distance."

There was a knock at the door and Simion called for the person to enter. A Revolution guard opened the door. "How can I assist you, President?"

"Same thing as always, but I'm not going to try linking my comm up. Can you just escort Officer Darcan to the med facility, please? They're expecting him."

"Yes, President Simion."

Simion clasped the bridge of his nose and sighed. "Still not fucking used to that." He shot a pointed look in my direction. "If you're sure you're going into active duty, Merq, then I want you to get checked out by Dr. Casas."

"I'm sure."

"Then make that two, Private."

The guard held the door open and waited for Armise and me.

Simion walked around the desk and circled his arm around Armise's shoulders as we started for the door. "Welcome to the synth club. We'll catch up when you're out of recovery."

Armise was a head taller than Sims and even with a missing arm could have pounded Simion into the ground for that brazen touch. But he didn't.

I would continue working to earn that right.

5

"Officer Darcan, you can enter through the doors on your left," the private instructed as we passed through a set of double doors. "The team has been notified you're on your way. Colonel Grayson, follow me."

Armise broke away from me and I grabbed his biceps and pulled him to a stop. The Revolution guard paused, and when I shot him a look to back the fuck off he moved farther down the hallway and out of listening range.

I kept my hand wrapped around Armise and tried to figure out what I wanted to say to him. This was the first time I'd intentionally reached out for him since our fight on the boat. It was the first time I'd touched him with care instead of anger since he'd been lying on that bed bleeding out in the safe house, and yet my message hadn't changed.

"Don't die, okay?"

Armise stared at where my hand was wrapped around him. "Can you...?"

I flinched, my stomach churning as I realized he still didn't want me to get that close to him.

I started to walk away, to respect that he wasn't ready, when he called out for me to wait. I turned around and he was digging in his pocket, pulling something out that he offered to me.

"Do not lose these," he said. He dropped his watch and bracelets into my open hand. I stared at them, a slash of hope knifing through my defenses. I hadn't known he'd kept the bracelets I'd retrieved for him, let alone carried them all this time.

"And can you"—Armise cleared his throat—"take the others as well?"

He lifted his hand and placed it palm up, exposing the flame tattoos on his forearm, holding himself still as I removed the matching set from his left wrist. Because he couldn't take them off on his own. What the fuck had I done to him?

I couldn't force myself to say anything out loud through the sorrow and regret that overwhelmed me.

His wrist emptied and my hands full, he opened the door and disappeared inside. I closed my fingers around the stone and wood beads, the strap of his watch pressing into my palm in the shape of a perfect circle, and I slid them all into my pocket.

"Take me to Dr. Casas," I said to the private. I followed when I was sure I could move without stumbling.

* * *

"So you stole President Simion away from me only to abandon him exactly when he needed you?" Dr. Feliu Casas accused.

On the heels of leaving Armise, only seconds after entering Feliu's clinic, the doctor's words cut into me with a venom I would've usually been able to ignore.

Yes, I'd chosen Armise over the Revolution and I wouldn't apologize for it. I didn't need to be reminded—again—that Armise was facing months of rehabilitation to get back to normal.

"He's better off than Armise. Still think Simion would have been okay with me here? Just fucking do your job and clear me for active duty. Where do you want me?"

Feliu pursed his lips, pointed to a table against the far right wall and picked up his med scanner.

I sat down on the table and decided the best course of action was to gloss over how much of an asshole he was being and treat this as if it were any ordinary checkup.

He made verbal notes as he progressed through scanning my vitals and there wasn't anything I could hear that was out of the normal range. I kept my eyes trained on the door, expecting at any moment to have someone show up who would tell me Armise hadn't made it through the procedure. The chances of that happening were slim, but I couldn't let that fear go.

Shit. I was frightened—just as Armise had said. I hadn't tapped into the fear until now. No. Since Ahriman's assault on Armise, all I had been was afraid.

"Merq. Chin up and look at me."

There was a frustrated bend to his voice, and I realized that probably wasn't the first time he'd instructed me to do that. I ripped my gaze away from the door and complied.

Feliu stared at me with a frown, the wrinkles on his face deepening as he studied me. "He'll be okay. The procedure is the easiest part."

"Don't try to pacify me when you're the one who attacked first."

He went silent. He set his medical scanner down and picked up a thin light that he tapped against his hand. "I'm sorry. I didn't understand. I do now."

"What?" I raged. I couldn't hold my anger in, not with how raw and vulnerable I was. "What the fuck do you understand now that you didn't when you threw that bullshit at me when I walked in the door?"

49

"That he's the most important part of your life."

I slumped forward. I hadn't even been able to admit that out loud to Armise.

"Why aren't you performing Armise's surgery?" I asked instead, then cringed when I realized what I was doing.

I was getting too damn used to deflecting anything and everything that had to with Armise. The choice to erase his role in my life wasn't passive, it was actively pushing him aside each time I denied who he was to me. I swallowed against the burn in my throat from keeping this truth unsaid for too long. "He is."

Feliu nodded in recognition and moved on in his assessment of me. "There are other, much more qualified doctors who specialize in neurology. Open your eyes wide, so I can take a look."

"What's your specialty then?"

"Genetmods."

"Of course it is."

He peered into my eyes, the light blinding me. "What's around your eyes?"

I blinked and he pulled back. "I don't know."

He gestured with the light in his hand. "There's a defined circle around your irises. It looks like an implanted lens."

My stomach dropped. "No," I said. I went for a mirror on the other wall. I opened my eyes wide and tried to see what he was seeing, but I didn't have to to know what it was.

I remembered Dr. Blanc saying to Ahriman that he had to be careful with my eyes because the lenses hadn't fully implanted yet. But I'd been so out of it, so unaware and unsure of what was real and what wasn't. I hadn't thought again of what he'd said. But there was only one thing it could be.

They'd implanted a memory projector inside my eyes. And with not knowing if there had ever been a mental tripwire, or how these memory projectors operated—solely from the user or accessible remotely—Ahriman or anyone he let in on this could have complete access to everything I knew about the Revolution —base locations, weapons caches, background on Simion, Jegs, Armise.... Fuck. Ahriman could have all of it already and this op Simion was planning could be a trap.

I pushed past Feliu even as he yelled after me to tell him what was going on. But I couldn't stop.

I had to talk to Priyessa. Now.

* * *

I SAT in Armise's and my quarters thrumming my fingers on the table, getting more and more agitated as each second ticked past that Priyessa wasn't answering her comm. I didn't want to go to Simion yet with my theories, or—more accurately—with my fears. I didn't have enough information to know whether there was anything to be afraid of.

When I'd heard nothing from her after ten minutes, I connected with the analysts in the capital of the States and asked them to track her down. Fifteen minutes after that none us had heard from her.

"Fuck!" I yelled and began to pace.

I'd been outfitted with this device months ago, but now I was in a Revolution base. I had talked with Simion about classified operational details. I had walked through enough of the base for Ahriman to learn the layout if he had access to my head. For him to guess how many staff and soldiers were at hand.... Shit, he would be able to find out that they weren't using shields.

I had to know how much could be ripped out of my brain with the tripwire and the memory projector, and if anything in my memories could be accessed remotely, or only if I was in front of him. Seconds counted, and I was tipping into half an hour without being any closer to knowing just how much of a threat I was.

I dropped into the chair and activated the comm again. The other end of my transmission was a black screen with yellow letters at the top that read "Neveed Niaz." This aircomm request was a long shot, and right now, my only shot.

"Fuck, he is dead," I muttered to myself just before the comm activated from the other end.

My head snapped up and I breathed a sigh of relief when I saw Neveed's copper eyes staring back at me.

"Things must be really bad if you're calling me."

I ran my fingers over the piercings on the shell of my ear. "You have no idea."

"Oh, I think I do," Neveed insisted. "I have a teenage girl who is going through a way worse transition than I ever thought I would have to help her through. A chipper and yet really fucking snide Singaporean hybrid who refuses to leave the back guest house. And a mother who specializes in psychological and physical torture, yet is so fucked up by what she's learned in the last six months that she's come to her overly sensitive son for help. I think I know bad when I see it."

Against the push of my somber mood, the corner of my lips curved into the beginnings of a smile. "I'll give that one to you."

He leaned forward. "So. Now it seems I've added a disheveled and distraught ex-lover, ex-Revolutionary hero to the mix. How can I help you, Merq?"

"Not quite ex on that Revolutionary part yet. I've told Simion I want to go back into active duty. But I've run into a complication."

"And you love those so. Is it Armise? Manny told me what happened. Well, as much as he knew before coming my way."

I settled, breathed in, and let a long exhale go. Neveed knew me. He knew more about my life than anyone else besides

Simion or Armise. I could trust him and he was offering to help. I had an ally in him when I had wondered at one time if he and I would ever be on speaking terms again.

"Thank you for picking up my aircomm, Neveed. You didn't have to."

He gaped at me. "Appreciation? Wow. This is bad. Now talk."

"I think I've been compromised like Wensen Kersch. Maybe Priyessa's already told you about the tripwire Ahriman possibly put in Armise's and my brain—"

"She did."

"Well, turns out the fabled encryption chip is very much real and now situated in Armise's neck with an explosive device around it that prevents it from being removed. And I've also been implanted with something called a memory projector."

"Shit." Neveed fell silent and looked away from me and off screen, his features clouded. He pushed back his dark curls and secured them behind his head. "I don't know if I can do this again."

I furrowed my brow. "Again?"

Neveed paused then looked at me. All joviality was gone from his demeanor. The set of his features was the same as when he'd broken off our affair.

"Neveed. I don't know what's going on. What can't you do again?"

He stared off into the distance as he spoke. "Kersch told me he'd been compromised and Armise was coming for him. And he told me I couldn't stop Armise in what he needed to do. I could have obscured the shot—stepped in front of Wensen and into Armise's sightline. But I didn't because he knew he was going to be killed and that it had to happen. And I trusted him enough that if he thought that was best then I wasn't going to figuratively or literally stand in his way."

My stomach sank. "You knew—"

He nodded. "And that's why I quit. I couldn't go through watching any more friends die. Watching Wensen drop to that stage was one of the hardest things I've ever done. Allowing Chen to leave my house for Kash is almost as high up on that list."

I wasn't asking the same of him that Wensen had though. "I'm not asking you to let me die, Neveed. I want to know what's happening so I can live. I need to get to your mom so she can work this through with me."

"That...."—he took a deep breath—"that I can do."

I couldn't end our conversation like this. I was much too attuned to the thought that I'd left a permanent stain of anger and hurt on every relationship I'd attempted over the entire fucking course of my life. I remembered the moment in the DCR when I'd joked about us hooking up again, of the unfettered smile he'd given me when he realized we were going to be okay.

I smirked. "And leaving me is somewhere on that list too, right?"

He lifted an eyebrow. "Do you want me to lie to you?"

I gave him my best scowl. "No fucking point, Neveed."

Neveed chuckled, his features rearranging to something that reflected pain, but not as immediate. Not as...unresolved. "I joke, Merq, but that's not the truth of it. I was supposed to watch you die on the platform in the stadium when you killed the premiere. Walking away from you after what we went through on your great-grandfather's island...that doesn't make my list because you were alive, healthy, and not under threat."

"I'm not under threat now. I am the threat, just like Wensen was. And I don't know what to do about it. But I won't give in like Wensen did. There has to be another way to fix this. My death would be the easy solution, but I've never done anything the easy way."

Neveed laughed, and I felt lighter hearing the sound.

"I'll rouse the PsychHAg from her bed and send her your way. She can answer your questions plus some you didn't know you should be asking. You have coordinates for me?"

"Transmitting them now. Thank you."

Neveed thrummed his fingers on the table. "How is Armise, Merq?"

"That's another complication."

"Fix that one too."

I nodded. "Give a hug to Chen from me, and my gratitude to Manny. Tell him I said he can stay with you as long as he wants. And keep avoiding Simion. I can't hide the reason for Priyessa's presence here, but let's keep you and Chen out of the line of fire."

"You'll get no argument from me on that. See you around, Grayson."

* * *

"I NEED you to trust me here, Sims," I implored as we stood in the transport room and waited for Priyessa. "What she may have to do to me isn't going to be pretty."

"Don't bullshit me. There's more to you not wanting me in the room than PsychHAg tactics. You know how much I can handle."

"There is more," I conceded. "Hence the trust part."

"You'll let me know—"

I cut him off. "I'll notify you when there's something you need to know."

Simion crossed his arms. "Have they given you an update on Armise?"

Regardless of him being my president, I snapped. "I wouldn't be doing this if I didn't know what his status and timeline were."

"Jesus. Okay. Got it."

Before I could say anything else that would piss him off, Priyessa appeared on the platform. Her hair was twisted into a braid that hung over her shoulder and the worry lines around her mouth and eyes were deeper than I'd ever seen. For the first time in all the years I'd known her, she looked her age.

She stepped off the platform and took Simion's hands in hers. "Thank you for allowing me entrance to and use of your facility, President Simion."

"I don't know what the fuck it's for 'cause this one is holding on tighter to his secrets than usual, but I trust that you understand your original orders for treatment of Colonel Grayson hold."

I quirked an eyebrow. "And those would be?"

I didn't expect an answer but Simion said, "No permanent damage."

"Of course," Priyessa acknowledged. "I have requested that my favorite chair be transported over as well. President Simion, could you afford me a room where my work will not be disturbed by concerned citizens?"

I huffed. "No permanent damage. Right. I think she means there's a chance of my screams drawing an unwanted crowd."

Simion frowned. "You sure you want to do this, Mig?"

I glanced between the two of them. "I don't want to. I have to."

"THE CHAIR IS for your protection just as much as it's a tool for me," Priyessa explained as she strapped me in.

I attempted to pull my hands from the restraints and couldn't. "I remember you trying to convince me of that over twenty years ago. I still don't buy it."

"Merq. You asked for my help. You know how I operate."

"And you know I've always been obstinate."

That brought a smile to her face. "Yes. An accurate choice of words."

She took a simple wooden chair that had been left in the corner of the room and slid it across the floor next to the torture seat I was strapped into. My heartbeat kicked up a notch at her proximity and the memories that flooded me.

"You remember what comes next, Merq?"

I did. There was no way I could ever forget. I nodded.

She laid her gnarled left hand on my right forearm, just above the spot where my wrist was bound to the chair. She tapped her pointed fingernail on me and slid it up and down my skin. The gesture was a warning of what was to come and also a psychological prompt. I knew what came next—her tearing at my flesh with her fingers until I was focused solely on what she was asking of me, so desperate for the pain to end that I would remember things I wouldn't be able to otherwise and would only speak the truth. That pain—both remembered and present —wasn't just one PsychHAg device for centering my thoughts with pinpoint accuracy. It was *the* method that had always been most effective with me.

"Tell me what you know about what Ahriman did to you."

It was an opening that delved into my conscious memories. She wouldn't do anything yet to sharpen those memories, she was merely probing for what remained on the surface, and her query mimicked the movement of her hand. Just as her interrogation and movements would continue to be in sync for however long this took.

I closed my eyes and remembered. "He said that it was something I'd done to myself and he didn't have to do anything to me. He said that I betrayed myself or that I was my own enemy, I don't recall the exact wording. He said Kersch had done the same. But then he said that he had done something to me, that chaos was occurring in my neuro-pathways. I remember that phrase distinctly. Those two scenarios didn't seem to coincide with each other. I found out later he was using this drug to control paralysis and consciousness. He never said anything to me about Armise being mentally influenced."

She continued to scratch at the surface of my arm, the rest of her body still. "Think about who else was around you. Who else was in the room with you during those four months?"

"Armise, Ahriman's father Dr. Calum Blanc, Dakra—the first of the hybrids—and Chen Ying. Neveed told me you would be able to answer my questions about her."

"I will. We need to focus here first."

I swallowed, tried to remain patient. "Okay."

"What did Ahriman say to the others?"

I shook my head. "He made no sense. He was contradicting himself with each thing he said. I couldn't decide what was lies, what was the truth, and what was fiction—created or forced memory. I still don't know."

Priyessa dug her nails in, and I could feel the first beads of blood running down my arm. That trickle would gush if I didn't answer her in a way that satisfied her.

"He said that Armise and I were weak but that we were useful," I added.

"Was that something he said to you or to someone else?"

"Me."

"Why would he think you were useful?"

This was where her interrogation shifted from memory to critical analysis. She carved into my flesh more with each second I hesitated and I clenched my fists and my jaw trying to stave off the pain shooting up my arm.

"I didn't give up any of the Revolution's secrets."

I snarled as her nails dug in deeper. "That's not the information I asked you for."

I sucked in a breath and tried to focus. Ahriman's building had smelled of wound pitch—the battlefront mix that kept blood from pouring out of cuts—and smoke. But that wasn't what she'd asked me either.

I opened my eyes. Her pointer finger had dug into my flesh up to the first gnarled knuckle on her finger, but instead of centering me, the pain ripped me away from the memories she was trying to get at and brought me to the present. To Armise.

Armise and pain were now inextricably linked in my head. The more I hurt, the more I thought of him. I wanted ecstatic agony from Armise. The pain of rough sex and powerful hands bruising me. And in complete opposition to that, I craved destroying all possibility of pain ever coming to him again. I wanted to take all of Armise's pain away and have him feed it to me, fuel me, over and over again until he was purged and I was filled.

This pain was wrong. It was only Armise who had the right, my permission and my desire, to hurt me—and her intrusion into what was suddenly so intimate made me furious. I didn't want to fight her, and I didn't even want to give in. This wasn't working and I wanted to get the fuck out of here. I didn't want to be here. I didn't want to do this at all. Fuck the Revolution. Fuck Ahriman. I would wait for Armise to get out of surgery and we would leave. We were no longer a threat if we weren't here.

Priyessa dug in even deeper. Blood streaked from my arm where her other fingers held on to me and agony lanced up my arm and I remembered this torture—could pull it from the depths of my memory and it would still make me cry out—but I'd felt worse, endured worse, survived much worse, and at least I had a fucking arm for Priyessa to tear apart. Armise didn't even have that.

59

"This isn't working," I ground out between clenched teeth.

"You've said that to me before in very similar circumstances, Colonel Grayson. And this method worked then."

"I was sixteen at the time. I know myself better now."

"Do you?"

I laughed and the movement made her grip tighter to me. "No. But I have a better understanding of what drives me, and your brand of hell isn't it anymore. Maybe your methods ensuring I didn't break under torture worked better than you ever thought."

"Then how did Ahriman take control of you?"

"I don't know!" I screamed at her.

"You do, Merq," she insisted as she dug her nail inside me and twisted it. "If you can't tell me why you and Armise were useful, then what did you say to him?"

She wouldn't stop until she got something from me, because I had given her permission for this. My stomach lurched with the realization that I'd allowed her to get too deep inside me again. I had to end this. I took a deep breath and searched through everything I could recall from those four months, realizing that all of my verbal replies to Ahriman had been sarcastic. Biting. Fighting him each step of the way.

"Nothing. He got nothing from me."

"Even what you don't remember?"

I set my feet on the floor and tried to pull back from her. "How the fuck am I supposed to know that?"

"I went through Tiam's records. The supposed tripwire Ahriman used with Kersch only held for so long. The brain buries what we want to forget and has a way of revealing what we force ourselves to remember. Simion also gave me access to Kersch's personal logs. He had an idea of what was happening."

I shook my head. "That hasn't happened to me. I don't have flashes of there being anything else or anyone else in my head."

She stilled her hand. "That's because there was nothing there to allow him access. The threat of the tripwire was used to lure you in, nothing else. Do you remember what the drug was called that he used on you?"

"Sleepsense."

"I thought so. It's also a hallucinogenic."

"And the memory projector? Am I a threat because of it?"

"He likely fitted you with the device because he couldn't get you to break any other way. I'm betting he failed in that objective as well."

"I don't remember it ever being activated."

"You would. The wearer has to actively control the memories for them to be accessed."

"Then the only reason Armise and I survived is because Dr. Blanc modified the levels of Sleepsense we were given until I could control my actions again."

She removed her finger from the recesses of my arm and wiped her hand clean. She retrieved a pouch from the table next to her and opened it, showing me a white dust. "Localized nanos to speed healing. No surge involved."

I nodded my approval for her to go ahead.

She poured the powder over my wound then undid the restraints around my wrists. "Don't think too highly of Dr. Blanc. You are a test subject for him. He saved you and Armise simply because he needs to gather more data from you. Tiam's records confirm Dr. Blanc's role in his work."

I flexed my hands. "The Anubis project?"

Priyessa nodded. "I was one of the original members. What do you want to know?"

6

I sat at Armise's side and waited for him to wake from the seda-tive. Unlike his wounds after Ahriman had taken his arm, the juncture where Armise's synth met his shoulder was clean and already healed. When Dr. Blanc had treated him the nano-laced surge hadn't been enough to stave off the enormity of his injury, but his surgery today had followed a prescribed set of steps intended to minimize the trauma. At least that's what the doctor had explained to me when I asked.

I was alone with Armise, having been reassured that the time it would take for him to emerge from the anesthetic would be considerably less than other patients they'd worked on. He wouldn't need two months of a medically induced coma in order to heal. Maybe my recovery would have been drastically different if Neveed had allowed me to get a synth after the DCR attack. Or maybe this was just further proof that Armise would always be stronger than me.

Armise's eyes went from closed to open in one breath. He pulled in a long inhale and blinked, eyes fixed to the ceiling.

"So you didn't die," I goaded him in a soft voice. "Going to have to try harder to put you down the next time."

Armise licked his lips and turned his gaze toward me. "Is it morning?"

"Evening. You get to start tomorrow with a new arm and a rehab session with Simion. He's already set it up."

"Of course he has." Armise frowned, a flicker of frustration crossing his face.

"Moving it will take time," I told him, gesturing to his new right arm. "The physical damage is repaired but the muscles have to be strengthened and the neurons have to be given a chance to reconnect."

"You're an expert now?"

"I ask a lot of questions. It's useful at times."

The corner of Armise's lips tipped up at that.

"What did you tell them about the encryption chip?" I asked.

He frowned. "Nothing. I can assume they didn't try to remove it since I am still here."

"They probably thought it was one of Ahriman's shield chips, and they already know not to touch those. Let's keep its value between us for now." I didn't care if it stayed there, untouched, forever. There was much more I valued in him than would ever be found in that chip.

He lifted his head and surveyed his new synth, eyebrows stitching together with the effort.

"You want to see it?" I offered, yet remained seated so he would have the choice to say no.

"Yes," he answered in a gruff voice.

I stood and circled around the bed. The skin itself was synthetic—similar to human skin but not the same. I set my hand under his and he flinched at the first touch, which made me freeze.

"What's wrong?"

"It just feels off. Go ahead."

The synth was unmarked—of both scars and ink—and that

63

lack of history made me starkly aware of how much had been taken away from him. I held my palm to his, thumb resting next to his, and set my left hand under his elbow. The skin was soft, hairless, and was neither hot nor cold...just normal.

I lifted the appendage for Armise to study. "Tell me if any of this hurts you."

Armise glared at me in silent reply.

His jaw clenched and unclenched as sweat started to gather on his forehead.

"Stop trying to move it, Armise. Give it time."

"I do not have time," he snapped.

I eased his arm to the bed and leaned over him. "This is your only commitment now. Approach it with the same determination you have everything else in your life and it won't take long."

"I would choke you if I could."

I had to smile. This was the Armise I hadn't seen for months.

"When you're ready I'll be waiting." I hoped my answer would be heard for the two meanings it held. "Do you need to sleep?"

"I do not want to sleep anymore."

"Then work?"

He shifted on the bed, frowning when he couldn't sit up. "What about it?"

I slid my hand under his shoulder and adjusted the pillow behind him so he wasn't lying flat anymore. "I spoke to Priyessa about Anubis."

Armise paled at that. "What did she say?"

I sat on the edge of the bed so he could look me in the eye. I needed that connection too. I could feel that link between us in a way I hadn't been able to in months, and I didn't want to let it go.

"Chen was dead. Neveed buried her, so he had no idea that she'd been taken. Apparently the new hybrid transition serum is strong enough to revitalize organs and repair damaged tissue. Priyessa and Neveed still don't know if there's a lingering effect to Chen's brain."

"That is frightening."

"I know. Priyessa was one of the people who restarted Anubis, but she's been out of it for decades because she didn't like the direction it was headed in. Franx Heseltine from the United Union helped with funding. Dr. Blanc is in on it too. PsychHAg Tiam as well...." I paused. This was the name that I still couldn't believe no matter how reliable I thought Priyessa was. "And Dr. Sarai Kersch."

Armise swore in Mongol. "Wensen Kersch's wife?"

I nodded. "She was a virologist. I had no idea. Anubis was what my great-grandfather and his contemporaries originally called their work, and the Nationalists did destroy the archives because they hoped to end it. But Calum Blanc and Sarai Kersch restarted the project. They wanted to take my great-grandfather's approach to disease eradication and alter it to eradicate other types of human weakness. At least that was their original agenda."

"But they ended up using genetic modification to weaponize human beings instead."

"Exactly."

"If Sarai was involved then Wensen..."

I swallowed. "He was too. He tried to get out after Sarai was kidnapped, and that's when Tiam programmed him. She thinks that Ahriman didn't stop you from assassinating Kersch because he was actively working against Anubis. Ahriman was brought into Anubis by his father but he branched out and took the project to the Opposition—hence the falling out between father and son. She also told me that our role in Anubis is as test subjects. We're the first generation and the hybrids are the second. But you already knew that, didn't you?"

"I did. And Chen is third gen in a way we cannot anticipate."

"Shit. I didn't think of it like that."

"Is that all Priyessa told you?"

I bit at my lip piercing. "It's more than enough for me to attempt to sort out at the moment."

"I think we both need sleep."

"And food. I'll go see if I can find you some genetmod meat to get your stamina back up."

Armise grimaced. "Nothing genetmod for me. Not after hearing all of that."

"Except for me?"

Armise grunted.

I got up from the bed. "I'll see what I can uncover for you."

"Merq?"

I turned to face him. The tips of his synthetic fingers were raised slightly off the bed.

I stared at him in disbelief and started to chuckle. Five minutes into recovery and he was already operating his synth in a way that shouldn't have been possible.

"Yeah, Darcan?"

"Thank you."

I circled my hand around the back of my neck, digging at the tension there. "I've heard you say that more in the last two days than I have in fifteen years."

"I have to restart somewhere."

"Tomorrow. You restart tomorrow. Tonight we eat and sleep."

* * *

I WOKE UP TO SILENCE.

I'd gone to sleep with my belly full and no worry about what today would bring. The sun was rising over the desert outside my window—hazy lines of mist lifting off the sand as the sun rose bright and hot. The light within the room shifted from blue to red to yellow-white. I lay in bed overwhelmed with uncertainty. Armise's restart began now—today—and there was only quiet to usher in the shift. An easy calm that hinted at safety and security when I knew that wasn't the truth. It was an engulfing silence that threatened to drive me mad.

I blinked, then closed my eyes and tried to see if I could feel the memory projector lenses implanted in my eyeballs. I used my forefinger and thumb to search around the bones of my hand for what Grimshaw had used to activate his implanted device. When I moved past the chip that identified me as a man who lived a much more inconspicuous life than I ever would, I found a minuscule lump—a rigid circle—that protruded between my thumb and forefinger. I didn't push it.

I scrubbed my hands over my face then flipped onto my stomach, burying myself into a pillow. The cloth was soft. And that was enough for me to understand that I wouldn't be able to stay here long. I wasn't meant for a life like this. I wasn't comfortable in a life like this.

The reality was I *wouldn't* be here long. I was to begin combat training today while Armise was with Simion. It had been six months since the attack on the hybrid camp in Kash, with time and circumstance wearing me down instead of inaction. I was looking forward to stretching my body to its limits again, holding a knife, and balancing a rifle on my shoulder. All of these things were familiar. That Armise wouldn't be at my side while I trained—or when I went into battle—wasn't familiar anymore.

I dragged myself out of bed and into the en suite to piss, get cleaned up and dressed, then get out of this room so I would be doing something to fill the suffocating silence.

I was due to report for breakfast first, and my training session immediately following, but I went to Armise's room before I did either of those. His bed was empty already. I scrunched my eyebrows together and went in search of him. Someone would have come to get me if anything had gone wrong with him—that much I was sure Simion would've orchestrated—so I was searching for a man who wouldn't be put off by the advice of his doctors, or me, that he needed time to heal. He'd likely hit the gym as soon as I'd left him the night before.

"Fuck no!" I heard Simion exclaim as I walked into the training wing of headquarters, then he prattled on, the up-and-down lilt of his shifting accent all I could make out. His tone was light, teasing, and Armise's rumbling laugh shocked me to a stop.

I hadn't given Armise the time he said he needed while we were on the boat. Maybe he needed it now.

I bypassed their training room and headed for the galley instead.

* * *

"SOME THINGS NEVER CHANGE," I heard a familiar voice say just before a plate was dropped in front of me.

I turned toward Exley as he took a seat next to me. "What the hell are you and President Simion doing in the same place?"

"Good to see you too, asshole," Exley replied and pushed the plate in front of me closer. "Food heals all."

"Believe me. It doesn't." I took a bite and grimaced. This food was more likely to kill me than heal anything. Exley may have been delivering the food but he definitely hadn't made this. "Should I be congratulating you on the promotion?"

Exley shrugged and swiped a handful of errant braids over his shoulder. "I believe in Ricor. Super easy decision."

While phrased with a casualness that spoke to Ex's laid-back persona, that was a sentiment I was getting used to hearing. It made me proud of the man I'd grown up with.

"You didn't believe in Kersch?" I asked. I tried to force another forkful of the bland mush in front of me down my throat.

"Trainees," Exley explained, cocking his head to indicate he was talking about what was theoretically food on my plate. "Can't be in control of all the details anymore. And it wasn't that I didn't believe in Kersch. I just didn't trust him."

The only thing that bothered me more than Armise's distance was how much my perceptions of Wensen Kersch had changed since his assassination. It had taken his death for me to learn who he really was, and I had the sinking feeling that I still didn't know it all.

"Your instincts were on with that one. You—" I cleared my throat, set down my fork and pushed the plate away. Eating right now had no value except to build my strength. I'd deal. "Have any of the jacquerie kids from the camps made it home yet?"

"Some. Very few, really. The transition isn't smooth for them. It's all a process."

I definitely wasn't going to be able to stomach anything now. "They know violence in a way that can't be forgotten or erased. Maybe it's better to teach them how to use that anger."

"You would know."

There was no judgment in his statement, just an awareness of my core identity that I couldn't refute. Exley tried to form a smile, to push past the darkness that had taken hold of his features when we talked about the camps. He likely didn't realize what he was giving away—just how much he himself was bothered by violence—but he'd always been one of the easiest people for me to read.

"So what are you doing in the DCR? I heard on a newsfeed

that you and Simion were leading divided fronts—him in the DCR and you in the UU."

Exley's eyebrows shot up. "No one told you? Singapore is our only front anymore. The Opposition has been beaten back everywhere except Singapore-held areas. We're moving on the island soon. Ricor figures that if we take the heart then there won't be much life left in the body. I disagree with the metaphor but his strategy is sound."

"Wait. You're sending Revolution troops into Singapore's capital?"

Exley nodded. "Same time that we move on the last hybrid camp in Moscow. We take Ahriman, and we take their capital, there's not going to be much of a power structure anymore. To add to that, we've already secured the approval for the attack with Premiere Pearce. He's too pissed about not getting his stash of goods from the UU to pretend to protect Ahriman. It's going to be a long time before there's any change to the leadership and restructuring of the five countries but it's happening."

"A process." I repeated what he'd said earlier.

"We have you to thank for the addition of the Nationalists. That was the turning point. Nationalists, jacquerie, Revolution.... When we collectively got our heads un-assed things started to move."

"I had nothing to do with Grimshaw."

"You're the one he brought in—not us. You gotta learn to see your own value, Merq. Now if you're finished with that shit, you and I have training to do."

I raised my pierced eyebrow. "What could you possibly teach me?"

"Not a thing. But apparently Ricor thinks it's time for me to learn how to shoot a gun. Thought you might be just the guy to do it."

* * *

I<small>T WAS NEARLY</small> nightfall before I made it out of the range. Exley wasn't the worst student I'd ever worked with. He had a chance of becoming competent one day. Perhaps enough to not flinch each time he fired. I made a note to send a report to Simion and let him know that his second-in-command needed to have a bodyguard with him at all times. I ran my fingers through my hair and inhaled the lingering scent of gun oil and firing powder on my hands. It was intoxicating in an unexpected way, the memory of firefights humming with an insistent pulse through my veins.

The door to Armise's room was cracked open as I walked by but it was dark inside, so I left him to sleep. I'd see him tomorrow.

Tomorrow still wasn't guaranteed, but it was a hell of a lot more likely in a place like this. In the morning I could find out just how hard he'd driven himself today, and how much progress he'd likely already made—

I came to a dead stop in the hallway and set my hands on my hips, hanging my chin to my chest and closing my eyes.

No.

My tomorrow wasn't guaranteed, and neither was his. I'd already spent too many years thinking that if each last time was really the last then I would be better off for it. I now knew that I wouldn't be. And I believed that he wouldn't be either.

I didn't need to avoid him or give him so much space that I wasn't present at all, did I?

"Fuck," I mumbled out loud and turned on my heel.

I pushed open the door to his room and waited for my eyes to adjust to the darkness. Armise was crowded into the edge of his bed, lying on his left side facing away from me. The meeting of stark, unblemished synth and his scarred, inked back was a

71

visual representation of his old life versus the new. The easy, rhythmic up and down of his breathing told me he was deep in sleep.

I picked up a chair, carried it to the side of his bed and set it down with as much care as I could with my shaking hands. I was so unsure of myself.... Shit. Like a five-year-old struggling to walk after my home had been destroyed and my parents had abandoned me to the States.

I sat down in the chair, leaned forward, and scrubbed my hands over my face. When I looked up again he was still asleep —peaceful, relaxed, and yet like an impenetrable wall protecting me from the world outside that door. Something inside me settled—no, broke open—and allowed me to take a full breath for what felt like the first time in my life.

I grasped on to the reality of who Armise was to me.

I was drifting off course without him. Not lost, but lacking a destination. For two years, since the tunnel under the Olympic stadium, Armise had been vocal about what he wanted from life. Unwavering from his ultimate goal. Armise knew what his destination was, and now I did too.

That the final stop was us—fuck this war, fuck the dates of our deaths—was a truth it was beyond time for me to embrace.

7

I sat in the back of the briefing room, tapping my fingers against the table and trying to keep my focus on the general at the front who was running through drone aerials of the hybrid camp again. It was early in the morning on the third day we'd been at the details of our attack and I'd lost patience for her repetitive nature two days ago. If the soldiers in the room didn't have the plan of attack down by now then they shouldn't be on the ground. Period.

Neveed never would've approached an op of this importance with such a lack of decisive leadership. He'd had an inherent trust in his soldiers because he knew—without a shred of doubt —that each person in that room was capable, driven, and intelligent enough to accomplish what he set out for them.

I'd been a valuable asset, trained and led by the best Kersch had to offer, but every soldier deserved to be led by people of the highest level of capability. When the strategy session ended I thumped out of the room and up to Simion's office, giving two hard knocks and pushing through the door as soon as I heard Simion grant access.

"Your general is incompetent," I said without preamble.

Simion sat back in his chair. "Are you asking for a promotion, Colonel?"

"Fuck no. Even if I was eligible it's not a job I'd want. That woman may be eligible but that doesn't mean she's capable."

"So you're questioning my leadership then."

"No," I sputtered.

"General Nissim has two children who were victims of the hybrid camps. She's careful about this op because it matters. She has a personal stake that gives her emotional drive to get it right. Some people become more detail-oriented when they're emotionally compromised rather than less."

I bristled. "What the fuck does that mean?"

"You have a personal stake in this op that's emotionally compromising you. Don't become so wrapped up in the need for revenge that you lose your view of the op as a whole. I'm granting you Ahriman's death because you asked for it. Because you earned that right. But he isn't the only objective, so don't lose sight of that."

"I know exactly why my rifle sight is trained where it is."

"That's my point. You've got yourself so focused through the scope that you're missing everything else around you. You have to become less myopic or I'll pull you out of this."

I seethed. "You won't."

"Get the fuck out of my office, Colonel," Simion dismissed me. "I have real work that requires my full attention."

I WAS SET to meet Exley in the range for another lesson, one that was sure to ignite my frustration instead of cooling it down, so I told the guard outside Simion's door to notify Exley we were rescheduling and I headed for my quarters instead. The hallways were as quiet as usual. Too serene. Too seemingly oblivious to the fact that the Revolutionary movement was standing at the edge of a precipice, about to dive head first into the toughest, most critical moment in the war. Everyone was either too confident of success or too sure of their place at the top of the food chain. But either way, no one had enough of a sense of just how much we teetered on the knife's edge of failure. That lack of urgency was driving me mad.

I threw my door open and slammed it shut, the reverberation thudding in my ears. I froze as soon as I realized I wasn't alone.

It had been three days since I'd last seen Armise, when I'd fallen asleep in the chair next to his bed, waking up before him only to slip out before he'd known I'd been there at all. Since then I'd been so wrapped up in preparation for the attack on the hybrid camps and so consumed with my own frustration that I'd sequestered myself from anyone I didn't need to be in contact with. It wasn't as if I hadn't tried to see Armise. Every morning he was gone, no matter how early I woke, and every evening he was asleep by the time I was finished for the day.

He was sitting at the table, boots propped up, synth lying in his lap, head tilted back, and eyes closed with the morning sun streaming across his face, highlighting every scar on his forehead, cheeks, and neck. The crash of the door faded away and Armise opened his eyes, looked to me. At me. Into me.

"What are you doing here?" I asked and immediately wanted to take the question back. There were too many things I wanted to take back when it came to what I'd said and done to Armise.

He drew his lips into a thin line. "I have officially been discharged from the medical facility."

"Good," I replied. "It's been different—"

I stopped myself.

This was his restart. Old versus new. Unmarked skin next to

ink and wounds and permanent reminders of so much pain. We had an opportunity to change our pattern.

I had to find a way.

I ran my fingers over the piercings on my left ear and took a breath. "It's been hard not having you in bed with me."

His eyebrow lifted at that and he dropped his left foot to the floor.

"Not just for sex," he said.

My eyes drifted to the open vee of his legs before focusing back on him. I shook my head, confirming what he was saying even though it hadn't been phrased as a question. I couldn't hold his gaze and I looked to his boots instead. "Who tied your shoes for you?"

His lips tugged into a frown. "I tried this morning...."

"It won't take you long."

I was standing just inside the door, too far away from him to reach out. Too far to be close, and I couldn't maintain that distance anymore.

"Armise—" I started to say and cut myself off, trying to formulate what I wanted to say before the wrong thing came out of my mouth again. "It's not just about sex. It's not. But...." I had a flash of a memory—Armise sitting at a table in Bogotá, sliding the key to a hotel room to me. With everything I knew now, that memory was different. He had been coming to me for sex, but also something more. I repeated to him what he'd said to me that day. "It's been too long."

The frown disappeared from Armise's face and he went still, that unnatural quiet that meant he was focused inward. I waited to see or hear how he would respond.

Finally he flexed the fingers of his left hand, closed them into a fist, then used his thumb to pop the joint of the first one, second, third.... Drawing attention to that missing fifth finger just like he'd done that day in Bogotá. I didn't know if that action had been conscious then, or if it was now, but it was a reminder that he'd always been the one to push in our relationship, to move us forward. That shouldn't have been only his responsibility to bear and it couldn't be anymore.

"Fuck this."

I crossed the room to him, grasping his face between my hands, bringing his lips to mine. I wondered how he would respond to me, if he would respond at all, but I didn't have to wait. Armise's skin was warm to the touch and he opened for me as I breathed him in, tasted him. I lost myself in him, only him. My memory of how he tasted, how his tongue slid against mine, could never match the reality. He pulled back just a fraction and lapped into my mouth, then bit at my lower lip and sucked my piercing between his teeth. The moan he ripped out of me couldn't be controlled.

It had been months since I'd last kissed him and I never wanted to stop. His hand circled my thigh, pulling me in closer to his body. I straddled his leg and he palmed my ass, fingers digging in and holding tight. He bit at my bottom lip again as a hitched breath stuttered out from between my lips.

I drew back and looked him in the eyes. "Tell me you don't want me and I'll stop, Armise. But I want you. Not just a fuck. You."

"I'm here," was all he answered. It took me seconds of searching his face, waiting for him to say something else, before I realized what he was telling me.

Come to me when you're ready.

He could've gotten his own quarters after leaving the med facility, but he hadn't.

He was here. With me.

"Okay," I responded, his presence heating me more than the sun coming through the window falling hot on my face. Armise's skin was warm under my hands, the chill of detachment gone, and that haze of the last two months—that sense of wrong, *this is all wrong*—began to lift, dissipate.

I stepped back and set my right hand under his, against the synth, and curled my fingers around him, trying to coax him to his feet. "Come on, Darcan. I know you've probably already learned to do things with this arm that no one should be capable of this soon."

He smirked and his brow furrowed in concentration as the fingers of his synth tightened around mine.

I pulled him up until we were face to face, hands locked between us. "That's what I thought. You've always been driven, almost to the point of madness."

"I learned from the best," he replied in a low voice. I felt the rumble of his bass with how close he was to me. Finally.

My body responded to his proximity, his heat.

And yet, I hesitated.

At one time I'd thought he was my drug, my fatal addiction. But he wasn't that at all. He was just as vital as the air in my lungs or the water that slaked my thirst. Just as solid as the ground beneath my feet. He was the fire that kept danger away, yet held me within his protective circle. He was warmth I'd never expected to find in the chill of his skin and standoffish demeanor.

I hesitated because the enormity of who he was to me had little to do with his size or his strength.

There was ease returning between us that hadn't been there since the steppe, a back and forth that spoke of history and connections, but I hesitated because there was still so much pain. So much we hadn't talked about and hadn't said out loud. So many things I was just beginning to figure out, let alone give voice to. And he deserved to hear it all first.

Armise cocked his head. "Let it go for now, Merq. Whatever you want to say can come later."

"Don't fuck with me, Armise, and don't try to placate or distract me. I don't want to put this off any longer." There wasn't any anger in my tone, no judgment. I just.... I had to be sure. There was too much I'd passed over because opening my mouth for his dick was infinitely easier than opening it to talk.

"It's been too long," I repeated, but with a slightly different intent behind my answer this time.

Armise sighed. "I do not think that conversation is as impossible as I once thought it would be." His eyes raked over me, from lips, to cheeks and back to my eyes. "There is little I would care to admit you have been right about, but this"—he clenched his jaw as he let go of my hand and grasped my hip, slowly and deliberately, with his synth—"this physical connection is us." He set his forehead against mine, his breath coasting across my lips. "Fuck me, Merq. Let me fuck you. Anything. I am here."

He had come to me when he was ready, so I had to trust that he didn't need anything more from me for the moment than exactly what he was telling me. I took his synth and guided his fingers under the edge of my shirt so he could touch the skin below. He bit at his bottom lip, brow creased in concentration.

"What does that feel like?" I asked.

"It is not the same. Much more sensitive. Much more...."

"Overwhelming?"

"Yes."

I took his left hand in mine and guided it under my shirt, my thumb grazing over the edges of the scars on his forearm. And we stood there, his stubble scratching at my cheek, his breath in my ear, his hands unmoving, locked to my side as if he was afraid to move.

I didn't want Armise to be afraid.

I rubbed my cheek against his, kissed up the line of his jaw until my lips were at his ear. "Think you could hold on to my hips while I fuck myself on you?"

S.A. MCAULEY

Then I drew back, cataloging his reaction, needing to see it all.

The corner of his lips tipped into a smirk. "I believe that would be considered rehab for the day."

I let go of his hand and circled my arm around his waist, lips finding his earlobe, nipping at it. He exhaled and the fingers of his synth curled in, pinching and digging to the point that I winced. He drew back, concentration pulling his jaw tight as he released me.

"I am going to hurt you, Merq. I cannot control it well enough yet."

"Nothing I can't handle. Nothing I don't want. Come on. Off with your clothes first, then mine."

He stepped back and I eased his shirt up so he could slip his left arm through and I could pull it over his head and off the other side without him needing to move his synth. I dipped my head down and took his nipple between my teeth as soon as his chest was bare, pulling at the nub and licking as Armise threaded his fingers through my hair. I held on to him with one hand while I used the other to unbutton his pants and push them to the floor. I kissed down his chest, dropped to my knees and buried my nose in the curl of hair at his groin, mouthing at the base of his shaft and licking up. Armise groaned and rocked into me. I was as hard as he was, and I needed to feel him, to fit myself over him so every part of us could touch. I reached between his legs, set the flat of my palm at the base of his spine and dragged my hand over his ass, just a hint of a touch at his hole, then grabbed on to his balls as I licked up him again. I was palming myself through my pants, my cock thick for him, and I reluctantly dragged my hands off him.

I unlaced his boots and there was a sharp inhalation from above me. I hadn't been allowed to touch him on the boat when we went through this ritual twice a day, but now....

He gripped my hair in a ferocious hold and pulled my head back so I was looking at him. His pupils were blown out, his dick was hard, and I waited for a dirty plea to fall from his lips, but instead he said, "Thank you, Merq."

I shook my head in disbelief. He had nothing to thank me for. "Get on the bed. Just the scent of you is going to make me come."

I stripped as fast as I could, yet gave him time to get situated however was most comfortable for him. He wasn't fucking breakable. He wasn't weak. But I wanted him to get just as much out of this as I was going to. I needed this first connection between us to be more than just another fuck.

I had to dig through my pack to find lube. It had been so long since Armise and I had done anything that I found the bottle buried at the bottom. I dug it out and tossed it on the bed next to Armise's left hand.

He shook his head and set it to the side. "Not yet. Let me lick you open."

I'd give him anything he wanted.

I kneeled on the bed and straddled him, facing his feet. I bent at the waist and swallowed his cock down as he bit into the flesh of my ass. He palmed my ass cheek and spread me open with his thumb and I had to pull myself off his cock from the intensity of the first touch of his tongue to my hole. He could barely lift his synth yet, he struggled to bend it at the elbow, but he curled his fingers around my knee and held me in place with that hand while he kept me wide open to him with his other. His tongue was hot against my hole and he fucked me with the tip, circled around the muscle as I rocked back into him. I sucked his cock in again and moaned, letting him hear and feel the vibrations from what he was doing to me. He spat, pushed a finger inside me, and I ground back then forward, taking him deeper into my mouth, both of us getting more heated, more frantic

S.A. MCAULEY

with each touch that had been too long coming. Neither of us could last long like this.

I slid my lips off his dick and looked over my shoulder at him. "Get me wet, open me just like that. Need it to take you. Fuck, it's been too long."

Armise finger fucked me, spread me wide, and slicked my hole. "Forgot how you taste. Makes me want more." He bucked into my mouth as I swallowed him again.

He dragged his fingers out of me and I turned to face him. His cock was slick with my spit, my hole with his, and I worked the tip of his cock in—with pressure, and pain, and the need for more—then stilled with him barely inside me. I lifted his right hand and placed it on my hip, keeping my hand over his as his jaw ticked and the fingers of his synth tightened with a painful bent into my skin. I would have bruises. Dark, circular patches where his fingertips were digging into me. That thought made me harder—Armise's marks on me again.

So much had changed, so much was different. But this undeniable attraction, this possessiveness—more shared than I'd ever understood before—was the same.

I bore down just as he was thrusting up, burying himself inside me. My breath caught with the rent of pain that followed, a sizzling wave of warmth closing in behind that, flowing through my blood and to every nerve in my body. I sat up and forced myself down again as he fucked into me over and over. I jacked myself as he hit me inside perfectly with each thrust, a sheen of sweat on his chest, his forehead and above his upper lip as he licked at his mouth, tasting what was left of me.

I clamped my eyes shut but I couldn't hold off anymore. I shot over my hand, onto him, and the only thing that kept me up was his steady hands on my hips—so much strength—holding me to him as he fucked into me and came with a rumbling moan.

I gasped for breath, the heat of the sun washing over my sensitive skin. Even before I could look at him I knew Armise's eyes were on me. I rotated my neck, set my hands on his forearms, and met his eyes.

There was only one thing I had to know. Had to ask. "Are you here for good or just for now?"

He licked his lips, seemed to be considering me. The grip of his hands on my hips relaxed and he slid them down to cup my ass. He was softening inside me, our sweat-soaked skin cooling. "My answer is the same as it has been since before the DCR."

I swallowed. "You love me."

It wasn't a question, but he answered anyway. "Yes."

"And some days you want to kill me."

The corner of his lips tipped up. "That as well."

I held on to him. Didn't want to let him go. I bit at the piercing on my lip and locked eyes with him. "I'm here for good too."

8

No matter how much I wanted to stay in bed with Armise, to sleep away the day because I finally felt as if I *could* sleep for days, I was leaving for the attack on the hybrid camp tomorrow. There were final details, weapons checks, and more fucking repetitive briefings I had to attend.

I left Armise in bed, his left forearm draped over his face and legs sprawled out, taking up so much of the space that I would've fought for room anyway. Instead I showered for the second time that day, surveyed the purple and crimson bruises spreading on my hips, and tried to steel myself for the battle to come.

For leaving Armise just when I'd gotten him back.

I dressed in a new Revolution uniform, that bright orange sunburst emblem like a target on my chest. At least the designers had placed it in a spot that would probably be nonfatal if a soldier was ever shot there. Armise stirred as I thumped the heel of my boot against the floor to settle it into the right spot. I began to strap my knives to my forearms and I looked up when I could feel his eyes on me.

"When do you leave?" he asked.

"Twelve hours."

He flopped onto his back and draped his arm over his face again, blocking out the sun. "Then I have more time to sleep."

"You don't have to see me off."

"I know how vengeance clouds a man's abilities and negates the most effective training. I will be with you until the point I cannot follow. Simply let me sleep first."

He'd slipped into speaking Mongol halfway through his statement and I didn't think he'd realized he'd made that shift. Armise was more tired than I'd ever seen him.

I walked over to him and lifted up his arm to look him in the eye—and annoy him a bit. "If you're not down in the next nine hours I'll send someone to wake you. But nine hours is all you get."

He opened one eye and glared at me. "I will need two."

"Take nine," I insisted and dropped his arm back into place.

* * *

"GENERAL, could I have a word with you?" I requested after our final briefing was completed and the room had begun to empty.

General Nissim was shorter than I, but not by much. She was slim, and had around a decade more years on me. She carried a weariness that I'd only been able to pick up because of what Simion had told me about her.

"Colonel Grayson," she addressed me and offered her hand. "I was surprised to see your name appear on the active duty roster. Thank you for taking lead on Ahriman Blanc."

"President Simion informed me that you have a personal connection to the camps."

The general hung her head as she nodded. "We all do. Ahriman was a man I helped train. I advocated for his rise through the ranks with the States. The hybrid camps are a crime against morality and basic fucking human decency. It's personal for all of us."

"Some of us in much more individual ways," I pressed her.

"My children weren't nomads or part of the jacquerie Underground. He targeted them because of who I am. But I'm here to focus on who we can save instead of those we've lost."

"I need you to know I don't have the same goal, General. My sole focus will be infiltrating his safe house and ensuring he doesn't emerge from it alive."

"Understood. That's why every other part of this operation has been hammered into the floor with a clear plan of attack for the soldiers—"

"Shit," I said out loud, cutting her off. "My apologies, General. What I said to President Simion was more of a reflection on me than you. I'm sorry that got back to you because it shouldn't have been said at all."

"Your apology will be accepted when Ahriman is dead. As for more important business, your path to him will be as clear as we can make it. President Simion instructed me that you were to be on your own once you cross a certain threshold."

"Those are conditions I've worked under before."

"However, operating without a team for something this critical is shortsighted and arrogant. Major Jegs and the two newest members of her team are waiting for you in the armory for their own briefing."

"Thank you, General."

She gave me a curt nod of acknowledgment and stalked away.

Well, at least Simion hadn't pulled me completely. Jegs I could work with. I left the briefing room and went to meet up with her to find out who the other two members of my team would be. There was no way I was letting control of this operation go to someone else.

I'd opened the door to the armory, my anger starting to take hold at the idea that I would have to learn how to work with two new people only hours before embarking for Moscow, when I saw Athol and Elina in Revolution uniforms, surveying a wall of guns with critical eyes.

Holly Jegs appeared next to me, already outfitted as well. "How much of the real story do I have about what happened to you and Armise?"

Even if Jegs had heard everything I'd told Simion, she was grossly uninformed. "Not a lot."

"Is me not knowing going to get me and the twins killed?"

I shrugged. "It might."

"But you're not going to tell me."

"There's always been things I didn't tell you. It's your choice if you decide to transport out with me. While I'm in this uniform, keeping you and my entire team breathing is my top priority. As it always has been."

"And once you're out of it, Armise becomes the top."

I stared at her. "Was that a joke?"

She scrunched her eyebrows together and stared at me for a second. "Not intentional, Colonel."

I faced away from her, tried to hide the smirk on my face. "Any chance someone was able to retrieve my rifle?"

She shook her head. "No idea where it is."

Which meant that Manny or Armise's aunt still had all our equipment. Either way it would be put to good use.

"How's Armise handling not heading off to battle with you?"

I cocked my head in the direction of Armise, who I'd spotted across the room sifting through pistol choices. It had been less than four hours since I'd left him in bed. My guess was that he'd stuck to his two-hour window of sleep and been down here since then. "Ask him yourself. He refused to let me leave without checking over my weapons first. Something about revenge and a lack of attention to details."

"He's right."

I couldn't deny it or make a sarcastic remark. "He is. It's been a long time since I led a black ops team. I'm going to rely on you to tell me if I make a call that's stupid, not just dangerous or risky."

"No problem there, Colonel."

I watched the twins amassing an arsenal on their bodies. Elina was yanking on the straps of a shoulder holster Athol wore, making sure it fit right while Athol nodded gravely to her. "Any issues with Athol and Elina that I need to know about?"

"They've taken to training faster than anyone I've ever worked with. They've got each other's backs first but, so far, have always stayed on mission. They are prone to violent outbursts."

I clapped Jegs on the shoulder. "They'll fit right in."

I'D NEVER BEEN a part of a mass troop movement via transport. The logistics of it were staggering. A cadre of fifty or more analysts was tasked with routing the simultaneous signals so that each battalion would arrive either in Moscow or on the main island of Singapore at the exact same second and no two people would land in exactly the same spot. The desert around the Revolution headquarters was a swarm of movement as everyone took their place, but there was little noise besides quiet conversations and the *thump-swish* of boots on sand. Presidents Simion and Kariabba Tivy stood at the floor-to-ceiling windows on the top floor of the headquarters watching the final arrangements, having already made their way through each group in the hours previous to wish them a good fight.

There were more faces that I didn't recognize than I did and the sea of black uniforms with that blaring Revolution seal on their chests swirled around me. Jegs, Athol, Elina, and I were off to the side of the fray—set apart since our destination wasn't one that any other soldier would be going to.

Armise stood next to me, the gray in his hair and stubble glinting in the sun. He wore a Revolution training uniform of a fitted shirt and loose pants and his feet were bare, the top edges of the tattoo of Manny's transport chip number peeking over his right instep.

"By the time I get back I expect you to have the shoe tying thing down," I goaded him, crossing my arms and waving a dismissive finger at his feet.

Armise grunted.

Neither one of us knew what to say. We'd fought against each other and with each other, but we'd never had one of us go into battle without the other. I felt off—wrong—leaving him, and just as suddenly realized why personal connections of any kind had been highly discouraged when I was deep undercover.

"Armise—" I started.

He cut me off with a gruff, "Don't."

I felt Armise's hand covering mine where I was holding on to the pistol at my hip and my hand stilled. I hadn't even realized I'd been clicking the safety of the gun on and off over and over again as we stood there.

"The safety stays off," he said and pulled his hand away.

The voice of General Nissim came over my comm, giving her troops a warning to be in place. There was one minute left until transport.

I turned my head to look at Armise and took in the stiff set of his shoulders, the grinding of his jaw and how he kept licking his lips as he stared at the scale of the massive operation unfolding in front of us. There was only one thing I had to say to

Armise before I left that could encapsulate everything I wanted to say that would have taken hours.

I tipped my chin up. "If I get the opportunity to tear him apart one vein and artery at a time then I will."

Armise kept his eyes trained on the other troops as he nodded his head up and down slowly. I wondered if he would say anything before I disappeared from his life for an unknown length of time, then Armise ran his hand over his stubble and looked at me.

"Don't be gone too long."

WE APPEARED in Moscow at the edge of a river, with tall swaths of switchgrass separating Jegs, Athol, Elina, and me from one another. I gritted my teeth through the aftershocks of the transport and forced my head to turn to make sure everyone else was okay. Athol and Elina were already closing in on my location—apparently not bothered one bit by the painful effects of transport—but Jegs was going through the same struggle I was.

The sounds of a firefight erupted in the distance, a cacophony that wouldn't let up until the camp had been destroyed and all the Opposition soldiers guarding it had been killed. I hoped for a quick, decisive win, but one that lasted at least long enough for the four of us to make it into Ahriman's underground hideaway without too much of a fight.

Athol and Elina had insisted on taking point because they were much harder to kill than either Jegs or me. I couldn't argue with their logic. Having them leading the way gave me a greater chance of being able to actually get my hands on Ahriman. He would still be shielded, so the only way I was going to kill him would be to physically rip him apart.

We followed the bank of the river north—away from the

battle—moving at a quick clip and keeping as low as we could. All of the surveillance systems in the abandoned city were disabled, as far as we knew, so it was a matter of taking us to the fight before Ahriman was even aware there was another threat against him than the one raging above his head.

"One thousand feet," I heard Elina say in my comm and I ticked off our progress step by step.

Athol dipped low, disappearing into the switchgrass, and seconds later I heard a pained cry that was abruptly aborted. Elina kept ticking off the remaining distance as Athol slid into his position next to her again.

We were close enough now that I saw the arch of broken stone leading to the stairs that dropped into the earth. I couldn't see any guards and there were no lights or movement coming from the cavernous opening.

The analysts had told us that at one time this had been the entrance to a mass transportation center, but it had been shut off from the rest of the city for at least a hundred years before Moscow had emptied out due to a massive earthquake that decimated the infrastructure. This part of the UU was still rocked by violent tremors. Ahriman's safe house wasn't remotely safe. But he hadn't left it in two months—since he'd transported out of the building where he'd held Armise and me.

We descended into the darkness with as much quiet and the least amount of light we could use without plummeting down the steep stairs. The walls were water-stained and cracked, and there were hints of paintings on the few smooth patches that remained. When we got to the bottom we crept past statues in various stages of disintegration. At one time, this had been a place of pride and artistic sanctuary.

Elina continued to count off the distance over the comm. The stone structure of Ahriman's safe house—built of crumbling blocks in a haphazard manner between high concrete walls—came into view.

We circled around the edge of the house and there was no sign of anyone being here. Had our intel been wrong?

The four of us took the steps warily, inching closer to the unsecured opening at the front that led us into a high-ceilinged room with rusted metal fans lazily spinning above our heads. I gave the signal for us to break apart and search the house. I slid to the left and Jegs to the right, Athol and Elina heading to the second floor overlook together.

I searched through each room I came to. Nothing. No one. There was evidence of someone recently living here—footsteps in the dust and fresh food in the kitchen. I met up with Jegs and the twins at the front and they confirmed that their parts of the house were the same.

"He had nowhere to flee," Elina said.

"He could have gone above ground," Athol pointed out. "But there are a hell of a lot of bullets flying around for him to pick any space out there that would be safe."

"You think there's any chance he transported and we didn't catch it?" Jegs asked.

"No, he's here," I replied. I kept my pistol in my hand with the safety off. Ahriman had pulled this same shadow act on me before, hiding in the abandoned PsychHAg building when I'd gone in to rescue my parents. He was waiting for just the right moment to appear.

The floor behind me creaked and I whipped around, pointing the gun at Ahriman's head. He was alone, hands raised in the air.

"I invoke the protections prescribed under section two hundred eight of the Consign Treaty and hereby surrender to your custody," he recited. A ghastly smirk pulled his features into arrogant angles intensified by the lack of direct light.

I holstered my pistol and unsheathed one of the knives on my forearm.

"Fuck the treaty," I snarled.

I barreled down on him, thrusting the knife deep into his belly. I could've sliced up. I could've gone for his heart. But I wasn't going to kill him so easily. He deserved to suffer—to be left screaming, and begging for death—before I finally granted him his place in hell.

Ahriman sucked in a surprised breath and circled his arms around his stomach, wheezing as he doubled over and began to laugh.

"What the fuck do you have to laugh about, you pathetic fuck?" I screamed at him.

"Did I forget"—he spat blood and winced, but the sneer never left his face—"did I forget to tell you that if I die the chip in Armise's brainstem explodes?"

My blood ran cold. "You're lying."

He released the grip on his stomach and his blood poured onto the floor. "Let me bleed out. We'll see what happens."

* * *

"ALL TRANSPORT SIGNALS are blocked until we have full control of the camp," the analyst said to me over the comm.

We were running for the place where all of us had transported in, Athol and Elina carrying Ahriman while I tried to maintain pressure on the wound. Blood didn't seep through my fingers, it gushed, and I knew we had minutes until Ahriman started losing consciousness, not the hours it would take for Revolution soldiers to D3 the camp and open up transport again.

"Fuck you," I spat out. "Patch me in to Neveed Niaz. Make sure he knows it's me calling. And don't give up contacting him until he picks up."

93

Jegs, leading us with her pistol drawn so we had some protection in case we ran into Opposition forces, looked over her shoulder at me. "Neveed? What the fuck is he going to be able to do for us?"

I shook my head and struggled to keep pressure on the gaping wound in Ahriman's stomach. "It isn't Neveed we need. It's Chen."

Jegs stumbled for a moment then continued forward. "She isn't dead."

"Not so much. Where the fuck is my connection?" I yelled into the comm at the analysts.

"We're attempting to connect...yes, sir, General Niaz. We have Colonel Merq Grayson on the comm.... Patching him in now."

"Get the fuck off my line," I said to the analyst. "I need this channel secured to only General Niaz and my team."

"Yes, sir," the analyst replied, and I let only a half-second of silence pass before I started speaking to Neveed.

"I need Chen on the line now. We're in Moscow with Ahriman. He's bleeding out and all transport signals are jammed for the op. I need her to get us back to the DCR now."

"Let that death-dealer finally meet his end, Merq," Neveed growled out on the other end of the comm.

I gave a dark laugh. "Can't. He says if he dies then he takes Armise with him."

"And the encryption chip," Neveed clarified.

"If that's what's going to make this happen then, yeah, save the fucking encryption chip. He dies, that goes too."

"You know that if Ahriman's that bad off he may not make it through the transport."

"I'm really fucking aware of that."

But we have no choice. There's no real choice.

"Chen's here, Merq. Already working on it."

"Neveed? I also need you to comm in Armise."

"Merq. He doesn't need to know what may be about to happen to him. He can't affect the outcome."

"Just get him on the fucking line."

Jegs came to a stop. "We're at the transport coordinates. Chen can lock on to my chip."

"I've got you," Chen said through the comm. "Working through the blocks now. Merq, I've got Armise on the line now too."

I swallowed. Froze for a moment while I tried to figure out what to say. "Armise. I need you to go to the medical facility right now. We're transporting in with Ahriman. He says if he dies that the chip inside you explodes...." *He's dying right now.* "Let the doctors know they have an incoming critical case."

Armise hummed. "And if he does not survive the transport they need to be prepared to put my head back together."

"If he's telling the truth. You getting us out of here, Chen?"

"It will only be a minute. Hang on.... Maybe two."

I stared down at Ahriman's belly. So much blood on my hands. Too much Darcan blood if Ahriman didn't survive this transport. "I'm sorry, Armise."

"At least you weren't gone long. I will see you here soon."

I fisted my hands in Ahriman's shirt, tightened the torn cloth strips around his torso and watched the bleeding continue.

"I'm through, Merq. You ready?"

No.

"Yes. See you in less than a minute, Darcan."

I closed my eyes, Ahriman's blood was warm beneath my fingers until that moment of nonexistence flashed through me and back out and my feet were on the ground in the DCR and Ahriman's heart skipped, sputtered, and the organ thudded to a stop under my hands.

9

"Stand back!"

"Out of the way!"

I was being pushed back from Ahriman's body, my hands shaking, blood running from my fingers to the floor as I tried to search through the chaos around me for Armise. Ahriman couldn't be dead. I hadn't killed Ahriman only for Armise to die. He couldn't be dead.

"We've got a heartbeat," I heard, and all sound rushed back to my ears as I spotted Armise standing in the doorway to the transport room. I was being jostled, pushed to the side as the medical team rushed Ahriman away, leaving my team, Armise, and me alone.

"He was dead," I said to no one. To all of them. To Armise. "I felt his heart stop."

Armise palmed the spot at the back of his neck where the encryption chip was. He grimaced as his eyes raked over me and I looked down, taking in the crimson coating my skin. My uniform stuck to me and I shuddered with the realization that I was covered in that psychopath's blood.

"One of you," Jegs growled from where she stood, head

swiveling between the two of us. "One of you tell us what the fuck just happened."

I sat down, hard, on the transport floor and set my forearms on my knees, watching the blood drip onto my boots as I tried to clear the static from my brain. I didn't know where to begin or how this would end. Ahriman could still be dying, there could still be a threat to Armise and he was right there but still too far away and too fucking at risk.

"We have to get that chip out of you," I said to Armise, ignoring Jegs' flare of anger.

Armise crossed the room to me, offered his hand to help me stand, and I reached up to take it then realized that would put Ahriman's blood in contact with Armise and I couldn't...I couldn't touch him like that. I flinched back, away from him.

Armise crouched in front of me, putting us eye to eye. "Not now."

I couldn't tell if his answer was meant for me or for Jegs.

"No," Jegs seethed, and came at Armise and me. "You owe us answers."

Armise's synth came up. His hand was the only barrier between her fury and us but it was enough to stop her cold.

"Not now," he repeated with a threatening depth of calm.

"Leave them," I heard Athol say and I looked up at Jegs.

Her face was contorted in rage, lips moving as if there were accusations running through her head that she wouldn't give voice to. I stared at her, all fight gone from me.

Jegs was pulled from the room at Elina's urging and Armise stayed where he was in front of me.

"He lied to you, Merq," Armise said when we were alone. "All of what he told us was likely a lie. This may not even be the encryption key inside me."

I shook my head. "I couldn't risk that."

97

Armise's features sharpened at that and I realized what I'd said could be taken two ways.

"I couldn't risk *you*," I clarified.

He held his hand out to me again. "Let's go clean his blood off of you."

I held my hand up and peered at it, my stomach rolling. I was so tired of all this blood.

I sighed and took his hand in mine, letting him help me to my feet. We stood in almost the exact same position as yesterday when he'd come back to me—with hands clasped together between us. I dropped my forehead to his and closed my eyes, breathing him in.

"We get this chip out of me and we go," he said.

I butted my nose against his, ran my cheek over his, his stubble grating against my shaved cheek, and circled my arm around him to pull him closer.

"I'm done," I replied. His hand tightened in mine.

He kissed my jaw, lips dragging against my neck as he answered, "*We* are done."

* * *

I DROPPED face first into the bed and buried my head in the pillow as I sprawled out naked across the sheets.

"Burn them," I heard Armise say to someone at the door. He must have been handing over the soaked remains of my Revolution uniform. There was a muffled voice from the hallway and Armise replied with a succinct 'thank you' before the door clicked shut.

"Ahriman will live," Armise said as he padded to his side of the bed and sank down next to me.

I draped my arm over his chest and tried to pull him closer but he didn't budge. Impenetrable. Immovable. This man next to me was a fucking mountain and I was the earth shaking at his feet. I slid my hand under his shirt, running my palms over his skin, and he obliged my urging, scooting closer so I could fit my leg between his and was half lying on top of him.

My eyes remained clamped shut, and I wanted to drift off to sleep to wear away just a piece of my exhaustion but I wouldn't be able to find any moments of respite today.

"What do we do next?" I mumbled against his chest.

Armise inhaled and my head moved with him. "I do not know."

"We can't disappear yet." That chip had to come out of Armise before we could make any kind of move.

"We will not be able to disappear at all," he said. "There is nowhere in the world we will not be found."

I thought of my great-grandfather's home in the Northern Territories and Kersch's assertion that no one else knew it existed. That place was our only chance at peace.

I set my chin on his chest. "There is. We free ourselves of every obligation holding us back and tying us down, and I know a place."

"Then that is what happens next." Armise set his right hand on my hip and peered down at me. "Simion told me you were implanted with a memory projector."

Fuck. I'd completely forgotten about that complication. "I don't know if it can be removed. Or if it even has to be for us to be free of surveillance."

"That is not why I brought it up."

I huffed and pushed myself up to sit next to him, rubbing at my eyes, an unconscious movement that I stopped when I realized what I was doing. I blinked. I couldn't feel anything in my eyes but that didn't mean it wasn't there.

"Then why?"

Armise pushed himself up against the headboard. "Show me what you remember from the months with Ahriman."

"No," I answered immediately. There were many memories I could have shown him but I knew exactly which one he wanted to access and I didn't want to relive that day.

"I need to see. I need to know what happened."

I gave a pointed look to his synth. "You know what happened."

"I know the aftermath, not the event."

"Event? Are you fucking with me? There's a lot of damn good reasons you were unconscious for most of it or your mind blocked your memories. It was horrific, Armise."

"It changed you."

I rested my hand on his synth, tracked my fingers over the line where his flame tattoos had been. "Those months—not just that day—changed both of us."

"Each day changes us, Merq."

"No," I insisted. "I won't do it and you shouldn't fucking ask me to."

"I have a right to ask things of you that I would of no one else."

"You do," I granted him. "But I don't want to revisit that day. I don't want to lose you to silence again. I can't go back to where I exist only when you want me to and as an inconsequential part of your life at that."

Armise stared me down. "How I lived for many years."

My anger rose. "That's now how it is anymore."

"How is it then?"

'*What am I to you?*' I remembered him asking me years ago in the dirt of the Underground outside the PsychHAg headquarters. I couldn't answer him then, but this time I could.

I ran my fingers through my hair and took a moment to think before I opened my mouth. "You—"

My chest ached. My fingers were going numb where I yanked at the hair on the nape of my neck. My tongue was dry and I swore I could feel the tattoo on my back.

I knew exactly who he was to me.

"You, Armise, are the only part of my life that matters."

Armise's eyes widened and he opened his mouth to speak, but I stopped him. If I didn't say it all, every thought that had been coalescing in my head for the last two months—or two years, or shit, maybe it was all of the fifteen years we'd been together—then I'd never get them out again.

I had to stop being afraid.

I scooted closer to him, dropping my knee onto his thigh. I needed that physical connection to him. "You're the only piece of my history that I regret massive parts of and yet would change nothing because we are here—alive and together. I feel sorrow I shouldn't because you make me wonder how things could have been different for us if we'd been born in another time, brought together under different circumstances.... You have changed me, Armise. I'm not a better person for having known you, neither of us is. You're an addiction, and an anchor, the balanced handle of a lethal knife. You are all of these dark and dangerous and threatening things and yet also their counterpoints at the same time—passion, stability, and protection. My life was irrevocably altered when I fell in step with you." I poked my finger into his chest just as he'd done to me in the tunnel of the Olympic stadium. "I can't, and won't, go on without you. That is how it is."

Armise dropped his chin and looked up at me. All desire, and want and...*fuck*. Happiness. Armise fucking Darcan was smiling. "You use my words against me."

"You asked and I answered. I don't want to show you that day because experiencing it again will only enrage us, give parts of us over to Ahriman that he doesn't own." I shook my head. "No —parts of us that we've had to fight to get back. He's alive but we can be free of him now. You once let go of vengeance for me, you can teach me how to do the same for Ahriman."

"It is not the same."

I scoffed. "I hope to fuck not."

"Then show me something else."

I got off the bed. "I don't even know how the fuck this thing works. If it works." I slid my thumb over the spot in my hand that I thought was the way to activate the projector, curiosity lighting me up. "Like what?"

Armise shrugged with one shoulder, but already I could see the right one beginning to respond to his command. He set his left forearm behind his head and crossed his feet. "Pick one."

"A good one or a bad one?"

He huffed. "One, Merq."

I closed my eyes and my thoughts immediately returned to the Olympics. Where and when everything had changed for Armise and me. The night he had come to me before the Opening Ceremonies.

I closed my eyes and pressed the button that sat in-between the vee of bones beneath my thumb and heard the same crack as when Grimshaw had activated his. My eyes themselves didn't feel any different, but there was a contrasting lightness and darkness on my eyelids that I'd never experienced. Like a vision of sun pouring through a window before you've fully woken, but as if that sun were inside my head.

I turned away from where Armise was sitting and opened my eyes. All I could see was darkness. I took a breath, waited for something else to happen, then clamped my eyes shut. What if the lenses hadn't fused right and I'd just damaged my vision?

"That was the night before the rifle competition," Armise said in a low voice.

I kept my eyes closed but turned toward him. "You could see that? Everything was black for me."

"I was standing in a hallway in my Singaporean training uniform. It was me," he chuckled. "But not the way I see myself in a mirror."

"The way I see you." I opened my eyes again and showed him what I was thinking. "I watched an electrical storm rolling in over the capital as you slept next to me—"

"Tried to sleep," he interrupted gruffly.

I couldn't see anything from my eyes, but that night was so clear in my head. "There were these marks your fingernails had left on the headboard and I remember looking at those and thinking they would last longer than either of us. Me for sure because I was dying that next day."

He huffed. "Always so melodramatic."

I flipped him off and he chuckled. "You forced me down, made me sleep. And I did it because I thought it was the last night I'd ever spend with you. We've had too many of those nights by now, Armise. I don't want to have another."

He was quiet for a moment, then, "Same."

I swallowed, tried to keep my eyes open so he could see it all. "You were gone when I woke up. Then I saw you on the range and in the tunnel.... So violent and yet so human. I'd already gone past the moment of you becoming more to me, but I didn't understand that then. I do now. The way I see you, Armise, this memory projector can never show that for real. It's everything— your voice, the way you carry yourself, your strength, and your intelligence. Fuck, the way you smell, the way you touch me...."

I clicked the button in my hand, blinked, and looked to him.

He was still on the bed but he was leaning forward, watching me with a clarity and intensity to his gaze I'd never seen before. His lips were parted as if there were words on his tongue that he wanted to say.

I knew what those three words were.

But I didn't need to hear them, I already knew.

"You are so much more than I ever saw back then, Armise. But I see it all now."

* * *

I WAS SITTING at the desk watching a newsfeed on the BC5 when there was a knock on the door. Armise sat on the edge of the bed, his back ramrod straight, as he focused on figuring out how to make his synth move. He and I looked to each other then to the door at the noise. It was well past sundown. Well past when anyone would be coming to us for normal business, but the knock lacked the urgency of a crisis.

"I will get it," Armise said. He was tentative for a second then the door was opening wide and Exley was walking in, followed by Simion pushing a cart into the room. Simion clapped Armise on the back as he walked by and stopped the cart in front of the table.

I pushed myself up and wiped at my eyes. There wasn't any lingering discomfort from using the memory projector earlier in the night as far as I could tell, but what I was seeing didn't make sense.

"What the hell is this?"

"Food and booze," Exley said as he dropped onto the padded bench that ran the length of the window. "It's been a helluva day. Thought you two could use this as much as we could."

"Know you two don't usually drink but if there's any time to start it's now," Simion added, filling a glass.

"What do you hear from the two fronts?" I asked and took the glass Simion offered me. "They D3 the camp yet?"

"It's gone," Simion confirmed. He produced more glasses from the cart and handed them over to Exley and Armise before filling his own. "Combat in Singapore is still happening but that's a matter of time more than the fight left in them. The news that Ahriman is in custody was a direct hit to the motivation of the Opposition troops."

"How the hell did you even get that news through?" Armise asked.

"Premiere Pearce," Simion explained.

I'd jumped to that conclusion immediately because of the conversation I'd had with Exley in the galley. Armise had been rehabbing with Simion for a week so he should have known the same things I did. But maybe they didn't talk business.... So what the hell did they talk about in those sessions?

I pushed the thought away and tipped my drink back before looking to Exley. "So if things went so well what are the two of you doing here?"

Exley counted out each point on his fingers. "We have the leader of the Opposition in a holding cell instead of dead. A child prodigy who is supposed to be dead and is a hybrid in hiding instead...."

"And an ex-Opposition officer who may have the key to freeing the world's knowledge implanted in his neck," Simion finished.

"It may be a mere three things," Exley continued, "but those three all have the potential to be world-shifting."

I held up my glass, most of which I'd downed as they'd talked. "I'm going to need a lot of this tonight, aren't I?"

Simion shook his head and started unloading plates from the cart onto the table. "We're not going to talk about any of those items. We're here to eat and drink and straddle that line of fucked-up and happy where you wake up the next morning fuzzy-headed but fine." Simion gave a stern look in Armise's direction. "In short, the only rule is no more war talk."

Armise smirked. "Yes, Pres. No war talk."

"Is that one of your rehab rules?" I ventured.

Simion and Armise traded a look that was all camaraderie and conspiracy and Armise answered, "Yes."

I scowled at his non-answer. "Which means that either it's the only rule the two of you have in rehab or that there's at least two rules, maybe more, and you don't want me to ask what the others are."

"He's getting good at reading you," Simion said to Armise, smiling over the lip of his glass.

"He has always been good at it. I just never gave him enough feedback or answers either way to let him know that."

Exley guffawed as he looked at me. "You realize how dangerous you encouraging this relationship is, right?"

A knock came at the door and the room went quiet.

"Shit," Simion mumbled. "I told my guards to leave us the fuck alone unless the world was exploding around us."

I set down my glass and strode for the door, opening it to find Jegs with a monster-sized bottle of thick green liquid in her hand. "I'm here to make amends for losing my shit earlier. Room for one more?"

I smiled and stepped back to invite her in. "Always."

Jegs set her bottle on the table in front of Simion's outstretched hand, made her rounds to say hello, and dropped onto the end of the bed next to Armise.

"Is that Somali?" Armise asked her.

"Your favorite. Figured we may as well do it up the right way before all of us leave here."

Simion poured her and Armise a tiny amount out of the huge bottle and I took note to steer clear of that stuff. Whether she was being sarcastic or not about it being Armise's favorite, if this was a drink that Jegs and Armise could only handle in small amounts then I needed to avoid it all costs or risk not getting out of bed tomorrow.

"No twins?" I asked Jegs as I sat down again at the desk and took a healthy swig from my refilled glass, a satisfying burn lighting up my insides.

She had a half-smile on her face that was more casual than anything I'd ever seen on her. "They're too innocent to handle this crew."

"Come on," Exley said, getting to his feet and going to the cart. "Eat up too. Don't need a crew of slag-offs tomorrow morning because your stomachs are empty. And no excuses on this meal, Merq. I made all this myself."

"Fuck yes," I hissed in contentment and swiped a plate off the cart.

"So, Darcan," Jegs began, her eyebrow tipping up. "Merq giving you enough opportunities to work out that new hand?"

I choked on the food in my mouth and Simion and Exley lost it laughing while Jegs knocked her shoulder against a scowling Armise.

By the time they left our room hours later, Simion was draped over Exley while Jegs—stoic despite the impressive dent she'd made in that bottle of Somali liquor—propped up Simion's other side since Sims was too bleary-eyed to make his synth work right.

I pushed the cart into the hall for someone to clear out the leftovers of their impromptu invasion of Armise's and my space. And when I closed the door behind me, a pleasant quiet enveloping me, I found Armise lying on the bed, pants pulled over his hips, palming himself with his synth as he watched me.

"Time for more rehab," I said.

I pulled my shirt off and crossed the room to him.

10

I was first to fall asleep that night. As I slid into unconsciousness I felt Armise awake next to me but I couldn't fight the draw to close my eyes. My dreams were a jumbled mass of confusion. Images I couldn't place, emotions I couldn't grasp on to. I was fevered, hot, then suddenly just as cold, shaking, begging for unseen help. Then Armise's voice—low and calm—came to me, urging me to wakefulness.

Our room was dark despite the window not being covered. It was the middle of the night and I was slick with sweat but not the sheen I'd had on my skin last night after Armise and I had gotten each other off.

"What time is it?" I asked, because I knew he was awake. I heard the echoes of his voice in my head and that had been real enough to grasp onto and draw myself out of my nightmares.

He shifted next to me. "Late. Or early."

"Why aren't you sleeping?"

"You."

I flipped onto my back and stared at the ceiling. "I'm sorry. I'm unsettled after yesterday. It followed me into sleep."

"No, Merq. Not that. You are always a restless sleeper. I have become accustomed to your patterns. It is what usually drives me out of bed before the sun."

I didn't know that. Of course I'd never really had a bed partner long enough before Armise for anyone to have time to identify a pattern. Armise knew things about me no one else did.

"Then what about me is keeping you awake? Besides all the usual."

Armise didn't chuckle at that and I realized I'd become used to his response to my inborn sarcasm. There was a heaviness to the silence that followed.

"What?" I pressed.

"We received a message last night from Simion after you feel asleep. He wants us to interrogate Ahriman."

"And that's what's keeping you awake? Fuck him. He's not worth the lack of sleep."

He flipped on the light and sat up. "There is something you need to know before we see him."

I covered my eyes to keep out the light. "We don't have to do anything Simion asks."

"We will do this and you know it."

We would. Simion had known that when he made the request. I turned on my side and faced him. I'd already asked this question three times and he hadn't hesitated like this to answer me—or outright deny me an answer—in a longer time than I could remember. My heartbeat kicked up. "What is it, Armise?"

"Ahriman knows something about you he will likely try to use against you. You did not break with him and he wants to see you shattered. He is at the end of his fall and now is the time he becomes desperate."

I rubbed my eyes. "And you know what it is too."

He nodded.

It took me a moment to piece together what he could be

insinuating, then it hit me. "This is the thing you said I didn't need to know yet. When we were in Grimshaw's camp."

"It is."

I laid my palm on Armise's chest and left it there. He gripped my wrist, holding tight.

"I'm not going to sleep any more tonight, am I?"

He ran his thumb over the inside of my wrist and kept his eyes locked to me as he shook his head. "Priyessa was correct that you and I, and many of our contemporaries, are the product of the Anubis project. But what she neglected to tell you, or that she may not know if she did legitimately leave the project, is that you hold a unique place in the first generation genetmod proto-types. You are not genetmod at all, Merq. You are the control."

My blood thundered in my ears. "I'm what?"

"You have no genetic modifications."

I pushed up and Armise held tight to my wrist, grounding me as the room spun around me. My blood went cold, an uncomfortable chill that started in my chest and spread through my veins until I was shivering. I stared at Armise and he held on to me, amped up his temp and gripped me tighter, holding me together.

Dr. Casas insisting he'd never put anything inside me.... The months I'd spent in recovery after the DCR and the attack on the bunker.... Wensen saying he'd asked too much of me.... Ahriman joking that I was the son his father had wanted.... Dr. Blanc, who knew everything about me and wanted to end genetic modification....

Then there was Priyessa. Abiding by decades-old orders that no permanent damage could be done to me.... Because I didn't have any of the genetic modifications to speed my recovery.

Because I was the control of an experiment and they couldn't harm their product.

Shit.

I sucked in a breath. "Simion told Priyessa her original orders stood—that she wasn't allowed to do permanent damage to me. Does he know?"

"I do not have an answer to that."

I stared at Armise, searching him for a reason to believe this wasn't real. Because—just as he had warned me—it changed everything about how I viewed myself.

I dug my fingernails into his chest then tried to pull away from Armise, but he held on. Maintained the physical connection between us.

"You're sure?"

"I am. Your parents agreed for you to be a part of the trials when she was pregnant with you, but you were never given any genetmods. Only those at the highest levels of the project knew that you would be raised with the same training and the same access to teachers and doctors. But your role was always to give them a baseline to understand how much of their success was the modifications and how much was environment."

My parents had gone to their grave believing I was a man I wasn't.

"And you are—?"

"Heavily modified."

I winced.

I wasn't impenetrable or unstoppable. I would never be stronger than Armise, no matter how hard I tried. That I was faster than him was a fluke—a genetic advantage that could be usurped with one shot of the right nanos into his body. Then I remembered Armise yelling at me in the Singapore safe house that I never would've been able to survive the trauma he'd been through....

"I'm not your equal."

Armise grimaced. "Fuck you. You are not because you are stronger than I will ever be."

"Armise—"

His features went hard in an instant. Angry. "No human being should have survived the physical toll you have wrought on your body. No person would be sane after experiencing what you have. You have driven yourself hard, to the point of breaking, over and over again for years. No, decades."

"You've done the same," I argued.

"In a way, yes. But I was programmed to survive. You were not. And yet, you did."

I circled my fingers around his wrist. Ran the tips over the lines of his flame tattoos and the scars underneath. "Who else is modified? As a part of Anubis?"

"Holly Jegs, Neveed Niaz, and Ricor Simion on our side. Ahriman. Maniel was even before his transformation into a second generation hybrid. There's less than a handful of others that exist on either side, or no side at all. And you know as well as I do that genetmods have gone public on a larger scale, but not as a part of Anubis. Our food supply is modified. Your DNA was chosen for the second gen because you didn't need modification in order to keep up with, and surpass, other first gens with your abilities."

I took a deep breath. "Grimshaw Jegs isn't?"

"He was never part of the project. But that's the reason he's the only other person who has a memory projector besides you. Genetmod eyes will expel the device as if it's a wound to be repaired."

I quieted. I paid active attention to the beating of my heart and the warmth of my skin against Armise's. My blood was different than his. My body. Everything I'd thought I knew about myself was wrong.

Armise had known that and yet nothing about his decision to be with me had changed.

I gritted my teeth and steeled myself for what Armise and I

would face—together—in the morning. "Ahriman would've used this against me."

"He cannot now. Despite not having mods, you are psychologically stronger than him."

No. I was stronger because of Armise.

"Who else knows about this?" I asked.

"I cannot answer that definitively. It was Dr. Blanc's BC5 I discovered this information from. I do not know if your parents ever discovered the truth or whether President Kersch did, but from what Priyessa told you I suspect he did. His wife Sarai.... I didn't know she was involved at all until you told me."

"Is there more?"

Armise gave a low chuckle. "Is that not enough?"

He released my wrist, laying my palm on his chest and covering my hand with his.

We were so alike, and yet so different. Knowing that, he'd chosen to stay with me, to fight with me and for me.

That was the only thing that mattered.

"I've had my world upended more times than I ever could have anticipated. I've survived each time. I'll survive this too."

* * *

"WE'VE CLEARED him as much as we can, but he's still shielded," Feliu informed Armise and me outside Ahriman's holding cell. "Allow me to clarify that. He has the shield chip like the hybrids —the one that protects from sonic and real bullets—but this shield is on top of that. Same type of thing I saw with Armise when we scanned him."

Armise frowned. "I believe it is a long-acting injection into the bloodstream. I do not know how to get around it. From what I know it fades with time. I do not know enough to guide you on how to counteract it, just what I was able to glean from Dr. Calum Blanc's records."

Feliu nodded as he took that information in. "That's helpful but not right now. Just want you to know you need to keep on guard because we don't know what he could be hiding, if anything."

I scoffed. As if we would be anything less than on guard when it came to Ahriman. Because of what Armise had told me last night, Ahriman wouldn't manipulate me again. Everything he'd told me so far had turned out to be a lie. I wouldn't hesitate to slice his heart out if he threatened Armise again.

"You mention Dr. Blanc," Feliu said. "Do you have copies of those records, by chance? Those would be helpful too. Especially with my research on how to safely remove yours and the hybrids' shielding chips."

"I do not."

I bit down on my lip piercing. "I'm sure he has them stashed somewhere where we'll never get to them again."

Feliu's eye widened. "He's alive?"

"Unfortunately. Let's get this over with, Armise."

Armise nodded to me and a guard opened the door for us to enter. Armise and I were both outfitted in our Revolution uniforms as a blatant show of solidarity. If Ahriman wanted to wage psychological warfare then details like that mattered in how we approached him.

Ahriman was strapped to a chair when we walked inside. The chair he'd held Armise in when he took his arm. As much as I despised transport, it was supremely useful at times.

There were cameras in each corner of the room, recording Ahriman's every movement and word. The feed was being monitored by Simion and Exley where they waited in Simion's office, but only the five of us would know what happened in this room unless Simion decided to bring anyone else into it.

Ahriman's chin was tipped up, black eyes trained on us as we approached him. He remained silent and still in his restraints. His skin was a waxy yellow in tone. The doctors had done just enough for him to recover from the gutting I'd given him yet not fed him enough surge to thrive. He was in pain and uncomfortable, and that satisfied me.

Armise stopped at Ahriman's side and used his left hand to roll up the sleeve of his uniform over his synth. Ahriman watched the movement with a smirk that was wiped away when Armise was able to repeat the same motion with his synthetic hand to roll up his other sleeve.

It was a complex movement that shouldn't have been possible this early in Armise's recovery, and by Ahriman's response he knew that too. But nothing of how resilient Armise was surprised me anymore.

Armise kept quiet as he moved behind Ahriman to a spot where Ahriman wouldn't be able to see him and I stood in front of him. I gave Armise a clipped nod.

Armise pulled a strap out, circled it around Ahriman's neck and pulled it taut, restricting Ahriman's supply of air, but not enough for him to lose consciousness.

I smiled. "That is fun," I said to Ahriman, echoing his words back to him. "An answer for a chance to breathe. You ready to play?"

Ahriman made a strangled noise as his face started to turn red. He wouldn't be able to answer anything with how tightly Armise was squeezing his neck, but that wasn't the point.

"Do you know where your father is?"

Ahriman's hands shook and his fingers curled into his palms as his body went taut.

I quirked my pierced eyebrow. "No? Well, I guess we'll have to skip that breath. How about this one? Have you heard that

Shio Pearce gave you up and that Opposition troops are surrendering across the globe?"

Ahriman's face was turning an oxygen-starved shade of purple as his lips opened and his tongue jutted out, drool dripping from the edge of his mouth.

I set my hands on his forearms, pressing down, and put myself inches away from his face. "How does it feel to be completely powerless? Impotent."

Ahriman gnashed his teeth together and I looked up to Armise, who let the strap go slack. Ahriman huffed in a huge breath. He coughed, his entire body tensing, and started to wheeze. It was only after a couple of seconds had passed that I realized the sound Ahriman was making was laughter—a grating sound aggravated by the damage that had been done to his windpipe.

"I won't make it out of here alive so you may as well kill me now."

I tsked. "Now where would the fun be in that?"

Armise circled around the chair and came to stand next to me. "You will make it out of here alive. We want you to see your empire fall."

I sneered. "You're done manipulating your way to a fucked-up agenda of sole control. There's no one left in power for you to manipulate. All of the five leaders signed a treaty this morning ending the Borders War and agreeing to a plan for reformation of geographic boundaries. PsychHAg Tiam is all but dead. Irreparable. We've seen the recordings of what you and Tiam did to President Kersch. You won't have anyone at that level you can use like that again."

Ahriman's pupils widened, dilating from fear, as his fists clenched. I let go of him and stepped back, thrown by a reaction I hadn't expected from him.

"You don't know what you're talking about," Ahriman answered, his voice wavering.

I looked to Armise and he was transfixed on Ahriman, his focus set, picking up the same discord I had.

Armise caught my eyes. "He did not know the recordings existed."

"You didn't okay those transmissions, did you?"

Ahriman's features went blank. "I don't fear you."

"Because there's someone else you fear more. Your father said the same thing to me. It's him, isn't it? You're afraid of your own father."

Ahriman's neck went tight as he gritted his teeth.

"No," Armise said. "It's someone else."

Someone else? Franx Heseltine was a bumbling opportunist who chased the prevailing winds to maintain his power. Shio Pearce was only in his position because the more competent, and wicked, former premiere and leader of the Opposition had been assassinated by me. Kariabba Tivy was steadfast in the Revolutionary movement and Isida Agri had been the first of the leaders to break open the power structure of the AmFed and call for jurisdictional voting rights.

Then there was Ricor Simion. A man I'd known most of my life. A man whom I trusted my life with.

No. It couldn't be him.

But who the hell else was there?

Ahriman was attempting to shake my foundations even as he was the one tied to a chair, and I was letting him. He was the one left with nothing. But just as Athol had asked, was he stronger than us because he had nothing to lose?

"There's no one else," I said, a calm settling inside me. "Ahriman wanted to be the only one in control and now he isn't. He never will be. There is no one else trying to eradicate a fair chance at life besides him. His father turned his back on him because he was weak. He's not the son Calum Blanc wanted or deserved, and he never will be."

"Did he tell you?" Ahriman asked in such a low growl I could barely hear him. I turned toward him again. Ahriman's features sharpened and he glanced at Armise. "Did he tell you what you are?"

Armise barked out a laugh next to me. "You go right ahead. Tell Merq what you think he does not know. What you think I am hiding from him."

"Yes, tell us some more lies. Armise already told me I'm not genetically modified and that my role in Anubis was always as the control in that fucked-up experiment."

Ahriman's smile widened, he huffed out a laugh and I steadied myself in front of him, hands tightening around his forearms, restraining the urge to rip his throat out so I wouldn't have to hear one more lie from him ever again.

I was inches away from his face. Those soulless eyes no longer unsettled me. "There's nothing you can say or do to me that I won't survive."

Ahriman was biting down on his lip so hard that blood pooled under his teeth but his empty eyes remained transfixed on me. "That's where you're wrong, Merq. You're not just the control. You're the first generation of the kill switch."

He spat in my face and I punched him then reeled back, swiping at my eyes. When I opened them again, only a heartbeat later, Ahriman was convulsing, eyes rolling into his head as his skin broke open around his mouth, then up his cheek, tears rending down his neck.

"What the fuck—" I began to say and turned to Armise but my eyes began to burn, water, and a heat rushed through my veins that was wrong. I reached out for him.

"Merq—" Armise took one step toward me, grasped on to my wrist, then let go when he collapsed to the floor.

Kill switch.

It couldn't be true.

I stumbled for the door, ripped it open. I couldn't see but I had to get out of that room and away from Armise.

I closed my eyes against the uncontrollable burning and pushed forward, trying to get as far away as I could. There were hands grasping me, holding me back, and I screamed at them to let me go. There was only one way for me to save Armise. "Get me into isolation now!"

Ahriman had chosen this exact moment to finally give me a truth I couldn't deny.

Ahriman was genetically modified.

So was Armise.

And I was their kill switch.

11

"Is he still alive?" I asked as Feliu drew another vial of blood from me. My eyes were covered in a damp cloth, and the burn had subsided. But my body.... I felt the change in me in every movement, every heartbeat. Every breath.

"Yes," Feliu answered immediately. "We've got him isolated as well. We're pumping him full of a surge that will boost his immune response and help his body fight this until we know what it is. He's in a medically induced coma until we know the severity of what's inside him."

I sucked in a shaky breath. "He'll survive."

I had to believe that. There was no other option.

If Armise had lived and Ahriman had died within seconds then I had hope he would pull through this. He and I would take off as soon as we figured out what Ahriman had done to us. Ahriman hadn't been able to stop us before and he wouldn't now. Our path had been set before today, but now there was no wavering from it. No more bodily harm. No last assignments. No loyalty owed to anyone else.

We deserved to find peace.

Feliu cleared his throat. "You seem sure of that."

I fought back the bile building in my throat and willed myself to believe there was hope. "I am."

I peeled the wet cloth off my eyes and blinked, the room coming into focus. "How can you be in here with me?"

"It became clear pretty fast that this...whatever this is—was solely affecting people with genetic modifications. I don't have any."

I glared at him. "And neither do I."

"I always told you that."

I scoffed. "Very sure you didn't. Not clearly at least."

"I couldn't. It would have gone against the experimentation protocol set up by President Kersch."

So Kersch had known.

I sighed and slumped forward, setting my elbows on my knees and clenching my fists. My muscles were sore. My skin hot, then cold. "What the hell is it, Feliu? What did Ahriman do to me?"

Feliu set one needle down on a tray next to me and picked up another. "He's dead, by the way."

"Good. I don't give a fuck. I care what the fuck this is."

"We don't know. But I'm guessing it's a virus."

I stilled. "A virus?"

"What is it, Mig?"

That was Simion's voice. I whipped my head around. He couldn't be here. Couldn't be in this room since he was genet-mod. And I was his kill switch.

Feliu pulled the second needle from my arm and pointed to the camera in the corner. "If you're hearing voices it's probably President Simion. We attached your comm strap so you can communicate with him and anyone else who can't be in the room with you. Give me one more minute and I'll leave you two to talk."

"Let me know when you wake him up," I said to Feliu.

"Okay." The doctor finished packing up his supplies and cleaning up then exited the room, sealing me inside.

I stared up at the camera. "Anyone else on this channel?"

"Just me," Simion answered in my ear. "Exley's on his way down though. He can be there with you."

"You sure about that?"

"I wouldn't be sending him otherwise."

The door opened with a *whoosh* and Exley entered with a metal plate covered in a dome in his hands. He took a deep breath, then a second one, and crooked an eyebrow as he looked up at the camera. "Told you."

He dropped the plate on the end of the bed. He patted my chest, shook his head as he gave me a thin smile, then jumped up to sit next to me.

"You brought me food?" I said to him, staring at the covered plate.

He shook his head. "You were right. Food can't fix all. Maybe science can though. I brought my own stuff to run some tests."

"No offense, Ex. But isn't that a bit more complicated than making sure the rice doesn't stick to the pot?"

Simion huffed on the other end of my comm. "Well at least we know whatever Ahriman did didn't fuck with his stellar personality."

Exley outright smiled at that and reached for his equipment. "My passion is food but I studied medicine at the urging of President Kersch."

I snapped my head around. "And Sarai, the virologist."

He nodded. "Now you're getting it. Not many people knew her at all. Kersch was such a dominant force that she was overshadowed. She saw something in me and encouraged it. Kersch made sure I was taught by the best after she died."

"You mean after she was kidnapped," Simion said. "She only died the one time."

My stomach knotted as I realized that if Dr. Blanc had restarted Anubis with Sarai—if they had complementary but different knowledge and specialties—then he would have needed her alive. It was unlikely he would have allowed Ahriman to kill his partner when a virus that killed genetmods was his ultimate goal.

"Is Sarai Kersch really dead?"

Exley cringed. "You watched her get her head blown off, Merq."

"That's not an answer anymore," I pressed. "If it was then we wouldn't have Chen."

I was met with silence.

I looked up at the camera. "You still there, Sims?"

"I think he's gone," Exley said. He motioned for me to extend my arm.

I furrowed my brow. "What the fuck?"

Exley grabbed hold of my wrist and yanked me forward. His features had gone hard as he whispered, "You've put him in a shit place by not telling him everything that happened. If he's going to be able to protect you at all then be careful what you say to him that could be overheard."

I blanched and gave him a nod of understanding.

"Now." He raised his voice to normal. "I need to take more blood and some skin scrapings."

"What do you think you'll be able to tell me that Feliu won't?"

"I assisted Sarai when she was working on synthetic proteins. I may be able to tell if this virus is one of hers or, at the least, if it originated from her work."

"How bad are we talking here, Ex?"

He seemed to be weighing his answer. "If it is a virus then we need to figure out how it transmits, how virulent it is, if you're under threat at all, or a threat to any other non-genetmods, if you can transmit to other non-genetmods and make them carriers, if there's treatment, or a cure, or an inoculation—"

I clenched my fist, slowing the flow of blood into his needle so he would stop talking and look at me. "In other words, it's bad."

"Chin up, Merq. There's a lot we don't know and it's going to take time to figure that out."

I took that all in. It didn't matter how long it took Armise to wake up, it would be longer than a couple of days before I would see him again. Even longer before I could be in the same room with him.

"And for however long that takes, I'm stuck in here."

Exley pursed his lips and nodded, but when he caught eyes with me.... His back was to the camera, where it wouldn't be able to see his face. He whispered again. "We'll see what we can do for you, Merq."

IT HAD BEEN a little over seven days, as far as I could tell, which was hard to do in a windowless room. But I'd eaten a few meals and slept a handful of times. My internal clock had rarely been off.

"You're much calmer than I expected you to be about all of this," Feliu said.

I tightened my fingers around the edge of the examination table that had been brought in to make their tests easier.

"You don't know me well."

I wasn't calm. At all. Each day I was trapped in here, my frustration and need to move—to do something, anything—ramped up exponentially. I wasn't good at being solitary with my thoughts and that was all I'd had for a week. I was a prisoner for all intents and purposes. A prisoner of Ahriman when the bastard was dead.

"I want to see Armise," I said to Feliu and to the camera. To anyone who would fucking listen. I was losing patience.

"You know we can't let you out of this room yet."

I slammed my palm against the table and Feliu jumped away from me. "Get me a BC5 and a link to him. Now."

Immediately the door to my room opened and Exley entered with a Revolution soldier standing behind him with a gun drawn.

I narrowed my eyes and stared at them. Each day Exley had come to see me—to gather more blood or skin scrapings from inside my mouth, taking more and more of my DNA away with each trip that he and Feliu made outside this cell. And each time they spoke less and less to me. I hadn't heard from Simion in over a day now. There was a lot happening outside of that door that I wasn't privy to—including Armise's status. And I couldn't deal with the silence anymore.

"Tell me what's going on," I growled to Exley. "If Armise is dead just tell me now."

Feliu backed farther away from me.

"He's awake, Merq," Exley said as he inched closer to me with his palms raised.

I jumped off the table and stalked toward Exley. "So why the fuck haven't I been able to talk to him yet?"

The soldier trained his gun at my head but Exley pushed the barrel down.

"There's something we need you to understand before that can happen. You haven't transmitted the virus to me or to Feliu but this virus isn't behaving normally. Every vial of blood we've taken from you, the virus is slightly changed. We don't know if it's maturing or mutating, but it's different every time."

I didn't understand what that meant for my chances of

getting out of this room. For my future. For Armise and me. "What are you telling me? And be really fucking clear this time."

Exley backed away from me, the guard remaining at his side, and I knew whatever came out of Exley's mouth next was going to be bad.

"Unless we're able to find a way to kill the virus or negate its effects, you will never be able to be in close proximity with anyone genetmod ever again. And that includes Armise."

I slumped over, my legs going cold, then weak. I sat on my haunches and ran my hands over my head.

That couldn't be true.

"There has to be a cure," I whispered.

There was the sound of movement then Exley crouched next to me. "We can't cure what we can't identify. As far as we can tell, you'll be a carrier of this virus until you die."

Death or permanent separation.

They were telling me those were my only two choices.

I snapped. "Get the fuck out of here. Everyone! Out of my fucking ear, out of my face. You'll get nothing else from me until I talk to Armise."

Exley looked to the camera, at who I had to assume was Simion on the other side of it, but I didn't hear any kind of reply through my comm.

When Exley turned back to me his face was stricken. There was no other word I could put to it.

I didn't give a fuck how bad he felt. He could walk out of this room. He could see Armise. Talk to him face to face. Touch him.

And I never would again.

Exley said my name, but I couldn't look at him.

"I'll see what I can do, Merq."

* * *

I WAS LEFT ALONE for two more days. Two days in which I railed at Simion through that camera, throwing names and accusations at him that made me sick instead of ebbing my rage.

When Exley came to me again I was sitting with my back to the wall, facing the door, my throat raw from screaming.

"I'm here so you can talk to Armise," was the first thing he said to me. It was a peace offering that was too small a gesture and yet all I needed to hear.

I waved him in.

He sat down next to me and raised a BC5 screen from his wrist, settling his arm on my knee so both of us could see it.

"Armise."

I released his name from my lips the second I saw him. Armise's face twisted, his nostrils flaring and eyes closing as if I'd physically touched him. Something I would never be able to do again if Exley was right.

Exley cleared his throat. He was pressed against my side and I'd forgotten he was there until that small sound came from him. But I couldn't take my eyes off Armise.

"Ricor is in a tough spot here," Exley said to both of us. "There was no way he could keep what happened quiet from the other leaders, not with the new treaty and all. They want you dead, Merq. Armise too. They think there's a chance of stopping the potential spread of this virus if we cut out all living sources of it. You have to try to understand where this puts Ricor. There's absolutely no evidence that you are infecting Feliu or me. I've been able to leave this room and have contact with genetmods with no adverse reaction and our blood shows no signs of the virus. But we know for sure you will, Merq. Transmission is guaranteed through touch, but just being in the same room as someone genetmod is a huge risk. And whether or not Armise is a carrier now—regardless that his body fought off that first strain—is still unknown. They're not going to let either of you walk out of here."

"Let us talk to Simion," Armise said.

"I can't make that happen. He has to distance himself from both of you."

I winced.

Betrayed. I'd been fucking betrayed by the man I'd dragged out of a med facility when death was the Revolution's only answer.

I wanted to rage, needed to feel the overwhelming burn of anger lighting through me, but that was all I'd done for the last two days and this betrayal, this death sentence, had been President Ricor Simion's response.

Gutted wasn't the right word. I was shredded. Eviscerated.

I looked away and Exley reached out with his left hand and knocked a closed fist against my thigh. "I need you to listen to me, Merq. The needs of the citizenry as a whole have to be above the individual."

I snapped my head up and glared at him. That sentiment was against everything Exley had ever believed in.

"You're a fucking traitor to your people, not just to Armise and me."

When Exley didn't react to that, I knew I'd lost.

I was powerless.

"We can't just let you walk out of here."

His fist beat out a slow rhythm that matched with the cadence of his words.

Something dropped from Exley's hand and into my lap. I ran my hands over my hair, hanging my head. Then I caught sight of the black transport chip that lay in the groove between my hip and leg. I sucked in a breath, my stomach churning and heart speeding until it was a static drumbeat in my ears.

'...let you walk out of here...'

It was exactly what Feliu had said to me before I'd said fuck off to the doctor and taken Simion from that medical facility.

But Exley had said 'we.' Did that mean he and Feliu? Simion?

"He's right, Merq," Armise said.

I looked up at the screen, at Armise. The chip was an old gen one that would have one destination preprogrammed inside it. If I used it I didn't know where I'd end up or where Armise would be, but Exley was getting me out the only way he knew how.

I had to trust that Exley was going to try to get Armise out, to somewhere safe that wasn't near me but where we would be able to find each other again. Somehow.

Exley gripped my thigh one more time then pulled his hand away. "Feliu and I need more samples. It's the least you can do."

"Fuck the Revolution. I've already given it everything I have."

"And we'll ask nothing more from you after this." Exley pressed his shoulder against mine, and with that chip sitting in my lap I grasped on to the alternate meaning to his words.

If I got out of here, I was free.

It was the only hope I had left.

12

I let them take more of my blood, more of my skin, and more of my sanity as I waited for a chance to be alone.

I kept the chip in my pocket, unwilling to hide it anywhere else in the room and risk not being able to activate it in a split second if I needed to. Exley and Feliu went through the same routine they had before they'd left me alone for days. Both acted as if nothing had changed. Both acted as if I didn't have a death sentence looming over my head if I didn't get out.

I had to believe that both of them knew how much danger they were putting themselves in by facilitating my escape.

The amount of trust I was handing over to them—to even think of using the chip—was massive. It wasn't as if using that chip was my only option. I could stay here and die. It was a valid course of action. I was a threat and I was risking others' lives. I had to accept that fact and own that leaving this building meant I was putting my life first.

I'd led most of my life in sacrifice for the cause, placing all else aside—family, connections, a home, and stability—because I believed my life wasn't worth as much as theirs.

What Kersch had been trying to teach me all along was that

it was. What Armise had helped me uncover was the stark reality that I was not only human—flawed, fucked-up, and faltering at every step—but that my *life* mattered more than my death. What Exley's gift of that chip showed was that he saw that too. I had to trust that Exley saw the same value in Armise and would provide the same option of life to him.

It was a potentially crippling amount of assumptions, but I'd known exactly what I would do as soon as I saw that chip.

Their examination sped past because I was no longer thinking about the present. I was focused on what needed to happen next. Activate the chip, figure out where the fuck I was, find out how to contact Armise, then go in search of Dr. Blanc and a dead woman.

Whether or not Sarai Kersch was really dead was a thought that haunted me with this virus running rampant through my veins. Whether her invention of the virus was malicious or a protective mechanism—bastardized just as much as my grandfather's research had been—was something I wanted to know, but I didn't need the answer to survive.

Whether or not there was a cure was the only thing that mattered now. Because only that would bring me back to Armise.

When I was finally alone again I didn't spare a second on any more considerations, I slid my hand into my pocket and pressed the button.

I blinked out, phased out of existence then slammed back, and I was on my hands and knees gasping for breath on a wood floor. A real wood floor.

I rested my head against the knots and imperfections and tried to relax so that the waves of transport pain would pass quickly. I slumped to the floor and rolled onto my back, staring at the ceiling above me—a high pitch of the same golden slabs

as the floor—and I inhaled damp, hot air, listening to the nothingness around me.

I sat up and looked around the small cabin. Waning sunlight
filtered through a window, a silvery trail of dust wavering in the
beam. The cabin popped and settled around me like a dwelling
that'd been left alone too long and wasn't used to bearing the
weight of the living.

Armise wasn't here. By the depth of the quiet I could tell
there was no one besides me. For the moment I was safe.

For now, that would have to be enough to keep me moving.

* * *

Wait for me. I'll be there as soon as I can.
- Ex

THEN IN BLOCK letters below that—

Don't leave the cabin.

I stared at the note on the table and the plethora of food
stores surrounding it.

"Shower. Please tell me this place has a shower," I mumbled
out loud and went in search of the en suite.

The interior of the cabin was sparse and clean, if dusty from
disuse. There were no personal mementos or indications of
whom this place belonged to. I could have been anywhere along
the equatorial belt but the heavy, floral fragrance I only caught
whiffs of was uniquely identifiable. I was somewhere in the
Southern Territories of the Continental States.

The en suite was of a size that matched the diminutiveness
of the cabin. But the shower water ran clear a minute after I
turned the spigot and the water was bracing in its chill.

After I was done, I shucked my Revolution uniform for the clothes Exley had left draped over the graying sheets. It was an outfit not unlike the one I'd worn into the Underground so many years ago. I rolled up the thin sleeves and sat on the edge of the bed, the numbers of Manny's transport chip peeking above the curve of my bare left foot.

I saw the flash of transport before I heard Exley's groan from the main room.

"With Simion's permission or without?" was the first thing I asked him.

"With."

My whole body eased at that. "And Armise?"

"Ahriman's claim about Armise not being able to transport was bullshit as well. He's out of the DCR and safe. I've officially been sent to recover you. Jegs has been sent after Armise."

I raised an eyebrow. "They think you could take me down?"

Exley chuckled. "Ricor may have overstated my abilities. Apparently I'm a man who knows how to do just enough of just about everything. Keep this up, I'm gonna have a rep soon. But you and I know the truth of it. It's not like there's a whole lot of non-genetmods who would volunteer for this gig anyway."

"People, Ex. We're called people. Stop with the non-genet shit." I offered my hand to him. "Why the Southern Territories?"

"You're on the Niaz homestead—"

I groaned. "Ex—"

He cut me off. "It was the best option to make sure there wasn't any chance of someone running into you accidentally. They know to keep a safe distance. Your perimeter is tight until we figure out where we're going next."

"We, huh?"

"You want the cure and I want answers as to why Sarai's research is being used like this. Figured we could find that together. Armise is going after Calum Blanc. And before you can harass me about it, the answer is now. You can talk to Armise right now."

EXLEY TOOK APART a cabinet in the galley and extracted a hardwired BC5 screen that he set up on the table. I stood off to the side watching him, trying to figure out what I was going to say to Armise. There was this gulf in front of me that was so massive I had no idea how I was going to jump across it, or if it was even possible to get to the other side, and I was shutting down again. Returning to old habits and blocking myself out from the impossibility of my situation. It was how I'd survived in the past, how I'd accomplished what had to be done when no one else thought I could. Focusing on operational details, tactical plans, strategic moves, and discussions on how best to gather and vet intel instead of how I felt about it....

All of that disappeared when I saw Armise.

"Exley. Can you—" My throat closed up. I blinked and gritted my teeth around the building pressure behind my eyes as I sat down in front of the screen. As close as I would get to Armise for now. Maybe ever again.

"Yeah. I'll hike up to the house and let them know we're here. Be back in an hour or two." The door closed with a quiet click.

I stared at Armise and didn't know what to say. I couldn't be flippant or sarcastic. I couldn't taunt him about his superior ability to survive. I couldn't talk operational details or tactical plans.

I couldn't find my voice at all.

We were alive and strong. We were free of the Revolution. Free of all obligation to a greater master plan. We could disappear and live out the rest of our lives in peace.

Just not together.

That realization hurt more than any other injury or betrayal I'd ever experienced in my life. And the only reason I understood what that pain meant was because of Armise.

Always Armise.

Always.

I pushed my legs out and sat back in the chair, running my hands over my eyes and trying to get the sight in front of me to go away. But I could see the ghost of his image in the black of my closed eyelids and I knew it would be forever burned into my memory. Armise with those silver-blue eyes darkened, a storm lingering on a Mongolian horizon, and the fingertips of his left hand swiping at his cheek....

I couldn't hold the pressure back. I couldn't hold it all in.

This man was everything to me.

And I had to let him know before it was too late for me to tell him.

When I opened my eyes he was there, his cheeks wet, like that river outside his village—crystal blue and clear—cresting over a precipice and crashing onto the rocks below.

I broke.

I opened my mouth to speak, fought against the vise constricting my lungs that made me want to curl into myself, but all that came out was a strangled cry.

My head was spinning, too light, because there wasn't enough air and Armise wasn't fucking here and there was no way for Armise to ground me and bring me back to stability because he wasn't fucking here and he never would be again. When I finally found enough strength to speak, I couldn't recognize my own voice.

"I've never hurt like this before, Armise. And I know what that means. Fuck. I know exactly what that means and you should be here for me to tell you—" There was no oxygen left in my lungs to tell him that I loved him. No way I could say those words out loud and make them real and not have him here....

With me until the end.

I'd seen Armise in the heat of battle. I'd seen him slit men's throats with a sadistic sneer painted on his face. I'd seen glimpses of his ever-present calm cracking, but I'd never witnessed it shattering.

I'd never known it was possible for him to break at all.

Until he did.

His roar came through the screen to me. He toppled his chair as he surged to his feet. I expected to watch him tear the room around him to pieces—because anger and violence were the language we shared, but love...I was never supposed to love Armise. Instead of the rage I expected, that a part of me wanted to see—because that was something I could deal with, that was something I could understand—he dropped to his haunches and repeated *no, no, no* over and over again until the word ran into itself in a loop that became more real with each repetition instead of less.

'*No,*' his voice repeated in my head and in my ears.

This is all wrong.

And I didn't how or if we could make it right. But we had to try.

"There has to be another option," I choked out, a wetness coating my cheeks that had only ever been there from torture or the haze of Chemsense, but this...this was catastrophic to the point I didn't know if I could survive. "There has to be, Armise."

He swiped at his cheeks again but remained on the floor, his gaze fixated on a point that was probably years in the past because that's where I was, struggling to figure out how this all could have been different for us.

His reply to me was so low, so broken I could barely hear it, and yet it carried the only hope both us had left.

"If there is we will find it."

* * *

EXLEY and I used a split sequence designed by Chen so we could transport into Kersch's former safe house in the Northern Territories without anyone being able to track Exley or wonder why there was a man named Av Garratty traveling with him.

I had my rifle slung around my back and Armise was tracking Calum Blanc in some other part of the world with his knife at his side. It was a connection to each other, to who we were for each other, which I held onto even though I had their illustrated components tattooed on my back. I needed something tangible, with weight and a surety of existence, to carry with me if I couldn't have Armise at my side.

Exley wasn't any type of backup I could rely on if we ended up in a tenuous situation, but I didn't expect to face anything akin to danger in the NT as long as we steered clear of the animals. The safe house was dark when we appeared at its steps and I trudged up the stairs with the heaviness of old memories like a fog I couldn't dissipate and had to push through. The thick door wasn't locked—it never had been—and I entered the lobby to find Kersch's coat hanging from the hook where it had always stayed because gear like that wasn't needed anywhere in the capital.

I flipped on the lights as Exley and I tracked through the house. It was as if this house had frozen in place, preserved by the ice and frost of the NT—since the last time I'd been here almost, what? Fourteen years ago? I didn't think it was possible that trip had been the last time the president and his wife had been here. Then I remembered that Sarai had disappeared soon after that and this house, of all their properties and hideaways, had been her favorite. Her respite. Maybe Kersch had been unable to return here without her. I'd always known there was a significant part of Kersch that had died when she disappeared, I just hadn't understood why until now.

"You see evidence of anyone being here recently?" I said to Exley where he tracked behind me.

"No."

"Me either. It's strange. I think the last time they were here was when I was with them. That was on the downslide of two decades ago."

"You think Sarai would have left any of her research or work here?" Exley asked, hope tingeing his voice.

I steered us toward the part of the house where Sarai's art studio was. "If there was any place where it would have gone undiscovered for this long, it would be here."

I turned the corner away from the bedrooms and into the main living area, heading for the glassed-off art studio. The firepit that sat between the two spaces was dark and filled with the remnants of its last flames. There was a hint of movement in the studio, a ripple of shadow against the glass and I hunched down, dragging Exley with me. My heart sped and my adrenaline kicked in. Was it possible Sarai was alive and living here?

The fire flamed to life and the face that peered at me through the glass wall was one I wouldn't have guessed I'd ever see again.

Dakra was standing behind the barrier between the living area and Sarai's glass furnace. He was shielded from me for the moment but I didn't expect him to stay there. Now I understood what he'd meant when he said he'd come to me when I could kill him.

I shouldered my rifle and motioned for Exley to stay down as I spoke to the original hybrid. "How did you find me?"

"I didn't." His voice was muffled through the glass. He set his forehead against it. He tugged at his ear, shook his head as if trying to ignore a sound and set his palm on the barrier. "I've been waiting here for you. I believed you would come after her eventually."

"Is Sarai Kersch alive, Dakra?"

"I don't know. There is no one else besides us three."

"You're here for the reason you told me in Singapore."

He nodded and pushed away from the glass. He picked up one of Sarai's orbs, those spiky, fragile conglomerations of synthetic glass that meant something different to me now that I had her virus thrumming through my veins.

"It's time for you to release me," he said.

"My answer hasn't changed. I don't want to kill anyone else. I don't see the need to kill you."

"I can survive almost anything. They can bring me back from just about any injury. But there is no escape from you. I can't be their subject anymore. I need to lie in the darkness and be nothing. You can do that for me." He crouched by the edge of the firepit, the only opening between the two of us. He set Sarai's globe into the flames. "Help me be free."

I took a step back. "Help me first. What do you know about the virus? Is there a cure or a way for me to get rid of it?"

"There is no cure for the reclamation virus. It dies when you die."

My stomach sank. "How do you know that?"

He reached behind him and picked up a box that he held in his hands. "She told me to give this to you. But if you won't kill me then what incentive do I have to obey?"

My head was whirling. "She? Sarai? Someone else?"

Dakra's face contorted into rage and he raised his arms and started to drop the box into the fire.

"No!" I held up my hands and he stopped before he could set alight the unknown contents in the roaring flames. "Just give me a minute. I need to know where Dr. Blanc is—"

Dakra thrust his arm through the fire, his skin crackling as it met the heat, and he threatened again to drop the box he was precariously balancing in his other hand. He began a downward arc that would engulf the box in seconds and I dove for his outstretched hand, grasping his wrist before he could torch what was inside.

Dakra started to shake as soon as I touched him, a pink froth spilling from his lips as he raised bloodshot eyes to me. "Thank you."

I let go of him and grabbed the box as I fell away from the firepit.

Exley leaned over me and offered his hand so I could sit up. "You okay?"

"No." My heart was thudding so hard I could feel it in the tips of my fingers and toes. "Definitely not okay."

I turned that box in my hand, noting the blood tie lock on the front, and tried to piece together what could possibly be inside it.

We watched through the glass barrier until Dakra's convulsing body went still.

13

"He's nowhere I have been able to locate him before," Armise said through the aircomm as Exley flitted around the cabin making us dinner. "On the positive side, Jegs has not gotten sick, so I do not think I'm contagious."

"Nope. It could also be her immunity genetmod," Exley interjected.

My head whipped up to Exley. "If there's a genetic modification for immunity to disease and it's working with her then why can't we use it with me or any of the other genetmods?"

"Because Feliu and I already thought of that and tested it. Her genetmod isn't technically an immunity—it's a heightened ability to fight off disease. Her system has had decades to evolve and improve with each thing she's been exposed to. She may be able to fight the reclamation virus off but there's no other genetmod who could unless they had years to build up a stronger system. Even then we don't know if it would work. There's promise there, but nothing quick enough to make a difference now."

"What if you gave me the immunity genetmod?"

"You take on any genetmods and the virus will turn on you. We already tested that too."

"So we're back to the box."

Armise ran his hand over his beard. "I have nothing but suspicion for the contents."

"Same," I said. "Exley says he wants to take it to a lab in the capital. I prefer to keep it within sight at all times and since I can't go to the capital...."

"Agreed. It stays with you."

I set the tips of my fingers on the bottom of the screen. It was the closest I could get to Armise. "How much does Jegs know about what's going on?"

"Not much. She is not asking and I am not volunteering."

I looked to Exley. "And Simion?"

"Ricor knows everything I know, whether he wants to or not. That's not gonna change."

"Noted. The less people who know the better. We've already dragged too many good people into this."

Exley rested his hip against the counter. "Everyone has offered their help. You're not forcing us into anything we haven't willingly agreed to."

I had no choice but to believe Exley. I couldn't have contact with Simion. I couldn't drag Neveed further into this than he already was.

I didn't know what I would say to Chen if I did talk to her.

I had to know she was okay.

"What about Chen? She's helping, has been since Moscow but.... Just...tell me she's okay."

Exley twisted one of his braids between his fingers. "Some days she is, some days she's not. Neveed and Manny are taking care of her."

"You know Maniel?" Armise asked.

"We've had enough interactions to get friendly," he said, but

I could see there was more to that answer. Exley brushed past that topic. "You figure out how to open that box so we can see what's inside?"

I picked it up and toyed with the latch. "It's a blood tie lock. Only a person with certain DNA markers can open it."

"Since Dakra gave it to you then you should be able to open it," Armise said.

"I know. But do I want to?"

"What other choice do we have?"

Before I could waver again on whether I should or not, I put my thumb to the lock. I still wasn't prepared for the pinching sensation. I jumped when I felt the tear of pain up my arm, then the latch popped open. Inside were three syringes—one a deep crimson color, one bright silver like liquid mercury, and the other glossy black.

Exley peered over my shoulder. "Ominous."

I turned the box to the screen so Armise could see. "You have any ideas?"

Exley tapped me on the shoulder then gestured to his ear. "Be back. Have to take this."

I nodded to Ex. There was nothing else besides the three vials in the box so I snapped it shut and slid it across the table. "How you holding up?"

"The same as you are."

The wrinkles around Armise's eyes were more pronounced since I'd last seen him in person, the silver in his hair more prominent. He was aging in front of me—worn down by stress and fatigue. I guessed I hadn't fared any better, but I was loath to take stock of any of those changes in my own reflection.

I frowned. "I don't know what our next move is."

Exley came back into the cabin and didn't say anything to me as he finished up dinner.

"Our time is running short," I said to Armise. "It isn't going to be long before the Council decides they need to send in other people to try to track us down."

"You said you had somewhere safe to go—" Armise started.

Exley threw up his hands and covered his ears. "I shouldn't hear this." He peeked over his shoulder and lifted one hand carefully until he verified neither Armise nor I was talking anymore. "Need that buffer of deniability. Let me take the syringes up to Chen to see if she has anything I could run some tests with. It'll be out of your sight but technically still here. Give you two time to talk also. Deal?"

I set my hand on top of the box. "You're not going to run with this, right?"

"Yeah. Like I need you and Armise after me. I have a better sense of survival than that. You'd probably genetmod me just to kill me."

I unlocked the box and pushed it closer to him. "I'll put my comm strap on in case I need to ping you. Tell Chen.... I don't know. Just tell her I miss our lessons."

Exley gripped my shoulder as he grabbed the box, cradled it, and walked past. "Will do. See you later, Armise."

I waited for the door to close before I spoke again. "It's time to talk about my spot, Armise. If we can't be there together—and something happens to me—then you need to know where it is so no one can track you down."

Armise sighed. "I choose to not engage you on everything that is wrong with that previous sentence."

My anger took hold in a heartbeat. "Fuck that. Let's have it out. As it stands right the fuck now, you and I can't be together without me killing you. That's indisputable."

Armise ground his teeth together. "Correct."

"I want us to be together, that is a fact. Again, indisputable."

"Merq—"

"Fuck that. Hear me."

The corner of his lips tipped up. "I hear you."

I scooted my chair closer to the screen and leaned forward. "With our time to find Dr. Blanc or the very dead Sarai Kersch running low, we need to see what other options there are. First, we turn ourselves in—"

"And they kill us."

I nodded. "Second, we kill ourselves. You pop the encryption chip out, I pop off myself. You don't have to lie to me, I know the thought has crossed through your head."

"It has. We would be in control and not them."

"I still don't consider it a real option. Not yet."

Armise nodded. "I am of the same thinking."

I gritted my teeth when I caught that his speech was becoming more and more formal each time we talked. That either meant that he was hiding something from me or tightly controlling his emotions. Neither was acceptable.

"Don't fucking shut down on me here, Armise. This is as emotionally fucking invested as we get. If there's a time to bare it all, it's now. It's the only way we're going to find a way out besides those first two non-options. You feel me?"

"I will—" He stopped himself. "I'll try."

I held up three fingers. "Third is that we stay apart, on the run separately. We're likely dead anyway if we pursue that choice and let's be real, neither of us wants to be alone."

That one got a full-on smile from him. "Correct as well."

"The fourth option is that I take the fall and you take my safe house."

The smile was wiped away in a second. "Not an option either."

"You sure about that?"

Armise glared at me.

"Okay. Then we have four down. Fifth is whatever is in that box. We find out what that is and we move from there. No matter what, though, you need to know where the safe house is. I'm the only person in the world who knows where it is and you need my blood to get in. I'll give you the coordinates and make sure Exley keeps a vial of my blood just in case you need it."

"You can't transmit the coordinates to me. We probably shouldn't be speaking over this fucking aircomm about where it is."

He was right. "I'll figure it out. Let's try to sleep tonight." I hadn't slept well since.... Shit. Since Armise and I were in the steppe of Mongolia. I pressed the heels of my palms into my eyes. "Not the same in that bed without you."

Armise chuckled. "It's not the same. I can sleep a full night."

And he clicked off before I could protest.

But the grin his exit left on my face gave me another shot of hope.

* * *

"GET UP, MERQ," Exley called out as he flung the bedroom door open. "I called Armise. We have to talk."

I trudged out of bed and into the galley where Exley already had a half-lidded Armise on the screen. Wherever he was in the world, he and I were living off the same sleep schedule—taking our cues from each other, instead of our locality.

I was about to make a sarcastic comment about Exley's intrusion when I saw the sick look on his face. "What the fuck could possibly be worse since you left us?"

Exley thumped two chairs down in front of the screen. "We found a way to extract the shielding chip—and therefore the encryption chip—that won't kill the host."

"That's good, not bad," I said.

Armise scratched at his beard and yawned. "But?"

"The Council isn't waiting anymore. They've taken the news

of the virus to the press corps and have made a public offering to Armise. All of his tests have come back negative for the virus. He's clean. So they're offering to let him return to his village if he hunts you down and kills you first. They don't know that the two of you are.... Well, whatever...and Ricor didn't bother to clear it up for them. All they know is that you used to be enemies and they're playing off that history—betting that Armise will trade his life for yours."

Armise sat back and crossed his arms. "They don't care about me. They want the encryption chip."

"True. But that's not all." He set the open box on the table. "These syringes are the hybrid transformation cocktail. Not the one we found in the D3d camps. It's the one Ahriman used on Chen."

Shit. I'd thought that could be possible, but not really *believed*. My instincts had been on though. "How sure are you?"

"There's no room for doubt. I tested it."

I narrowed my eyes. "On who?"

Exley blinked and licked his lips. "Please don't ask. It's not important. What I want to know is how Dakra got that, Merq. That's the more important question. And whether Sarai is still alive."

I shook my head. "There's absolutely no evidence she is. None."

"Then what woman would have asked Dakra to get that to you?" he pressed. "Who else would've thought you might need this one day?"

I looked to both of them, hesitant to answer with the theory that had been drumming around my head for the last day, let alone the plan that I thought should follow. It sounded crazy even to me, and I had no idea how they would react to it.

Exley patted my cheek. "I see the gears spinning up there, Merq. You gonna share?"

"My mother," I said. "She had access to the camps and to Ahriman. She was always stronger than my father was. Smarter. She could've programmed that blood tie lock with her blood knowing I would be the only one who could open it. Not even my father could have. She said something to me that day in Priyessa's house about me having too many lives.... And she entrusted it to someone who could only be killed by me."

Exley's brow furrowed. "I don't get it."

I looked to the aircomm screen. Armise did. His jaw was clenched, his lips set in a thin line.

"If she found out I was the kill switch, if she knew about the reclamation virus, then she would've known the only way for me to get rid of it would be to die. And one of those syringes is what brought Chen back. I think she was trying to give me a chance at a new life."

Exley's opened his mouth as if to speak. Instead he swiveled his head between Armise and me.

"If it was her...." If it was from her, it was the only gift she'd ever given me. "One fucking thoughtful decision will never outweigh all of her heinously wrong ones."

Exley sent his braids swinging as he shook his head. "You think she wanted to give you a second chance at life? It's more likely that she saved it for you because she learned you weren't genetmod and wanted to change that."

Armise gave a low growl of disapproval. "Exley."

I slumped forward. I hadn't thought of that.

These syringes were a cure for my curse of humanity instead of a gift. I shook off the slash of disappointment that sliced through me. That reasoning fit more with her track record.

"Fuck her. Fuck whoever got this to me. It doesn't matter why." I met Armise's eyes through the screen. "We have our fifth option."

* * *

I HADN'T BEEN able to finish the meal Exley had made, let alone find enough equilibrium to not feel like the room was shimmering out of existence around me. Exley had left hours ago, pretending to head out on another scouting mission searching for me. He was trying to keep the Council at bay for as long as he could, but my death wasn't something they would rest without.

Because of the Council's offer, Armise had an out. Because of those syringes, I had one too. His was much more guaranteed than mine, and that made me want to take the chance more than anything else. I didn't want to die and I didn't want to be without him. I didn't want him to be alone. But I couldn't be okay with him dying for me.

We weren't being forced into this fifth and final option, not really. We had four other paths we could choose to take. If I was guaranteed that he would live, I would sacrifice myself in any one of them if Armise asked me to—but I knew he would never ask me to.

No matter how I spun it, finding a way to use those syringes was the only option I could stomach. It was putting my life at risk, not Armise's. And how big of a risk was it really? If I died, the reclamation virus died.

And one of those syringes could bring me back.

I held the box in my hands, closed, so that I wouldn't have to look at them and wonder what I would be doing to myself. I didn't have to look farther than the other side of this homestead to know for sure.

Exley had said that some days Chen was okay. Some days she wasn't. I didn't know what that meant and I had to know if I was going to move forward with this option. I tapped on the BC5 and opened the connection for an aircomm with her, hoping that she would be monitoring the channel and not Neveed or Manny.

Her face appeared on the screen and before I could say anything, she cut in with, "Give me twenty minutes. Put on your comm strap."

I secured the communication strap around my neck immediately, closed my eyes and slid down in the chair so I could lean my head back. With each second that I waited my breathing became shallower and my heartbeat sped another notch. I tried to fight the anxiety inching into my system and that only made it worse.

I needed chaos to think straight, and right now all I had was silence.

Then I remembered Neveed's forced mediation lessons on the island. I'd hated every moment of them before I'd listened to what he was telling me. Once I'd learned how to master quieting my mind, each time I tried to drop into that headspace became easier, each time more beneficial.

I got up, lay on the floor and closed my eyes again. Within minutes I was edging away from the precipice of panic. An untold length of time later I was finally still.

"Hey, Merq."

My eyes snapped open. I searched around me but I was alone.

"Chen?"

"I'm outside. Upwind. Took me a bit longer than I thought to make sure I'd scouted a safe spot and could slip away unnoticed."

I smiled and pushed myself to my feet. "He probably knows you're gone anyway."

"Probably."

I heard the scowl in her voice.

I walked to one of the windows. "You close enough that I can see you?"

"I don't know how close I can get."

There was a hint of movement through a copse of trees down the embankment that dropped away from the cabin. I dragged a chair to the window, grabbed my rifle off the table and set it on my shoulder so I could use the scope. A head of shiny black hair peered out from behind the tree. Where her fingers curled around the trunk she left deep grooves through the bark.

"That tree isn't a real barrier, Chen. Are you frothing at the mouth?"

"Um, no?"

"Then step out and let me see you. May be the closest we ever get again."

She pushed away from the tree and stood facing the front of the cabin. Her lips were pulled down in to a pronounced frown. She crossed her arms against her chest. "Merq—"

"Nope," I stopped her. We couldn't have this conversation go like this. Chen's and my relationship had always been one of the easiest for me—because we knew each other well enough not to have to say the things out loud that other people, people not like us, needed to hear. She'd never asked for reassurance, only respect. "No time for sadness. I need to talk to you before Neveed comes to hunt you down."

She swallowed, the black strap of her comm bobbing with the movement. "Or Manny."

"They taking care of you okay?"

She readjusted her comm strap before answering, "I think I scare them."

"That's what I need to talk to you about, Chen."

She lifted her eyes to me. Locked on to me with a clarity that felt as if she could see directly through the scope at my eye. "The transition?"

"Being dead."

"Oh."

I rested my cheek on the stock of the rifle. "Or maybe it's the coming back to life part. I'm out of my fucking comfort range on this one."

She put her back against the tree and slid down, facing me and draping her forearms over her bent knees. "Exley told you about the syringes."

"Why wouldn't he have?"

"I asked him not to."

I gritted my teeth, a flare of anger pushing through me. "My first reaction is to get pissed and ask why"—I took a deep breath —"but I think I already know. How bad is it?"

She rocked forward and crossed her legs under her. Her hair fell over her shoulders in waves and she tucked it behind her ear in a delicate swish of movement. She looked like a teenager, acted like a teenager, but she wasn't that anymore.

"I'm not the same as I was before. There's this...fog in my brain that I can't shake. How I see myself hasn't changed, but when I take a step back, when I try to see what Neveed and Manny do.... I realize I am different. And it's not just that there's this clanging noise when I run into a wall—which I tend to do a lot because of the vertigo."

"Vertigo?"

She nodded. "Honestly, that's the worst of the physical symptoms. But the mental parts.... There are these spots missing from my memories, or points where I can't remember a particular word, and trying to remember just gets worse the more I try.... If this hadn't been forced on me, I wouldn't have chosen it. I asked Exley not to tell you about the syringes because I didn't think you should choose it."

"You say that and it sounds like that's changed. That you think I should choose it now."

"It's not my call, Merq. It's not my life. I don't have the same vested interest in survival that you do."

Armise.

I hadn't realized I'd said his name out loud until Chen was replying. "Yeah, Merq. Armise. I'm young, but I'm not blind."

I let go of my rifle, ran my fingers through my hair and stepped away from the window. I needed to move. "Are there any positives?"

Chen's voice brightened with the question. "Well, yeah. Of course there are. I like being physically strong, not gonna lie about that. I like knowing that no one can hurt me like that again. The titanalloy skeleton doesn't bother me. I'm seventeen so I hadn't expected to get any taller as it is. My skin regenerates as soon as it's harmed so I'm guessing the whole wrinkle thing is out. I can cut my hair and that seems to grow back at a fairly normal pace, but I can't color it anymore. How weird is that? I may be frozen at this age for the rest of my life. There's no way for me to know yet."

But I couldn't share her lightness. I stopped cold when I realized what she was saying, that she may not have caught on to yet. Dakra's plea for death echoed in my ears. "You don't know what will kill you."

"Well, yeah—" She went quiet and I crossed to the window again. Her gaze was still locked to the window, but when I looked through the scope her eyes were vacant. She shook her head, then tucked her hair behind her ear again. "I hadn't thought of that. I guess I won't know until it happens. Shit, Merq. Does that mean that if you take this route you may stop aging while Armise—"

"Dies," I finished for her. I was so fucking sick of death. "I hadn't thought of that either until now."

"Death isn't the worst thing that can happen to us, Merq."

I didn't want to ask her what she'd experienced when her body had given up on her. And she didn't offer any more.

I cleared my throat, attempting to alleviate the tightness there. "Is Neveed giving you any self-defense or battle training?"

She chuckled. "He tried, but Manny's had to take that over. I broke Neveed's wrist in one of our first sparring sessions."

"You keep that training up. You'll be invincible in no time. They tell you about the encryption chip?"

She nodded. "Armise's life and your happiness aren't worth the same as that chip."

I thought about Exley telling me I needed to learn my own worth. Chen saw something in me too. I sucked in a ragged breath. "Is there any progress on breaking the infochip open?"

"Every day there's something new." Her eyes went wide and she jumped to her feet, clapping. "Oh my god, I can't believe I forgot. You know, you remember way back, when you first came back to Wensen's bunker from your op with Armise? I never got to tell you. I'd just unlocked the location of what I thought was a store of books stashed away by the Nationalists."

I remembered now. Chen had said there was something she wanted to share with me, then Simion had been the one to tell me, when I was set up on the edge of a cliff waiting to take out the last Committee member.

I smiled with her. "Did you find them?"

"We did—Jegs and I. And Grimshaw has shared more about possible locations. Despite the paper records we've uncovered, that encryption key would change everything. But maybe... maybe knowledge is something we have to work for to truly appreciate."

It was wisdom that I hadn't been capable of at her age. "I think you're right."

She flipped her hair over her shoulder. "Plus, I am the key."

"You'll crack it open one day."

"Soon, Merq." She paused, then, "I know you're the one who called me here, but I was trying to find a way to come see you anyway since talking with Exley. I know you and Armise are trying to find a way to disappear. And I have a fairly good idea of how I think you're going to accomplish that. I already talked to Armise, knew he would be the easier of you two to convince."

"Of what, Chen?"

"To let me send something with you. He says you have a safe house that only you know the location of. I won't ask you where it is. But I came up with something that can act as a secured link to me if you need it." She peered up at me, the sun streaming over her head—all light and internal fire—and I knew she was okay. The corner of her lips tipped into a smirk of confidence. "If I'm going to be invincible, I may as well use some of that power to help my brothers."

* * *

"We know what we need to do," I said.

I blew out a long breath, leaned forward and settled my forearms on my knees, clasping my hands together. Exley had been back at the cabin for less than five minutes, but I'd linked up Armise immediately so all of us could talk.

"You're freaking me out, Merq," Exley said from the chair next to me.

"I don't like where I anticipate his thoughts heading either," Armise replied from the aircomm screen.

"There is no other option," I insisted.

Exley looked between Armise and me. "You two definitely have some kind of secret language I'm not clued in to, because I don't see how Merq's conversation with Chen or these syringes leads to any kind of solution."

"It's simple, Ex. Armise kills me in a very public way to

satisfy the Council's agenda, the virus dies, you use the syringes on me, the encryption chip gets removed from him in a way that makes people think he's died and Armise and I disappear."

Exley gaped. "What the fuck, Merq? That's not simple! That is not a valid plan at all!"

I bristled. "Why the fuck not?"

"One"—he held up his pointer finger—"you may not survive the transition. Two. You're allergic to titanalloy! Three, four, five, to a fucking billion reasons why this is a bad idea, we have no idea what the correct dosage is, or timing, or what injuries will kill you yet you can come back from. And everyone who does know is dead or in hiding. Not to mention that we don't know how this could change you. You may not revive at all, or you may come back as someone who is not *you*. What it's done to Chen, Merq.... There are too many variables we know nothing about."

"It's our only option left," I pushed.

I turned to Armise to look for his support but he was shaking his head. "I will not do it."

I glared at him. "I'm allowed to ask things of you that I wouldn't of anyone else."

"Those are words you cannot use against me. I will not do it, Merq. Jegs is out chasing a lead on Dr. Blanc. We keep looking."

Then Armise shut down his connection.

I jabbed at the screen. "How do I get him back on the fucking line?"

"Leave him alone for now, Merq. Take a breath and think about everything I just told you. This is not a simple answer, nor an easy decision. What would you say if Armise told you he wanted you to shoot him?"

I started to answer and stopped. Frowned. "You're against this."

"I'm wary, not against it."

"And what do you think Simion will say?"

"Seriously? The only opinion that you should give a fuck about is Armise's."

I sat back in the chair and crossed my arms. "Sims will be for it then."

"You two were always more trouble than you were worth." Exley flicked me on the ear and I reeled back.

"Ow! What the fuck, Ex?"

Exley grinned and mirrored my position. "You know I still have the knife you and Ricor gave me when I snuck you out of Peacemaker barracks that first time?"

"You said you traded that on the black market."

His braids swung lazily as he shook his head. "Meant too much to me. I always knew I would lose you two one day. Had to hold on to something that couldn't just not-return after a mission."

I swallowed. "You're not losing Sims."

"Doesn't matter. You and I have never been as close as Ricor and me, but that doesn't mean I don't get to hate what I'm facilitating here. I'm going to lose you, there's no alternative ending to that, no matter which option you choose. You won't ever make me okay with that."

"And you think Sims will be okay?"

Exley leaned forward and placed his hand on my knee. "No way. He'll be lost without you."

"But you'll be there to help him through."

"I'm not planning on going anywhere."

He squeezed my leg—a gesture of familiarity and support. I had Exley's backing.

Now I just had to convince Armise.

I HADN'T TALKED to Armise since he'd disconnected from that

aircomm. I couldn't talk to him. I'd decided to give him time to think because there was no amount of pressure I could put on him that would make him bend. Exley was also set in his wavering non-decision of a hope for some other impossible solution, but he wasn't fighting me anymore. He'd transported back to the DCR to talk to Simion face to face.

I didn't think anything I said to Armise could change how vehemently opposed to this he was.

That left me with Simion.

I hadn't talked directly to him since being held in the DCR and I didn't know if I could reach out to him via aircomm and risk his status with the Council. But I needed to hear what he had to say. I brought the BC5 to life and sent through a click-check before I could think twice about it. Anyone else monitoring the channel would know it was me communicating, but they already knew I was alive. The click-check wouldn't give away my location and that was what mattered the most.

I sat back and waited to see how long it would take for Simion to answer—or if he would reach out at all. Hours passed, the sky outside lightening and a dense humid fog lingering in billows outside the window. Each minute that passed made me surer that Simion couldn't contact me, not that he wouldn't... because that just wasn't who Simion was. I resisted the urge to ping in again.

I was about to start pacing when the BC5 activated with a call and I picked it up. Simion's face filled the screen. "Sorry it took me so long."

"Tech issue?" I tried to joke.

His lips tugged into a deep frown. "This can't go like that, Mig."

"I know." I wanted to ask him about the delay, but the reason didn't matter. I didn't want him to feel guiltier than he already did. Exley had said Simion knew everything he did, and I could see the weight of that knowledge in his drawn features.

"Exley's still hoping there's another way to eradicate the virus instead of risking your life. He's coordinating with Armise and Jegs, trying to locate both Calum Blanc and Sarai Kersch. You think there's any chance she's alive?"

"I don't fucking care if she is. We're running out of time, and even if she is alive—which is a huge fucking if—she's been so deep no one has located her in over a decade."

"You have more time. Armise has officially accepted the offer of the Council."

I let out a sigh of relief. That meant Armise was, at the very least, considering what I'd said to him. "Good. Then at least they'll be off his back and Exley's. You can get that chip out of him without killing him, right?"

Simion nodded. "The extraction has been tested on over a dozen hybrids with success. Feliu is using your grandfather's research to do the removal. Something about targeting the cells in a perimeter around the chip so it doesn't register it's not connected until it's already removed. He's confident it will work for Armise as well. You need to know the price that was paid for this knowledge though. Athol and Elina volunteered for the tests. Athol went first. He didn't survive."

My stomach rolled. "Shit."

Simion stared off screen, shaking his head. "I don't know if any of us deserve to have that encryption key. Maybe it would be better if it disappeared with Armise. Maybe it would be better if citizens are forced to work together to resurrect that knowledge. Maybe it will be better if what's been buried for so long never comes to light."

It was exactly what I'd thought. Exactly what Chen had expressed. But maybe there was another way.

"Give the chip to Grimshaw when the time comes. He'll

protect it. Regardless of what happens with me, I need you to make sure that chip gets out of Armise. We need to be out, done, free with no chance for anyone to drag us back in. I always thought that would happen through our deaths, but there's another choice here, and I need Armise to agree to take it. I need you to talk some sense into him."

Simion flinched and jabbed his finger at me. "That's the fucking point of being together until the end, you jackoff. If he wants to die at your side then let him."

"That's the thing, Sims. He doesn't want to die at my side, he wants to live there. It's the same for me. And this is the only way we have a shot at that."

"Jesus, Merq. Listen to what you're saying. A chance at living by him killing you? You've been trained your entire life to fall on your sword. Don't discount how much that fucks with you."

I furrowed my brow. "I thought, out of everyone, you would see that this is our only shot."

"I'm not saying it isn't. I'm just saying...don't be myopic on this, okay? You should talk to Chen to find out what you may be facing."

I was surprised Exley hadn't told him about Chen, but maybe that meant Ex was trying to swing Simion to my side of things in the way he knew how. I closed my eyes and dug my fingers into the bridge of my nose. I was tired, hungry and there were so many possible complications.... And the truth of it was, "I already did. And what she told me scared the shit out of me."

Simion swore under his breath. "Hard to back you when I hear things like that from you, Mig."

"I need your backing now more than ever."

"You have it." Simion tapped his fingers against his desk. "Exley says you're not willing to bring anyone else into this. Let me talk to Neveed at least."

I shook my head. "Neveed can't know. If he thinks there's any other options left on the table he's going to risk his life. It's just who he is. But I can't let that happen. He's got Chen to take care of now and that takes precedence over my life any day."

Simion eyed me, but there was the hint of a smirk on his lips. "Are you passing judgment on my level of love for you and Armise?"

I bypassed his joke and went to the heart of what he was getting at. "I'm passing judgment on your ability to compartmentalize. You know this is best."

He nodded. "Yeah, I do. Look—" He drew his lips into a thin line and scrunched his forehead. When he looked up at me again there were unspilled tears in his eyes. "Shit. I just need to look at you for a minute. Memorize all that ugliness, you know?" He laughed, but the irreverence I was used to seeing in his face was absent. Wiped away. Simion cleared his throat. "Whether this works or not, whatever option you and Armise choose, whether you survive or not.... This is the end of the line for us, Merq."

I'd had this conversation with Ex. No matter what came next —my death or my survival—I would never see or talk to Simion...ever again. But knowing that and seeing Sims breaking down in front of me were two very different things. Pushing toward the ultimate goal of being with Armise, I hadn't really believed Sims would care that I wouldn't be a part of his world anymore.

I froze, a shiver passing through me that flooded into profound sadness when I realized the enormity of what Ex had meant when he said Simion would be lost without me.

"Sims—"

He shook his head. "You gotta let me tell you that I love you."

I ached—a tangible wave of hurt that registered at the ending of every nerve—because I loved him too. Different than Armise but with just as much ferocity. I'd lost Wensen Kersch before I'd realized he was a father more than my own. In Chen's death, I'd had the same awakening of her position in my life as a sister. Relationships built on trust and mutual protection that had nothing to do with a common lineage, unacknowledged until it was too late. The composition of blood—mine, theirs, of my victims, and my allies—had nothing to do with the makeup of our souls.

At least I was realizing this before my own death. And of course it was Ricor Simion—a man of greatness from humble origins—who brought me to that understanding.

"Yeah, you can tell me. You're my brother, Sims. In all the ways that are stronger than blood because we chose each other."

He sniffed, blinked, and threaded his fingers into his blond curls. "Just when my hair was starting to grow back. Just do one thing for me, okay? Don't let more time pass without telling Armise who he is to you. I don't think he understands how far you're willing to go for him. I didn't until right now."

"Fuck you. It's not that easy."

He shrugged. "Except for that it is. I'll talk to Armise. He's scheduled to come in to meet with me and Ex tomorrow. I'll make sure he knows you're looking for him."

A heaviness settled into my core. "I don't know how to end this call."

"We never know what the future holds, Mig, so let's do it just like we would any other. You're a good man, Grayson. I'll see you on whatever flipside we end up on."

I steadied my shaking hands and touched the screen. "Yeah, Sims. See you there."

14

I couldn't get back to sleep. I paced the main room and left the BC5 active, waiting for Armise to reach out to me. I was going into my second day without contact with him and that was too long considering the factors we had working against us. I pinged him over and over again, refusing to just sit back and wait for a response from him. There had been a time for keeping my distance—playing through a negotiation I never won or lost—but now was not that time.

When he finally called I was at the point of fear—fear that he wouldn't answer because he'd gone in to see Simion and Exley and had been executed. By the time I picked up his comm I was raw, and too vulnerable.

"So I hear you're going off on your own," I snapped. "Alone and without backup. Sounds familiar, right?"

Armise frowned. "It's not the same."

"It's not the same, because both of our lives are on the line here, Armise. Not just yours."

He sneered. "What the fuck do you think I'm doing over here?"

"I don't know because you've gone mute. Refused to speak to me as some form of childish protest."

He sat back and crossed his arms. "You're right."

I blinked. "What?"

"You're correct. I have shut you out. I don't give a fuck if they all die. Every single person on this planet, including me. I won't kill you."

I sighed. "In my death we'll finally have peace."

"I want peace in life."

"Fuck, Armise. I want the same goddamn thing. But dead men don't have missions. Dead men don't have complications."

"Dead men can't touch, Merq."

I quieted, the haze of my disconnect from him clouding my head. "I can't touch you now. It took me years too long to learn to trust you. I'm sorry for that. I need your faith that this is a risk I would only take for you. For us. I need you to trust in me."

His features were still hard. Closed off. "This is not our only option."

"It's not," I agreed. "But it's the best one out of all of the fucking awful possibilities. It's the best chance you and I have of getting free." I swiped at my eyes with shaking hands. I was so goddamn tired and I needed him to understand. "Fuck. I'm going about this all wrong."

I sat back in my chair and rubbed my fist over my eyes again. Simion thought Armise didn't understand the lengths I would go to for him, and he was right. I'd been incapable of telling Armise, let alone showing him....

But I had the capability to show Armise everything I thought now, plus getting him the information no one else could learn. I leaned forward. "You know that memory I showed you in the DCR?"

Armise furrowed his brow.

"If I gave you fifteen of those memories—places only you

and I could identify—could you piece together each one for the coordinates to the safe house?"

Armise cracked the knuckles of his left hand. "I remember every moment I've ever spent with you—the good and the bad."

"Same, Darcan. You remember the place where you taught me how to track? You go to the home site and I'll be waiting there for you, downwind, and at a safe distance. Bring your rifle."

* * *

I DIDN'T TELL Exley where I was going. I contacted Chen and had her devise a transport sequence to mask my and Armise's movements. It had been six months since Armise and I were last in the steppe. I settled onto the rocky hill, my stomach scraping against the outcroppings as I set my rifle into place and peered into the scope at the spot where Armise and I'd had the ger set up for those weeks where it was only the two of us. The ground where our ger had sat looked as if it has been untouched despite the weeks we had spent here.

It was the only place on earth I had departed without leaving some kind of permanent stain of my presence. One of the only places I'd ever walked away from peacefully.

The only place I'd never wanted to leave.

There was a burst a mile in the distance and I itched to move when I saw Armise appear. He was so close. We would never have the chance of getting closer again if this didn't work. Armise paused and lifted his face to the sky, closing his eyes. Then he secured his comm strap around his throat and turned unerringly in my direction.

"You could come closer," he said.

"I can't. Too hard." It wasn't difficult because I was too much of a risk. It hurt too much to think of being near him and not *next* to him. "Fifteen memories for the fifteen digits. You ready, Darcan?"

He settled onto the ground and set up his rifle. "Where are you going to project?"

"West. The memory from the DCR is your first digit. Give me a moment to conjure the second one."

I closed my eyes and cracked the button in my hand. I brought forth the memory of watching Manny and Armise interact with each other in the Wildes of the UU. It was the first time I'd met Manny. When I opened my eyes—my vision blackening when the projector went active—I had to force myself to only think of that moment instead of the last time I'd seen Manny in person. That memory would come later.

I opened my eyes. "You getting this?"

"I can tell it's me, but the other person...."

"Hang on." I closed my eyes again, refocused my thoughts, then reopened them, hoping I was bringing the image into starker clarity.

"Got it," Armise answered.

"You sure?"

He grunted. "I'll tell you if I don't."

"Next one."

I remembered Armise on his knees and the residual heat of a stove under my hands. He'd just finished making dinner when I'd interrupted him and the scent of genetmod meat was heavy in the tropical air. It was one of the only times I'd come to him before he could seek me out.

"That has happened a lot," Armise remarked.

"Yeah, but only once when I was left with circular stove burns on my ass. I'm surprised that hasn't been repeated by now."

"We don't get to eat often enough."

I paused. "Was that a joke?"

Armise gave a low chuckle that I could feel the memory of rumble through me. "Perhaps. I have that one. Number four."

It took almost nothing for me to snap the next memory into focus. Armise sucked in a panicked breath on the other end of my comm.

"Give me a fucking warning, Merq."

"It's not like I know how to perfectly control this!"

I closed my eyes, trying to wipe away the images of Ahriman stabbing a hot knife into Armise's shoulder socket from my own head. Of Manny's panicked face. Of Chen's shudders of pain and fear. If I could forget everything about that day, I would.

Armise sighed. "Next."

I realized that I was able to see a faint distortion of the memory in the seeming blackness of my vision. I ran through the next set with the intent of speed. Making the projector work was easier each time I used it, and these memories were so distinctive Armise would be able to identify them as fast as I pumped them out.

A machete.

"That scar is one of my favorites," he said.

"And the tattoo that covers it is one of mine," I replied.

Armise chasing me on a motorbike and me crashing.

"You still can't drive."

I barked out a laugh. "I don't want to drive. There's a difference, Darcan."

A well on the edges of an abandoned city.

"That rusty spigot? I can't believe you remember that. I was so thirsty—"

"And there was no water." I closed my eyes and paused. "I remember everything, Armise."

His voice was thicker, lower, when it came to me this time. "Next."

I opened my eyes and showed him Karachi enveloped in the

beige and red of an electrically charged sandstorm. I'd recognized Armise even with his face wrapped, because of the bloody knife in his hand.

"Such a beautiful city," I said.

"Such a fucking awful memory."

The next one wouldn't be any better. An old man with a timeworn face, gentle hands, and his skin burning off his skeleton.

"Torga." Armise breathed out.

If grief had a sound that was it.

I closed my eyes and rested my cheek against my rifle. "I never told you I was sorry about him. I wasn't then but I am now."

Armise was quiet for a moment and I listened to the sound of his breathing through the comm, then, "It was a different time. At least I have his knife."

He forgave me too easily. "Still not an excuse."

Armise and I had experienced so much violence. Perpetrated so much violence on each other.... Then we had changed our fate. Sneered at the expectations everyone had of who we were, and become more.

We couldn't end like this.

"Are you ready for the next one? This memory...this one isn't you, but it involves you. Another person I took away from you, and yet another name it's difficult for me to say out loud. I don't know if you'll want to see it."

"Vachir."

That Armise had known Tiam and that PsychHAg was the one to order my first kill.... That he steadfastly ignored the first of the five hoops on my ear marking the first five people I had killed, as if he knew what they represented when he shouldn't have.... "Yeah. He was the first one, wasn't he?"

I heard Armise playing with the safety on his rifle. "Go ahead."

"You don't have to, I take it you know where he was without seeing—"

"Please."

So I showed him, however little there was to show. I hadn't spent much time with Vachir, hadn't known who he was or what his life, and the end of it, would mean to Armise and me years later. But I showed Armise what I'd taken away from him when I'd slashed Vachir's throat—my first kill—in exchange for time on Tiam's biocomp. I'd been a government-protected sixteen-year-old child, already steeped in the language of violence. Unable to comprehend the gravity of how each life I took would change me. Stain me. And inalterably change the lives of the people my victims left behind.

There was so much blood on my hands. That Vachir had been the first and Armise taking my own would be the last.... It was a balancing act I hadn't thought the universe to be capable of.

Armise was quiet for a long time. I closed my eyes, cutting that memory off, and listened to his breathing. There was nothing I could say to make right what he'd just seen.

"That was not as bad as I'd imagined."

"Does that make it worse or better?"

"Neither. Simply more real. I forgave you long ago. Show me number eleven."

I took a deep breath. "This one isn't yours either. You know where I was when I learned who you were?"

"Not Bogotá," he stated.

"No. But you've been there before."

I showed him President Kersch's office in the capital. A room that was packed with analysts briefing him while I stood at the back and waited for my next orders from Ahriman Blanc.

Armise's face popped onto the screen at the front of the room and I couldn't take my eyes off him.

"I got it."

"And this one. Not just where I was, but where you were."

"How do you know I can identify this one?"

I showed him the decimation of the Sydney market after a terrorist attack. "Can you?"

"I never knew that you were there."

"You weren't supposed to. No one knew. I was there to kill you, outside of any orders."

"I was already working for the Revolution."

"And the only reason I didn't get to you was because of that reverb. If I'd been able to go through with it...." I shivered.

"It didn't happen. Give me number thirteen."

I showed him shooting a soldier of mine in the head and slitting his throat at the same time. Him disappearing with a transport a second later as that soldier fell to my feet.

"What I remember the most of that day was your face. You hated me."

"I did." Then I repeated what he had said to me minutes ago. "I forgave you long ago."

"Is fourteen any better?"

I showed me fucking him in a dark alley with my pistol drawn, lying on his back.

"Apparently not."

I'd been fueled by the violence of that encounter. Armise too. That was the first time I remember thinking that, in each other, we had finally found the way to incinerate our demons. A certainty intensified by the foreign scent on Armise's skin that day.

"You smelled different—like wound pitch and fire. You'd been with Ahriman before that, hadn't you?"

He clicked his tongue. "That is a name that has no need to be uttered aloud ever again."

"You'll have no argument from me."

I couldn't see his response, but his lingering silence said what he didn't.

"What is it, Armise? That memory isn't nearly as bad as some of the others."

Armise chuckled, a sound that was resonant of a time we had long since passed. That sound was the Armise of a rooftop in Bogotá almost twenty years ago. "Did you know that Simion calls that time the callous years?"

"What time?"

"The five-year span between when you returned to the States from Singapore and before the Olympics," he said. "You were playing the role of States soldier for hire and setting yourself up to be the one who would assassinate Kersch. I was left with the fragments of a man I'd traded everything for."

I sighed. "Callous is too tame of a word for how I treated you. I knew who you were to me but I couldn't accept it because your life was both a failure of my duty and the only thing I craved. I know and accept it now."

I closed my eyes. "This one, Armise. This one is the most important. I need you to have this coordinate down to the exact spot where we were standing when this happened."

"I understand. Show me."

This memory would be the easiest for me to bring to life—it was one of my most colorful in a life of shades of darkness. Me sitting on the red metal railing of the boat that had taken Armise and me from the States to the UU when we were on the hunt for Committee members. Armise had left the boat when we went into the port of Maniitsoq. He stood on the dock, alone, watching the same natural chaos erupt around us as I did.

The sky swirled with bulbous clouds of ash from the east

that were held off by an arctic electrical storm of crisp, cold blue approaching from the west. In the distance, the mountains were frosted in red and gold lava that poured into the ocean.

At this port, we were at the edges of the populated world. Caught between two warring fronts that mirrored the path he and I followed.

I'd worn his coat around my shoulders to stave off the cold and it'd smelled of Singaporean balms—of him. He'd had his back to me and he'd worn a black T-shirt, his arms vulnerable to the elements swirling around us. A frigid rain had begun to fall, pattering against the dock and adding to the low hiss emanating from the meeting of molten earth and water.

Armise had tipped his head to the sky, flashes of blue arcs from the clouds had lit his features. I'd dropped from the railing onto the dock and taken his face between my hands. We hadn't talked that day—we'd barely talked for days—but the moment I'd touched him, the moment the icy rain had hit me and it was warm in comparison to the grounding chill of Armise's skin, I'd had no more need for words. I'd kissed him.

Everyone else was either below deck or sequestered into their homes. Only Armise and I had braved the outdoors to view the spectacle unfolding around us. Only Armise and I had understood that this danger was beautiful. The world had been falling apart around us, consuming itself, but we'd belonged in the midst of that upheaval.

I clicked off the memory projector and placed my eye to the scope of the rifle so I could see him. I cleared my throat against the ache that had settled into my chest and spoke to Armise, saying to him what I hadn't that night. "It wasn't the first time I caught on that there was more to you than what I knew, but it was the first time I remember consciously thinking that your secrets didn't matter.

"I've gone back and forth on that belief a thousand times

since then. You're not my only option, Armise—never have been —and you are the furthest from safe that I could have chosen. But you're the only one I'll ever choose.

"We've always treaded where others were unwilling to venture. We can't just let all of this go. All of these years. Everything we've fought for and lost along the way.... Fuck, Armise. Everything we've gained."

He stared back at me through that riflescope. In the same position as almost twenty years ago, and yet everything was different. He sighed. "We risk losing it all with gambling with your life."

"We've already lost, Armise. It's time for us to breathe in the devastation, get off our knees, and take back what is ours."

I WAS MET with an eerie silence when I materialized where transport platform number four in the president's bunker used to be. The air smelled of oil and dust—with a fetid metallic bite that made my stomach lurch. I flipped on the light attached to my shirt and lifted my eyes.

It hadn't been just me who had almost died in this chamber. Two other soldiers had suffered career-ending injuries. Five others had died. All of our blood remained streaked across the debris.

As far as Chen or I knew, no one had been inside this bunker since it was abandoned after the Nationalist attack. I hung my head and breathed through my mouth as I waited for the aftershocks of transport to pass through me. When I finally found my way to my feet it was on shaking legs.

I sucked in a hissing breath through my teeth and tried to force myself to calm down. "Recalibrate, Grayson."

The sound of my voice was absorbed, dampened, and dulled

where it disappeared into the wreckage of concrete and collapsed earthen ceiling. I didn't need any further proof I was alone in what came next.

I was without my usual comm strap. Without any of my Revolution-sanctioned chips. Without Armise.

My fingers twitched and tightened around the two chips on my palm. One that brought me here and one that could take me away—back to Neveed's homestead—if I made that choice.

I dropped the transport chip that had brought me to the capital and ground it underneath my boot. I flattened my hand and stared at the other one. The second chip was just as utilitarian as the one I'd destroyed. Just as inanimate as every other technological tether that had kept me linked to the Revolution.

The only tether I wanted—needed—was to Armise.

His lips against mine. His arms wrapped around me. His gruff voice in my ear as his teeth nipped at my skin and demanded that I turn off my maniacal brain and rest for once.

I crushed the second chip into the bloodstained floor then faced the jagged, dark separation in the east wall where Chen had told me Simion had hid himself and me for a day after the attack.

If I was going to make it out of this bunker and to the remains of the stadium, then my only option for exit was through that hole. I crouched down, tossed my rifle inside, then tilted my damaged shoulder forward. I turned onto my side and slid into the dank space. Dirt cascaded down the walls at my intrusion and I fought back the panic that fluttered in my chest. The edges of my terror were like a hibernating beast fighting its way back to consciousness. There was no other comparison I could find that seemed quite as apt, since I was currently over the spot where my father had once compared me to extinct apex predators.

I heard his voice in my head. *'Dominant predator versus domi-nant predator...'*

It was as if he'd known how Armise and I would end.

I shifted in the tight space, trying to discern how Simion had managed to fit both of us in here at all, let alone with as much damage as we'd both sustained. But the visible marks were enough to tell me more than I ever needed to know. The concave spot in the wall where Simion had rested his head. Grooves in the floor where fingers had dug into the soil. A thick, dark line where I had nearly bled out while Simion waited until it was safe enough to move me.

I shuddered and shifted my focus to the right where the space became more cramped, my light unable to completely break through the pervasive darkness. Simion had had to traverse this section, to bash his way through another wall in a desperate bid for survival, with no source of light at all.

I detached the light from my shirt and held it up. Dribbles of water leaked down the wall onto my back as I pushed my rifle ahead of me and clawed my way through a space barely large enough for one man. My breath came out in billowing gasps that fogged my vision. I was cold in a way that wasn't familiar or comforting.

I followed distinct drag marks to a gaping hole that led into the adjoining room. The lines ended abruptly within a foot of entering the room. The boot prints I tracked were remainders of a man who'd carried a fallen comrade to safety. A year ago I wouldn't have known by looking at the prints that the man had a pronounced limp. Now I could recognize the signs.

Because of Armise.

I stumbled, caught myself against the wall and picked up my pace, the heat of movement—of action and determination—flooding through me like fire. The blown-out door to the bunker was gone, replaced with a metal gate that wasn't secured. But no one had lived in this section of the capital since the attack. Since the jacquerie had abandoned the Underground. Which was the biggest reason why Chen had advised me to transport in here.

But I wasn't alone when I stepped outside the bunker.

Jegs pointed a sonicpistol at my head.

All I had to do was take a couple steps closer to her for the virus to possibly infect her. I held my hands up. "I don't want to kill you, Jegs."

Jegs sniffed as if she was offended by the idea. "You think I'm going to sacrifice myself for you, Colonel? Good fucking luck on that one. As far as Exley can tell, you can't transmit to me without a whole hell of a lot of bodily fluid contact."

I smirked.

"Yeah, I told Ex he didn't have to worry." She slid the sonicpistol in the holster at her side. "Sorry for the hostile greeting. Had to make sure you weren't followed."

I frowned. "No one was supposed to know where I was transporting to."

"You can thank Av Garratty."

I recognized Dr. Calum Blanc's voice immediately.

I turned in the direction I'd heard his voice and trained my rifle on him. "What the fuck is he doing here, Jegs?"

With my sights trained on Dr. Blanc I didn't see Jegs' reaction but I heard an indignant huff of breath. "You're fucking with me, right? I started hunting his ass across the world because Armise told me he needed Dr. Blanc. But now I find out that Armise has accepted a contract to kill you and the only conclusion I can come to is that Dr. Blanc knows how to help you, so Armise wants him as dead as he wants you." She stomped over to me, close enough that I felt the reverberations of her footfalls as she approached. "I won't let you die, Merq."

I ripped my gaze off Dr. Blanc and glared at her. "Stay the fuck back."

She balled her fists but stopped in place. "What's that you said? Thank you? Well, you're fucking welcome, asshole."

I dropped my rifle out of position and faced her. She didn't know about Armise's and my plan. She didn't know about the hope that existed for Armise and me beyond my death. She couldn't know if we were ever going to be free.

I took a deep breath. "He doesn't want to help me. The only reason Dr. Blanc doesn't want me dead is because he doesn't have the data he needs for his experiment. Armise doesn't know that."

"What fucking experiment?" Jegs said.

Dr. Blanc cleared his throat. "The same one that gave you your immunity mod."

Jegs snarled. "You're the one who created the virus?"

"Dr. Sarai Kersch did," I clarified. Jegs' mouth gaped open.

"I don't have a cure for it," Dr. Blanc said. "But if you come with me, Merq, then we have a chance of replicating it and—"

"Fuck you," I spat out. He'd admitted that there wasn't a cure, so there was no ending to that sentence that would be acceptable to me. "I won't live to be used by the Revolution or by you. I'll kill myself before I let that happen."

"You're our best weapon against righting the wrongs of our ancestors."

I scoffed. "I never bought into that martyr thing the way I was supposed to."

"Your life doesn't have to end here."

"You don't want me to die," I said. "There's a difference."

"If you die, any chance of ending Anubis dies with you—"

"How many times do I have to say that I don't give a shit?" I yelled at him.

Dr. Blanc flinched back. "Sarai is out of control, Merq. She has to be stopped."

My blood went cold. "Sarai is dead."

"The Sarai you knew is dead. What she is now...." He pulled his coat tighter around his body. "The only thing I can do is uncover what she did to you and Chen and take it public. I destroyed every vial of her new serum that I could find.... But she's nearly indestructible now. The only thing that's guaranteed to kill her now that she's gone through the transformation is you."

I ran my fingers through my hair and paced away from them as I pieced together what Dr. Blanc was saying with what I already knew.

Sarai Kersch had created the virus....

Ahriman had supposedly killed her, but Dr. Blanc asserted she'd gone through the hybrid transformation....

Ahriman had activated the virus when he'd realized that someone had been monitoring his communications with President Kersch, as if he'd been betrayed....

It was now public knowledge that I was infected with a virus that would kill anything genetmod....

The only way for the virus to be killed off was for me to die, and yet those syringes had appeared just when I had no other options....

I'd been set up all along.

By forcing my hand into dying—so that the virus would die—Sarai was eliminating the only known threat against her.

She'd used me to save herself.

And I didn't give a shit.

I gave a dark laugh. There was nothing else I could do. "The Council won't allow me to live and I refuse to live as an experiment. I have a date with death either way, Blanc. You and your son ensured that. So I'm going to be in control of how I go out."

"I can't bring you back, Merq," he said. "Even if I did have access to her serum, I wouldn't use it. You die and that's it."

He wasn't aware that I had the new hybrid cocktail in my

possession. That he refused to even consider using it made my stomach roll with apprehension. "I know."

"I have to call this into Exley," Jegs said. "I don't know if what Dr. Blanc's told us will change anything, but I can't keep Ex in the dark on this."

I nodded an acknowledgement and Jegs stalked away. The grating rasp of her voice was rougher than normal when she began to speak.

I tried to tune her out, then her voice cracked and she tried to whisper, but I heard every word. "He's prepared to do what needs to be done."

I allowed her sorrow to wrap around me—to take it in and fully understand what it meant about my place in her life—as I listened to her update Exley.

I would mourn the loss of her in my life too.

"...there's no way to know how much more of the serum exists," she continued with Exley. "If Sarai really is alive there's no way to know how much more she's created or who she's testing it on—"

She fell silent as she listened to whatever Exley was saying.

"I'm sorry, Merq," Dr. Blanc said.

I pulled my attention away from Jegs and crossed my arms. "Don't bother wasting the last minutes of my life with lies."

Dr. Blanc opened his mouth as if to say something, then clamped his lips shut.

Jegs ended her call. She smoothed her hands over her uniform before she faced me again. "The Council's order to kill you stands. But Exley said to tell you that quote-unquote he and Ricor got this." Jegs frowned, the scars on her face pulling her lips down at harsh angles. "What is he really telling you, Merq?"

She was too perceptive.

He's keeping his promise, I wanted to say.

But I couldn't tell Jegs that.

Simion and Exley would take on what came next. As far as they were concerned, I was free.

But more importantly, I was finally aware of my limits.

I had no fight left in me. No more will to shoulder the issues of people who were crueler than I would ever be. I wanted a chance at life and I would never have that if I allowed myself to be drawn back in.

I didn't know how to answer Jegs.

She scowled deeper when the seconds of silence dragged on, then sighed as she looked to Blanc. "You don't have a cure for Merq?"

'For Merq,' not for the virus.

Dr. Blanc shook his head.

Jegs drew her sonicpistol, pointed it Dr. Blanc and pulled the trigger. His body thumped to the ground in a cloud of gray dust.

Jegs holstered her pistol without taking a second look at Dr. Blanc's form and pulled out a scanner from her pocket. "Shit. We've got to get out of here."

I paused, blinked, as I stared at Dr. Blanc's body. But Dr. Blanc's death wasn't my concern anymore. Whether Sarai was really alive or not wasn't my concern anymore. I readjusted my rifle so it was slung over my back. "What's going on?"

"The Council formed a team of hybrids to back up Armise and make sure you don't make it out of the capital alive. I've been tracking Elina since I found out about their plan."

"If she gets close to me I'll kill her."

Jegs shook her head. "She doesn't care since Athol died. But you know firsthand how deadly and brutal she is—she hasn't failed a mission yet. And she just transported into the capital."

"Where?"

"Less than two blocks away." She lifted her eyes to mine. "If you really want to choose how you die, then now's the time we run."

* * *

THE SOUND of our boots thundered off the alley walls as Jegs and I careened around a corner and headed toward the stadium. The footfalls behind us were too close—as if the hybrids had known where I was even though I should've been untrackable.

"Why can't we shake them?"

"Bet they're tracking the same fucking chip I was."

Fucking Av Garratty.

I whipped one of the knives out and dug into my wrist. My lungs burned, the dust in the bombed out streets of the capital made my eyes water and pain sliced up my arm, but we had to keep moving. I dug my fingers into the wound and ripped the chip out, tossing it over my shoulder.

"That should buy us some time."

Jegs huffed out a laugh.

I'd left Armise in Mongolia—unable to get any closer to him, but sure that he was going to go through with our last-ditch plan since he'd relented and agreed with me. Him killing me in a very public way was our only option. But that had been hours ago and I knew better than most that it took less than a second for the tides to completely shift. With Elina and her pack on our heels as we ran through the outskirts of the capital, I didn't know how I was going to get away from her.

I headed for the stadium, Armise's and my rendezvous point, because I didn't know where else to go if something had changed. We were still miles away from it. Even if I'd had my comm strap I wouldn't have called for help from Exley or Simion. I had to keep them untainted. I wouldn't call for Neveed, Manny, or Chen. They'd gone as far as I would allow them to.

I had Jegs at my back and it was a scenario I was used to— comfortable with in a way that made my heart ache because she knew exactly what ending she was assisting me toward.

Maybe Elina's pursuit was part of Armise's plan to give my death the credence it needed. A bullet whizzed past my ear and blasted a hole into a shop as I diverted around another corner. Jegs swore. I sneered.

Fuck. Maybe this wasn't an act.

Jegs was barely keeping pace with me. I'd always been faster than her, but if I took off then I put her life at risk.

"I don't know what to do," I yelled over my shoulder at her.

She stretched out her hand. "Where do you want to go?"

I stumbled and she gained on me. "The stadium."

"Done." She clasped my biceps and we flashed out in a burst of nothingness, slamming into existence into the center of the stadium.

I gritted my teeth against the pain and caught eyes with Jegs. She was grinning despite the tremors passing through her.

"That will buy you even more time," she said.

If I hadn't been covered in my own blood I would've drawn her close. Grasped the back of her neck and brought my forehead to hers. "You're a good woman, Jegs. It's been—"

"Fuck you," she interrupted. "We don't do this shit. We keep fighting. I'll hold them off as long as I can."

With that she transported out and I was alone.

I stood, surveying what had once been the grandeur of an Olympic stadium that held the hopes of citizens seeking peace. Now it was cratered earth filled with debris—the remains of the reverb Ahriman had ordered minutes after I assassinated the Premiere of Singapore. That the titanalloy structure of the stadium was mangled, just as torn apart as the cement, spoke to how violent the action had been.

There was a scream in the distance—the rending wail of a last breath. Apparently Jegs had made her way back to the hybrid pack.

I found my footing in the rubble and scrambled up one of

the two remaining walls. I didn't know where Armise would be in the stadium. All I knew was that I had to get to high ground so I wasn't as vulnerable. Every second counted now.

The buzz of low-flying drones came from the distance, the sound multiplying as it got closer. I didn't bother looking for the flash of Armise's transport into the stadium because I wouldn't see it. We were playing this out for the benefit of the drones we knew would latch on to Armise's location as soon as he made the call that he had me in his sights. That he was prepared to kill me.

Once again, Armise's and my faces would be plastered over the media, but this time I would be exiting this stadium as victim instead of victor.

A dronebot swept over the edge of the opposite wall then flew over me, circling back to hover. A second drone appeared and a third, and it was then that I realized these weren't all military drones—they were from the press corps. I had no qualms about being used this way. Each witness to my death would verify Armise's participation, ensuring his freedom.

I fought the urge to stop and search for Armise. It didn't matter where he was located, his sights would find me. The heavy tread of boots on stone came from above me and a cascade of debris rolled at me. I snapped my head up and caught eyes with Armise. He shouldered his rifle and trained it on me but didn't put his eye to the scope.

I pitched my voice low so the drones above us wouldn't pick up what I was saying to Armise. "If you don't pull that trigger then I'm going to be ripped apart by Elina. Pretty sure there won't be any coming back from that."

He frowned. He didn't fire.

My stomach churned with fear. Fear of Elina getting to me before Armise get a shot off. Fear of what came next. Fear of losing Armise forever.

That fear was the greatest of all of them.

"Get it over with!" I screamed at him. My heartbeat thumped through every nerve in my body.

Armise adjusted the rifle and settled his cheek against it. His hands were shaking.

I stood and held my hands up as if I were giving in. "Breathe, Grayson," I said to myself. "Inhale."

Armise sighed and the weight carried in the sound was like a palpable wave of sadness that crashed over me. I needed the ability to take that pain away from him again. But that wouldn't happen if he didn't take his shot.

"Armise—"

He cut me off. "You've always had to remind yourself to breathe, Merq. As if that basic function was worthy of overanalyzing. You simply have to trust yourself."

"I do. But I trust you more."

Armise's shoulders relaxed. "You've been repeating your mantra in your sleep for months now."

My mantra. I hadn't thought of that vestige from my time with the PsychHAgs in the same amount of time I'd apparently been reciting it in my sleep.

Inhale.

I looked to the lightening sky over the States' capital. The sun was rising into a sky I would never see again. "At one time it brought me peace."

"And now?"

The sounds of fighting drew closer to the stadium and the dronebots above our heads hummed with expectation.

Hesitation is my enemy.

"I'm ready to let that part of my past go," I reassured him.

A firefight echoed around us—inside the stadium this time. We were running out of time. "You ready for this, Armise?"

Solitude my ally.

"No," he answered. His gaze settled on me. Tore through me. The color of his eyes was so deeply burned into my brain that their intensity would follow me into an afterlife I didn't believe in.

He cocked the hammer of his rifle back. "I love you, Merq."

My hands shook with the need to touch him, to be with him. I had to believe it wouldn't be long until I could.

For now, I couldn't go into death without him knowing. "I love you too, Darcan. Come on then. You've always been a better shot than me. So prove it once and for all."

Armise adjusted his sights and put his silver-blue eye to the scope.

Death the only real victory.

I closed my eyes and held my breath.

Exhale.

He pulled the trigger.

EPILOGUE

May 2561
Merq Grayson's 37th year
Northern Territories

IF LONELINESS HAD a sound then this was it.

There was a ringing in my ears I hadn't heard before—or hadn't been aware of—since my world had gone dark. The silence I'd heard when I was alive wasn't a void. It was filled with the static of life, an unending background noise.

I'd simply never realized it.

Death had had a quiet that was total—unnerving in its pervasiveness. I'd had no concept of what that meant in the moment, but I did now. The memory, or lack thereof, of that complete silence was different than the quiet that surrounded me now. From Armise's bullet to my chest to the second my eyes had snapped open again—here in my great-grandfather's home —the gap wasn't bridged instantaneously.

There was a sense of loss, and of time moving forward, that

wasn't like when I'd been put under for a procedure or during recovery. In those moments of healing, the breaks in conscious- ness had been like picking up my rifle after being away from it— there was muscle memory, familiarity, and a recognition of every other time I'd felt that rifle pressed against my cheek. A sense of connection to my past that felt right, like *me*, even if I didn't know what had happened to me when I opened my eyes again.

Waking up from death was like waking up...new. Not wiped clean, not fresh, but not recognizable either. Six months on I was just beginning to understand how—besides the obvious heightened abilities that came with the transformation—I was different. I had nothing but time to understand.

With Armise.

There was a thumping of boots next to my head, then the *thunk* of a heavy bag, their entrance reverberating around me where I lay on the floor in the not-so-silent silence of the cage in our safe house. Our home.

My loneliness dissipated.

"You could've used the front door," I said to Armise.

I felt him move in close, looming over me, and his hand clasped onto mine to help me off the floor. But he didn't pull me to my feet, he simply held on to me, his skin cool from hours spent outside our hideaway. "Then I'd have to take more of your blood."

I heard the frown on his face.

"What are you doing in here, Merq?"

Instead of waiting for him to help me, I got to my own feet. He refused to let go, pulling me close, wrapping his synth around my waist.

"Listening to the silence."

He chuffed. "Is that like searching for the absence of something?"

It was a remnant from a conversation from so long ago that I should have been surprised he remembered. But he remembered everything. "I need to move. Been waiting for you too long."

He smoothed an errant lock of my overgrown hair off my forehead. "You'll be able to hunt with me soon."

I wanted it to be now. I pulled out of his arms, frustration ratcheting my energy up. "Then we need to practice. Hit the switch to close us in."

The room that had been my great-grandfather's lab was now a training room, stocked with items Armise had been able to ransack from Kersch's safe house and from the intermittent shipments we got from Chen. Armise had accomplished piecing together disparate items to create a facility that wasn't just passable, it was one of the best I'd ever trained in. We also had a library of paper books that grew with each delivery from Chen. But I relied on Armise completely to use that resource.

"The usual?" Armise asked as the door to the cage slammed shut behind him.

I didn't wait for him to settle in. I whipped my knife out and lunged for him, swiping across his belly.

Armise recoiled with a hiss. "I don't have that many shirts, Merq."

"I suppose one of us is going to have to learn how to sew."

I lunged again and heard the clash of metal with titanalloy, the reverberations of my knife hitting his synth rippled all the way up my arm. That his entire skeleton was now titanalloy since the transformation into a second gen hybrid had been completed—with my agreement and months after my own transformation had taken hold so we knew what to expect—was an advantage I'd never have. The serum had brought me back to life, but Armise had been unwilling to risk killing me, again, with an allergic reaction to the skeletal compound. His own transformation had been easy in comparison. Of course.

"That isn't fair," I grumbled.

He laughed. I was just enough distracted by the joyful sound that he found his opening. He grabbed my right wrist—the one circled with a set of bracelets that matched the set he wore on his left—and squeezed, forcing me to drop the knife.

"Since you don't have that titanalloy skeleton, I could snap your wrist," he baited me.

I took a step toward him and brushed my hand against the front of his pants. His skin warmed under my touch. I ran my cheek against his, speaking low into his ear. "Then you wouldn't have my hand on your cock for at least a day while the stitch mod did its work."

"*That* isn't fair, Merq."

I nipped at his earlobe. "Have to compensate somehow for the blindness thing."

"Compensate?" he scoffed, not for the first time. "I think we may finally be evenly matched."

He would always be stronger than me, but I'd accepted that well before his transformation. "Not equal, but...balanced. Like a lethal blade."

Armise set his palm on my back, tracing the edges of my tattoo with his fingertips. "Or compatible. Like the fit of a bullet into the chamber of a well-oiled rifle."

I chuckled. "I can't tell if that's a come-on or if you're being nostalgic for the times we hunted together."

"I do enjoy both of those with you."

I kissed the side of his neck and stepped back. "Food then sex. Hunting tomorrow. I think I'm ready to go out."

"Tomorrow then," he agreed. I heard footsteps then the sound of cloth rustling.

My stomach rumbled with the thought of a warm meal. "What did you bring home?"

"I don't know what it's called. Small, red fur. Should feed us for two days, maybe three."

"Clean it and I'll grab greens from the garden."

I started to walk away, reaching out to discern exactly where I was in the room, when he thumped the bag to the floor and stopped me. He pulled me into his grasp again, holding my chin in place so he could look into my eyes even if I couldn't do the same.

"How are you today, Merq?"

I wished I could see his eyes boring into me, but I could feel his gaze, stronger than I ever had before.... Before I'd lost my sight when the genetmods took hold and expelled the memory projector from my eyes. No stitch mod could repair organs that no longer existed.

I rested my forehead against his. Inhaled. No matter what he said to me, there would always be things I overanalyzed—the fragility of my and his existence being one of them regardless of how strong we were now.

"Today is a good day," I reassured him. "No headaches, no vertigo."

He let a beat of silence fall between us. "And you remember me?"

I answered him as I had for the last six months. From that first moment I'd opened my eyes to darkness but known he was with me. "I could never forget you."

Then he kissed me.

Possessive, and with aching surety. Slowly, and with care that was luxurious. I lost all sense of time and place, existing in this exact second with only him. I could touch the man I loved whenever I wanted for the remainder of the many, many years we had left.

There was nothing else I needed in life.

Safety, quiet, and the warmth of Armise.

ALL THAT REMAINS

AN ARMISE POINT OF VIEW SHORT STORY

03 December 2560
Armise Darcan's 41st year
The Continental States—the capital

Regardless of how many times Merq had been in front of my rifle, I'd been unable to pull the trigger since that first shot in Bogotá nearly twenty years ago.

This time had to be different.

I ignored the dronebots flying above our heads and focused on the man in front of me. Merq got to his feet, his hands raised as if he were begging for his life instead of his death.

I attempted to detach myself from the man I loved and focus on the details I had to be aware of to get this right. But I couldn't. I saw his throat move with the effort to swallow. I heard the scrape of his boots on the stones of the imploded Olympic stadium as he shifted nervously.

Merq was more frightened than I'd ever seen him. Yet I knew he would not back down from this course. I wouldn't back down either.

This shot, out of all of the shots I had ever taken, had to be the most perfect.

"You ready for this, Armise?"

"No," I replied, barely able to get that simple word past my lips.

I couldn't allow him to suffer. I couldn't allow him to go into death afraid.

He trusted me.

I gripped my rifle tighter.

"I love you, Merq."

"I love you too, Darcan," he replied with ease. As if those words weren't new to his lips.

My stomach knotted. I had to blink to clear my vision.

The steel of my rifle was cold under my synthetic hand. My overly sensitive skin registered every scratch and indentation in the metal. Just as I had felt everything on Merq's skin—every scar, every flex of muscle over bone, every shift in temperature, each of those unique pieces of Merq I would carry with me forever—when I'd last touched him.

"Come on then," Merq urged. "You've always been a better shot than me. So prove it once and for all."

It was one last taunt between soldiers who had spent nearly a lifetime against each other.

I wouldn't fail him in this.

I pulled the trigger and watched Merq's eyes go wide. There was a gurgling noise from his throat and he began to lift his hand to where his blood poured out of his chest. But I'd set my sights just above his heart, to rip apart an artery that would cause him to lose consciousness in seconds and bleed out in less than a minute.

Before his fingers could reach the wound, his legs gave out and he plummeted onto the jagged debris—his right hand trapped under him and head facing away from me.

I began to shake.

I'd never seen Merq motionless. He would toy with his piercings and bite at his lip when he was working through a problem. He would thrum his fingers against any available surface—his thighs or the palm of his hand if there was nothing around him—when he was lost to his thoughts. He would punctuate his few words with dramatic movements of his hands. He would thrash around the bed while asleep, sending all covers askew and, usually, dropping them to the floor until I retrieved them. His gaze had always been on the move, assessing his surroundings and taking in details I didn't pay attention to.

But now his eyes were wide yet blank. Fixed. Unmoving.

His hand and legs were strewn limp across the rubble.

His mouth was open but there was no sound. No breath.

He was still.

I shivered.

I was so cold.

Agony ripped through me. A pain greater than anything I'd experienced in my life. I would allow Ahriman to tear my arm off a thousand times and it wouldn't match the anguish—the grief—that doubled me over and left me gasping for breath.

A choked, nearly silent cry came from my lips and I dropped my rifle.

I looked to the dronebots above the stadium. Merq would have flipped them off just to fuck with their decency standards.

I didn't know what to do.

So I waited. I had to be sure he was dead before I got anywhere near his body. Both of us would be lost if there was any of the reclamation virus alive within him.

I tried to count out the seconds that passed, but my thundering heartbeat pushed every number out of my head. My hands were shaking too much for me to tick off the time. I couldn't look at my watch because I didn't want to know the exact time of Merq's death.

That was a memory I couldn't have access to.

I dropped to my haunches, scrubbed trembling hands over my face and rocked back and forth, desperately trying to find my equilibrium.

There was nothing anchoring me to the present. Merq wasn't here to ground me. All we had was an unchangeable past, and a future that was uncertain. I didn't want to exist in this moment, in this exact second, because there was no longer a reason for me to exist at all if I couldn't bring him back.

There was the sound of boots clambering up the debris and I lifted my head to see which of the Council's mercenaries had made it here first. Elina strode up the rocks, sure-footed where others stumbled. Blood gushed down the side of her head and over her shoulder.

But no amount of blood would ever be more than what I'd rent from Merq's chest.

She didn't slow as she approached Merq's body. She didn't hesitate to grasp on to his biceps and flip him over. She touched the side of his neck then extracted a scanner from her pocket and ran it over him once. A mad grin split her face and she lifted her boot as if she was going to bash his skull in.

"I will tear your head from your spine if you touch him."

I couldn't remember standing, let alone moving, but I had my hand around her throat. My knife was drawn, the tip of it digging between her ribs, pointed at her heart.

She brought her foot down slowly, away from his body. "Merq is the reason Athol is dead. If he'd never asked us to fight with him—"

I tightened my grip on her neck. "And now he is dead."

I released my hold and pushed her away with such force that she staggered, struggling to find her footing.

"You don't have the right to touch me!" she screamed. The hybrids closed ranks around her, rifles aimed in my direction. But none of them challenged the barrier I put between them and Merq.

Elina tilted her head, then replied to a voice I couldn't hear. "I'm here." She grimaced as if she didn't like what she was hearing from whoever was speaking through her comm.

"President Simion wants to speak with you." She dug into a pocket at the front of her uniform and pulled out a comm strap that she threw toward me.

I swiped it off the rubble and affixed it around my neck, speaking first because I knew there was only one thing Simion wanted to know. "It is done."

There was silence on the other end, then, "I'm sending a heli. Elina knows he's—his body—Shit. She and her team know not to fuck with him or you."

I took a deep breath. "Thank you."

The drones above us moved swiftly to the edges of the stadium, and the thump of a Thunder's blades echoed off the wreckage as it drew closer.

"None of you are allowed to touch him," I snarled. All of the hybrids, including Elina, took a step back.

The descending heli sent dust scattering across the floor of the stadium and whipping it into my eyes. I bent over Merq's body. His chest wound gaped open, his blood staining the hand that had been trapped under him. I could only hope I'd hit him in the correct spot and hadn't blown open his heart. I didn't know if that was a mortal wound he could come back from. I lifted his hands to his chest, covering the damage I had done to him. I ran my fingers over the hoops lining his ear, along his jaw, then over his lips, closing his mouth.

I left his eyes open, because thinking of them closed forever was worse than the blank stare I couldn't tear my gaze from.

I struggled to make my synth work the way I needed it to, but no one helped me. No one dared to come close. I cradled Merq's head with my left arm and was able to bend my synth enough to crook my right arm under his knees. I clenched my jaw and stood, having to use all my strength to lift him with me.

His body was already going cold, and I began to amp up my temp—in a response that had become automatic for me in the last six months—then realized he wouldn't feel the chill settling in his own bones.

I would never forget it.

I heard his voice in my head, *'Don't die, okay?'*

That phrase repeated over and over, cutting into me like no knife ever could. I had been the one to end his life. I wouldn't be far behind him if the serum failed us.

I refused to hand him off to anyone when we got to the Thunder. I refused to let him go when we landed at the Capitol Building. And I refused to let anyone else—especially Simion—take on the true weight of what I carried when I caught eyes with the president and his knees began to buckle.

I said the only thing I could think that would bring him some measure of hope. Hope I had to hold on to just as much as he did.

"He is at peace, Pres."

If we hadn't been surrounded by guards, by the other four Council members, and by Elina and her pack, I don't know how Simion would have responded. As it was, Simion grabbed hold of Exley until he seemed to find his strength again, then he stood tall—confident in the midst of his own grief.

Merq would have been proud.

Simion stepped forward and rested his hand where Merq's own lay on his chest. "He deserves that. And much more. Bring him inside."

* * *

I leaned against the medical facility wall with my arms crossed and watched Dr. Casas perform the tests necessary for the Council to glean as much information as they could about the status of the virus. I waited for them to okay the release of Merq's body to be burned. They weren't taking any chances, which meant I was going to have a very short window in which to disappear. An even shorter window until I couldn't deal anymore with the sight in front of me.

Every needle that was pressed into Merq's flesh made me wince. Every slice of the scalpel was as if it were cutting into me. I was on the verge of gutting the next person who put their hands on him.

Someone had closed his eyes after I'd finally relinquished his body. But I couldn't wipe the memory of Merq's death mask out of my head.

"Officer Darcan, may I speak to you?"

I ripped my gaze away from Merq and searched for the person who called out for me.

In the corner of the room the five members of the Council were gathered around a bank of BC5s that showcased the feed from the stadium that the press corps had captured, medical data, and situation reports. Kariabba Tivy, Franx Heseltine, and Shio Pearce were huddled together near the screens that pumped out readings from Merq's blood as it was analyzed. Simion stood off to the side, his lips pressed in a thin line as he listened to them speak. He glanced at me then focused his attention on the other Council members again.

Whatever they were saying to each other seemed to be of no interest to Isida Agri though. She was facing me, waiting for my answer.

I nodded to her and she sat forward, eyes returning to the footage from the stadium where it played on a continual loop.

"Sit, please," she requested. She motioned to the chair next to her.

The metal legs scratched at the floor as I pulled it out, the grating sound setting my teeth on edge. I dropped into the seat and tried not to appear as tense as I was having my back to the doctors and scientists who were violating Merq's body.

"You've been a soldier for a long time," she said.

She was the president of the American Federation and had likely been briefed on every detail of my life that was contained in operational files. That wouldn't be everything, but it would be enough for her to have a good idea of who I was.

"I have been."

She resituated the AmFed insignia pinned to her lapel and turned toward me. Her accent was thick around the Continental English that I assumed wasn't her first language. "There aren't many people left alive who know this, but I used to be a covert operative. Were you a fighter before the time of communication chips?"

I nodded. "I saw that technology years before anyone in my village did."

"I came from a similar place. Despite my height I was a good at what I did. I didn't need a chip to spy on anyone, just a clear line of sight and a good pair of binoculars." She shifted in her chair so that we were only inches apart. Her knees nearly bumped against mine. "Did anyone else know you loved him?"

I looked away from her, staring at the screen she'd been engrossed with. The press corps' drones were positioned behind Merq where his face couldn't be seen. But my features were clear. As was the movement of my lips as I'd said my last words to him.

'I love you, Merq.'

"I do not—" I began.

The door to the room burst open and there was shouting accompanied with the grunts of a physical altercation. I stood, putting myself between Merq and whatever threat was coming through the door.

Jegs barreled inside, her professional demeanor stripped bare, her gun in her hand. On her heels there were four Revolution guards, but none of them restrained her.

She glanced at Merq's body then quickly looked away—there was still so much blood on him that I knew she wouldn't be able to stomach the sight. She faced me, her entire body vibrating with anger.

"What the fuck did you do?" she whispered. She raised her gun and pointed it at my head. "All he wanted was to go out on his own terms. He was going to kill himself anyway."

At one time Jegs and I had respected each other. At one time, I'd thought maybe I could love her. For a time I'd cared for this woman. But never as much as Merq. I wouldn't have sacrificed half of what I had for her.

The only thing we still had in common was our mutual love and respect for the man who lay motionless on that table.

I couldn't explain to her what had happened or why, all I could do was beg that she wouldn't take my life. That she wouldn't take away the last hope I held on to.

That hope was the only thing holding me together.

"Holly—" My voice cracked as I said her name. "Please."

"He trusted you," she seethed between clenched teeth.

"Major Jegs—" Simion started to say.

She whipped her head around but kept her gun pointed at me. "Don't you fucking speak to me. Merq gave us his life and this is how you repaid him? Fuck you all. Don't think you can trust this Dark Ops piece of shit either. Let me do you all a favor and end Armise's life here."

"Major Jegs," Simion repeated, this time with more force. "If you do not relinquish your weapon immediately I will order you to be shot."

"You've betrayed *all* of us to save your own ass."

Simion didn't flinch or cower in the face of her attack. He stepped forward and held out his hand. "Your gun, Major."

Jegs ignored him and looked to me again. "Now that Merq is dead his order that I play nice with you is void."

"*I* order you to stand down!" Simion yelled.

Jegs started, and I did too. I'd never heard Simion speak with such fury. Jegs dropped her hand to her side, handed her pistol to Simion and stalked out of the room without another word.

President Agri stood and set her hand on Simion's shoulder. "I will speak with her."

Simion clenched his jaw, turned Jegs' pistol over to one of the guards, then acknowledged President Agri. "Let her know I'll catch up with her later."

"Are we finished here?" Simion said to Dr. Casas.

"I've taken the samples I need," Dr. Casas confirmed. "It will be another hour before I get all the results back. We have to preserve the body until then. You can escort Officer Darcan to the other med bay. I'll be right behind you."

Simion beckoned me. "Come with me, Armise. Let's get that encryption chip out."

* * *

There were only the guards at the door when we walked into the hallway. I didn't know where Jegs had been taken or why the president of the American Federation had offered to speak with her, but none of that was my concern. I was focused solely on the steps I needed to take to get Merq and me out of here as soon as I was free of the encryption chip.

Simion led me down the hallway and into another room that held an examination table. He closed the door behind us and slumped against it, all fight draining from him. "Thank fuck for Jegs' interruption. I had to get out of there anyway. I couldn't look at him anymore. It looks too real."

I leaned against the edge of the table, seeking stability. "It *is* real, Pres."

He winced. "Yeah, I guess so. How's the arm holding up?"

I held up three fingers on my synthetic hand. That movement was easy compared to carrying Merq's body. "Rehab rule number three—no evasion."

Simion gave a chuckle that held resignation instead of his characteristic ease. "Fair enough. How are *you* holding up?"

"I am...."

I struggled to find the right answer to his question. I pushed myself onto the table and collapsed against the wall.

I was tired.

I was cold.

No matter how much I ratcheted up my internal temp I couldn't take the chill from my bones.

I was vulnerable.

I'd had Merq at my side for too long to feel safe without him.

"I'm scared," I finally answered him.

"Me too," he admitted. Simion pushed off the door and took a seat across from me. He plopped down and stretched out his synth. "I'm invoking rehab rule number three, subset A."

I quirked an eyebrow. "Complete honesty?"

"Complete," he said.

"Go ahead."

He leaned forward and set his elbows on his thighs. "Did you ever think of not using the serum? Because of what it may do to him?"

"Of course. I considered every possibility."

"And?"

"Merq and I have a plan," I answered without hesitation. "It is my responsibility to execute this next step."

"'Execute?'" He grimaced. "Jesus Christ, Armise. You couldn't think of a different word?"

I balked at his response. "I don't know how to handle this any better than you do."

His features crumpled. "Oh hell, Darcan. I'm sorry. You're always so— I'm sorry."

He stood and began to pace. He held the same nervous energy—the inescapable need to *act*—as I did, but he excised it through movement, just as Merq would have, while I allowed that same directionless churning to tear me up inside.

To be torn apart was what I deserved.

"Did you and Mer— Did you two talk? Before?"

I frowned as I tracked his circles around the tiny room. "I don't know how to answer your question."

"Did he finally tell you what you meant to him?"

"He didn't have to, I already knew. But yes, he did."

Simion stopped moving. He sat next to me on the table, sliding against the wall. "Good. That's really good."

"And the two of you?"

"I'll never feel like I said enough."

His synth clanked against the table as he adjusted his position. His shoulder bumped against my synthetic shoulder. There were few people I allowed to touch me this casually. Simion's presence was comforting though.

"Is there anything you want me to say to him?" I offered. "Or a note you want me to get to him...after?"

"Come on, Armise," he scoffed. "If I was a fucking poet I wouldn't be killing people for a living."

I smirked.

He caught my eye and gave a sad smile. "Nah. He knows everything that counts."

Simion was heartsick, but not broken. He was a good man who owned the consequences of his decisions and continued to move forward, holding on to his humanity despite his position of authority.

There was so much more I could have learned from him if we'd had the time.

I unbuckled the strap of my watch, slid it out from under my beads and handed it to Simion. "Make sure this gets to Maniel Gloden, the hybrid and former Dark Ops officer. He's staying with Neveed and Chen. He won't believe I'm dead unless he sees this."

"It's a watch," he noted.

I huffed in frustration. It was a response Merq would have given. "You should know better than to assume something is only as it appears on the outside."

"So what's the deal with this then?"

"Maniel knows," I evaded.

"I see that rehab rule number three, subset A has been revoked in favor of rehab rule number four."

"Maybe you will ask the right question the next time," I chided him, trying to bring some kind of levity to the situation. There were few people whose happiness I cared about, but Simion would be always be one.

Simion toyed with the watch, examining the face and the coded markings on the back. He attached it to his wrist then hung his head almost to his chest. "Yeah, maybe next time."

There was a knock and Simion squeezed my thigh then dropped off the table. He opened the door and stood to the side for Dr. Casas and Exley to enter.

Dr. Casas waited for the door to shut, and for Simion to lock it, before he said anything. "The medical wing has been vacated per your orders, President Simion. The Council wishes for me to thank you for considering their safety."

Exley clapped me on the shoulder, then settled his hand on my cheek and patted it. He didn't say anything. He didn't have to. There were equal parts grief and gratitude written across his features. Merq had once told me that Exley was the easiest for him to read. I now understood what he'd meant.

"Are you ready for the extraction, Officer Darcan?" Dr. Casas said. He held a device in one hand and a scalpel, syringe, and capped tube in the other.

"More than," I answered.

Dr. Casas came to the edge of the table and Simion and Exley hovered behind him, watching over his shoulder. "Lie down on the table with your chin hanging off the end. It won't be comfortable but this won't take long."

I moved into position and held my breath.

"Exhale, Officer Darcan. I need you to breathe evenly for the next few minutes."

I shifted my position. I wasn't comfortable, but not because of how I lay.

"Please call me Armise," I said to him. "I'm no longer a Dark Ops officer."

His fingertips were warm against the back of my neck. "Okay, Armise. Now remain as still as you can but continue to breathe. I'll inject localized surge to numb the area so you shouldn't feel anything. Tell me if you do."

"I will."

There was the prick of a needle then the warmth of surge flooding up my neck, over my shoulders, and down my back. I heard Dr. Casas' movements but couldn't feel what he was doing. The sound of the stopper being pulled from the tube came from above me then the clatter of the chip being dropped inside. There was pressure applied to my neck then nothing.

Simion gave an audible exhale. "You remember what your instructions are, Feliu?"

Dr. Casas tapped my back. "You can sit up now, Armise."

I stood and rotated my shoulders, grateful to find that the localized surge wouldn't hamper my movement. I didn't want to waste any time now that I was free of the chip.

Dr. Casas nodded. "My report will reflect that the extraction was successful but the subject's shielding chip wasn't the same as the others, therefore the subject didn't survive the extraction. In order to protect the integrity of our facility, the subject's body was taken to the incinerator by me."

While Simion and Exley knew what came next, they—and Chen—were the only ones. Dr. Casas believed he was covering for my solo escape. I didn't understand why he was willingly putting himself at risk to give me a chance at freedom.

"Thank you," I said. It was the smallest of tokens, but the only thing I had left to offer.

"I'm sorry about Merq. He was—" Dr. Casas cut himself off. He swallowed and didn't finish that sentence. "I wish you good luck and safe travels, Armise."

"Thank you, Feliu," Simion said. "Hold on to the chip for at least a half hour then make sure it gets to Major Jegs."

I waited for Dr. Casas to leave the room before I spoke. "Are you sure she won't destroy the chip just for vengeance?"

"She won't. We've likely lost her to the Nationalists, but at least they're our allies now. Let's be real, Armise. There was little chance I could hold this team together with him—" Simion clamped his eyes shut, then slicked his hair back with both hands. "I can't hold our team together like Merq did."

It was the first time I'd heard Simion say Merq's name since Merq's death. He was a lingering presence in this room and between the three of us. I would be the only one of us who had any closure though.

Exley was balanced on the tips of his toes, as if he was restraining himself from going to Simion's side. I was fighting the same impulse. But Simion's battle was internal—one he would have to learn to fight on his own.

I hadn't fully understood Merq's place in the lives of Simion and Jegs until today. "He united you."

Simion nodded but didn't say anything else.

Exley stepped forward and handed me an old-generation transport chip that was connected to a small black box by a thin wire. "This will allow you to program the coordinates of where you're going into the chip, then you can destroy the device or take it with you. There will be no record of where you're going, even in transport station logs."

"Is it an encryption designed by Chen?" I asked as I set the device and chip aside. I wasn't going to tempt fate by entering those digits where anyone else could see them. Even men I trusted.

Exley nodded and handed me the other box from the bag slung over his shoulder. "You're going to need this too."

I took the box of transformation serum in my left hand, fearful that if I touched it with my right I wouldn't be able to control my synth and it would crush the contents. The blood tie lock was still engaged and only Merq's DNA could open it. I would have to wait for that, too.

I could feel Exley's and Simion's gazes on me as I cradled the box. The two of them were quiet in a way that made me uncomfortable. "What is it?"

Exley glanced at Simion. Simion stuffed his hands in his pockets, rocked back on his heels, then crooked his head in my direction. "Go ahead, Ex. Tell him. I don't know how else we're going to explain this."

"There's something else you need to know," Exley began. "I lied to Merq when I told him I'd tested the serum and that's how I knew what it was. You'll find every last drop of it still in there."

My heartbeat kicked up, a sick regret coursing through me that I had killed Merq and all of this had been for nothing. Already tipping over the edge of my patience levels, anger coursed through me at Exley's admission.

I glared at him. "How can you be sure of what it is then?"

"Because I received an encrypted message telling me what it was. Then another on how to use it," Exley said with complete calm.

There was only one possibility of who that message could have come from. "Sarai Kersch."

Exley shook his head. "There's no way to know for sure. Chen tried to track the message but we couldn't pinpoint *where* it came from, let alone *who*." He handed me a folded piece of paper. "This will show you exactly how to use the injections and in what order. Each syringe contains enough for two doses. So you're going to have leftovers."

"'Leftovers?'" Simion scoffed. "What the fuck is up with both of you and your word choice today? This isn't a meal we're talking about here, Ex."

Exley erupted, much like Simion had earlier. He tossed a handful of braids over his shoulder then poked at Simion's chest. "What the fuck do you want from us? Your scraggly ass doesn't get to hide behind some flippant remark because you don't know how to deal with your shit and force us to be uncomfortable."

Simion's jaw clenched and he balled his fists. I was sure Simion was going to take a shot at Ex, then a hint of a smile appeared on his face. "Isn't calling my perfectly fine ass 'scraggly' a flippant remark?"

Exley gaped and turned to me. "You sure you don't want to take him with you?"

I held back a chuckle. If nothing else, I would be able to tell Merq that Exley and Simion were okay. "We *are* going to have leftovers."

"I knew Merq letting the two of you become friends was going to be an issue." Exley flicked Simion's chest, then turned on his heel and crossed his arms. "Goddamn leftovers...."

Simion grinned for only a second then began to pace again, his lips tugging deeper into a frown with each step he took. "Okay, but seriously. Tell Armise why it matters that there's extra in there."

Exley scooted onto the table next to me. "From what we can tell, Chen isn't aging anymore. None of the hybrids are. At the very least, their cellular degradation has slowed to a crawl and their ability for regeneration is heightened. We won't know for sure what's happening to them for a very long time. What it likely means though is if you use that serum on Merq and it works, then the same principle applies. More importantly, what those leftovers mean is that you will have a chance to use the transition cocktail too if you want."

I kept my face blank. This wasn't news to me thanks to Chen. It was one of the main reasons why I'd agreed to Merq's plan at all. But neither Simion nor Exley needed to know that.

"I understand," I said.

Exley sputtered. "I expected a way bigger reaction than that! I tell you that you and Merq could possibly double your life expectancy, *together*, and you give me your understanding? A romantic you are not, Armise Darcan."

Simion raised an eyebrow at his second-in-command. "Not like you, Ex?"

Exley flipped him off. "You and your scraggliness can fuck off."

Simion leaned a hip against the table—bracketing me between him and Exley—and stared me down. "Still scared?"

I nodded. "That will not change until I see Merq's eyes open again."

Simion put a hand on my shoulder and squeezed. "It will happen."

Merq had always been the one to ask unending questions, but I needed to take on that role for now. I had new insight into just how much patience it took—and restraint I'd never recognized was there—for Merq to explore every option before he acted.

"And after?" I continued. "What have you been able to discover about the transition? Some of the hybrids are completely unstable. They are not—" *They're not themselves anymore.* "Yet Manny seems to have taken to the transition without those complications."

"That seems to be a function of age," Exley answered. "The younger the hybrid, the worse the transition. Older candidates seem to fare better. But again, we don't know for sure."

I gnawed at my lip and rolled my shoulders to keep any post-surge stiffness from settling in. The need to act was eating away at me—tearing me apart inside—with each second I was away from Merq. "I cannot delay any longer. The longer we talk and the more I learn…. My goal has to remain Merq, and getting him away from here. I need to get him home."

"I understand," Simion said. "The Council will be told your bodies have been burned—"

I clenched my jaw and raised my hand to stop Simion from giving me another placating statement that delayed me. I didn't want my friendship with Simion or Exley to end in a bad way, but now that the encryption chip had been removed, I needed them to know where my focus was. "I care about your welfare and your future but I will not be here to directly impact it. I am trying very hard not to tear through both of you to get back to him. I do not care what you tell the Council or what happens next. It is time for me to go or you may not leave this room with your vocal chords intact."

Simion recoiled. I had never spoken to him that way. Then Exley huffed out a quiet laugh, breaking the tension I had caused. "I don't know about you, Ricor. But I prefer silent Armise to deadly Armise."

"That you and Merq were enemies for such a long time suddenly makes so much more sense," Simion said. He took a step back and smirked. "Then we'll leave you to it. The med facility should be clear for another fifteen minutes."

I wouldn't need that long.

I jumped off the table and took a moment to memorize the details of two faces I would never see again, but would never forget.

I didn't know what else to say besides, "Thank you. Both of you."

"No thanks ever needed, Armise," Exley said. "But you're welcome."

"Just love each other well," Simion added. He slung an arm around my shoulder. "And that's an order straight from your president."

Out of every order I had ever received, that request would be the easiest to follow through on.

*　*　*

I had never wanted to kill, but I'd been too good at it to be left alone.

First by Vachir, when he'd learned I could hit the center of a target only years after I could walk. Then by the Singaporean Dark Ops after the DCR attack on my village.

There was no other evidence of my skill needed besides the man I loved lying motionless on the table in front of me.

My skill was inborn and they had all used it to their own advantages. *I* had used it to my advantage to keep me alive. I'd practiced until my aim was flawless, as natural as breathing.

'*There's no one else I'd trust with my death,*' Merq had said when I agreed to this insane plan. He'd laughed—a pained sound that had been removed from his usual sarcasm. A sound that had spoken to the inevitability of our end.

Then, I'd not only understood his viewpoint, I'd shared it. But now....

Now, he was dead.

And I was realizing the fault of our perspective much too late.

The mechanics of death were much too easy for us to accept.

The realities of life were much more complicated. Much more painful. Much more tenuous.

Lividity was setting into his limbs, and my legs shook. Anger welled inside me with every wound on his skin, but Merq felt no pain.

He was dead, and yet I was the one who was fragile.

I didn't hold back the tears that poured down my cheeks when I touched him. I took the set of beads off my right wrist and placed them on his. I whispered prayers over his form—for safe passage, peace, and gratitude—as I dressed him in the scraps of cloth Exley had left behind. They were muted fabrics that resembled the clothes of the jacquerie.

His skin was gray. His lips were as white as sun-bleached stone.

Wherever we ended up, I would never again take for granted the color of life.

I'd done a cursory search of the sector Merq's coordinates were leading me to. I knew it was in the Northern Territories but that was all I knew. I programmed the chip and put the device into my pack with the serum instead of destroying it—I had been the cause of too much destruction already—lifted Merq into my arms and activated the transport chip.

I locked my knees to remain standing when we materialized in the Northern Territories. The sun hadn't yet risen and the sky should have been black—void of all light this far from people—but there were streaks of green that shimmered above our heads.

It was silent. And cold.

And I was filled with hope.

There was a stone wall two feet in front of me with an electrical panel of some kind exposed. I understood with complete clarity why Merq had been so adamant about me getting the coordinates right. He had placed me *exactly* where I needed to be.

I used one of the packets of Merq's blood that Exley had given me, puncturing it against the edges of the blood tie lock on the wall. A door I hadn't noticed was there popped open. Light streamed into the night and I pushed inside carrying Merq's body, struggling more to hold onto him with each step I took. I'd barely made it inside when I had to drop to my knees to keep from losing my grip on him.

I was lost to the steps that I needed to take now that I had Merq here. My complete focus became the process on the piece of paper, written in a loopy scrawl I had to assume was Exley's handwriting.

He had documented every step in detail, as if I wouldn't be able to comprehend the most basic of functions.

1. Unlock the box using one pouch of blood. Keep the others just in case. For what, I don't know. Just do it.
2. Extract the syringes and place them on a clean surface.

3. Sanitize the needles with the included wipes (don't skip this step just in case, Darcan!)

4. Inject the red serum into Merq's arm, stopping at the mark on the syringe. This is the revival serum. It may take a few minutes. So now you wait. I don't know how long. Just wait.

5. As soon as Merq's heart begins to beat inject the black serum to the mark on the syringe. This is the one that will start the hybrid transformation process. Try to inject this one before he starts moving around too much.

6. DO NOT INJECT THE SILVER STUFF. IT'S THE TITANALLOY INJECTION. (It should be okay for you to use though.)

7. Wait some more. And pray if you're into that kind of thing. I'll be saying one on my end either way.

I read through the instructions twice, then a third time, preparing to follow them as if Exley were standing next to me. In a way, he was. Simion too. Because below Exley's list, in a jagged script that was different than the one above it, there was an additional step—

Give Merq a kiss from me (aka Sims). Or I guess it could be from you. Either way, he deserves one right now if you've made it this far.

I followed the first three steps, then took the first syringe into my left hand and slid the needle beneath Merq's skin.

"To live here will be the measure of peace we've been seeking, Merq," I said out loud. "Now you just have to wake up and see it for yourself."

Then I injected the revival serum.

I set the syringe aside and placed my synthetic hand on his chest, waiting for my overly sensitive nerves to pick up the first thrums of his heartbeat. I couldn't rip my gaze away from him. I couldn't move at all.

The first twitch could have been my own impatience, my own desperate need to feel anything, but the next thrum under my fingers was unquestionable. I left my hand where it was, pressed tightly to Merq's chest, when Merq gasped in a huge breath and began to thrash.

I propelled myself over his body, straddling his waist to hold him down, and plunged the second syringe into his arm. His eyes opened, rolled back in his head, then there was a gush of blood pouring from his eye sockets and I lost all semblance of calm.

I attempted to hold down his body as he writhed in pain and screamed out. The color returned to his skin, but it was a vicious purple-red, amplified by the crimson staining his cheeks.

Then he went completely, deathly still.

"No," I breathed out.

"No," I repeated over and over again.

I laid my ear against his chest and immediately heard and felt the steady thump of a strong heartbeat.

Wait, Exley's note had said.

I didn't want to wait anymore.

I couldn't pray as Exley had told me to do.

I couldn't think.

I slid off Merq and gathered him in my arms. The heat had returned to his skin and he was breathing, so I ripped the shirt away from his chest and studied the spot where my bullet had torn into him.

The wound that was now stitching back together as I watched.

Waves passed through Merq's body and his teeth gritted together with an audible scrape. The flow of blood from his eyes had stopped, and my stomach lurched as I realized what I had forgotten.

"The memory projector."

Genetically modified bodies expelled the memory projector. But if that's what had happened to him.... That meant the modifications were taking hold.

That meant there was more than hope.

I tore one of the sanitized wipes open and swiped at the blood on Merq's face. He curled into me, lifted his hand—the one with the wrist circled in my bracelets—and clutched his fingers into my shirt.

"Armise?"

Of course the first word coming from his mouth, even after death, would be phrased as a question. I cradled him closer to me—couldn't get close enough—and kissed his hair, then the line of piercings down his ear.

"You remember me?"

"I—"

My throat tightened as I waited for his response.

"I could never forget you."

I set my hand on his chest, at the spot where his wound was now closed. The skin had healed over and not even a scar remained.

"Why can't I see you?"

I grimaced. "The memory projector. I didn't think about it—"

He placed his hand over mine where it lay on his chest and squeezed. "It doesn't matter. It worked."

"Or maybe I'm not that good of a shot."

His brow furrowed then he winced in pain. "No, this is... different. It's...."

"Overwhelming?"

Merq shivered and I increased my body temp until he eased in my arms.

"We'll deal with it," I reassured him.

He nodded. "Together."

A NOTE FROM THE AUTHOR

Dear Reader,

In the summer of 2012 I was watching a rifle competition during the Summer Olympics and had this flash of an idea about guns that fired sound waves instead of bullets. The first iteration of *One Breath, One Bullet* was two thousand words. I thought that the story and characters had possibility, so I asked two friends to read it over. Both said they wanted to know more. (This series came to life because of you, Nik and Amanda!)

One Breath, One Bullet became twenty thousand words, then the originally published thirty thousand—only to land at fifty thousand in this most recent version. There was no going back once I'd let Merq have a voice.

No, let me rephrase that.

In truth, my real point of no return was the first time Merq said Armise's name.

From the very beginning I knew Merq and Armise would end up in their safe house in the Northern Territories—finally free of all obligation, and retired for all intents and purposes. I just had to get them there.

That journey took much longer than I could've anticipated.

The title of *Dominant Predator* came from a bumper sticker on a beat-to-shit pickup truck in a Meijer parking lot. I hadn't finished writing *One Breath, One Bullet* yet, but I couldn't get that title out of my head. While I struggled to piece together all of the intricacies of this new world in the first book, writing *Dominant Predator* was easy. I couldn't type fast enough every time Merq and Armise were on page together. The draw between the two of them was charged in a way I hadn't (and still haven't) experienced with any other characters.

I was desperate for them to be happy.

Which meant that ripping them apart in *Powerless* was beyond difficult. Yet I knew that Merq had to grow as a person before anything more could come of their relationship, and Merq was way too practiced at repressing anything emotional in his life.

That is something Merq and I have in common.

Powerless was written during a traumatic part of my life, when my daily existence was in upheaval—much like Merq's. Strangely enough, the outline of that book was finished long before I could have known what circumstances I would be writing it under. Merq's grief, frustration, and sadness—him being unsettled and not *whole*—was way too easy for me to tap into.

I healed with Merq during *Powerless*. But that healing process took much longer for me than it did for Merq, and I couldn't continue their story until I was ready to put everything I had into it. That break lasted almost a year and a half.

I started writing *Falling, One By One* under scarily similar circumstances to *Powerless*, but with a very different outcome this time. *Falling, One by One* was always meant to be a love story without the trappings of traditional romantic love. It was meant to be an homage to Armise, and also answer the question, "Just how far will Armise go for Merq before he doesn't know if this man is worth it anymore?"

I wrote the ending to FOBO while sitting in a restaurant with Jo Peterson. To give some context, I hadn't even written the *second* book yet, but Ahriman's brutalization of Armise was so clear in my head. Jo read the scene and promptly stated that I was the worst human being on the face of the earth and that she hated me. That was more than fair. I hated myself.

Strength of the Rising Sun followed right on the heels of completing *Falling, One by One*. I pretty much spent the entire six-week process repeating *fixitfixitfixit* over and over in my head. I hadn't lost sight of where Merq and Armise would end up, but it was a battle to get them there.

Merq and Armise have never done anything the easy way. Maybe I share that with them too. I may have never gotten to the end of this series without the help of an incredible support crew.

Thank you to my sister for bringing life to Merq's tattoo and to the symbol for the Revolution. Your ability to create is a gift to this world. Never stop pursuing the next shiny thing.

I owe the world to Jo for sitting next to me and forcing me to write these books. For feeding me bourbon and praise and pushing me forward. Your unfailing support of me is more than I deserve.

To Abi, my insomniac sister in writing, for treading through hour after hour of sprints at all times of the day. I think I won one, maybe two, of said sprints! You're a brilliant machine, lady. If I could manifest surge, genetmods, and synths for you I would.

To T, for putting up with an endless stream of screaming face and speak-no-evil monkey emojis over text. You've always been solidly in my corner, and whether you realize it or not, that support is one of the major reasons I keep writing.

To Nic, for asking me how Armise would tie his boots.

Thank you for helping create one of my favorite moments in the entire series.

To Ely, for well...everything. You've been my partner in crime from the very first words. You've helped me see both Merq and Armise in ways that weren't possible for me to pick apart. We'll get those AUs someday, even if we have to write them ourselves.

To Teresa, for picking up the series from the beginning and giving me the fresh perspective I so badly needed. You've been the stone that the sword was sharpened on.

To Abby, for your tweets and emails sent from locations all over the globe. For your words of encouragement sent exactly when I needed them most. Thank you for trusting me. I hope we're able to meet in person someday.

To every reader.... Your messages keep me writing when I want to burn every pen and piece of paper in existence. You are my Armise. I'm sorry for torturing you. I hope this journey was worth it.

The Borders War wasn't written as a political statement, but dystopia is a genre that lends itself to examining our current environment in a new light. I realize some overlap of present political instability will be unavoidable, but there was only one statement that I purposefully sought out to explore. The word "gay" or mention of any sexual orientation is absent from The Borders War. The entire series. From the beginning I wanted to build this world that was falling apart, destroying itself, and yet the gender of the person you slept with or fell in love with had no impact on how you were perceived. Just a hint of utopia in a dystopic world.

As for the future of this world, Merq and Armise's arc is complete. It's time to give them the peace they've earned. But that doesn't mean I intend on exiting The Borders War completely. I, personally, need to know Neveed is going to be okay. He wasn't meant to make it out of this series alive, but I couldn't kill him. He has so much more to tell.

Then there's Simion. I plot the hell out of books, but Simion was a character I couldn't plan for. Unlike Merq and Armise, I can't tell you where he's headed, but I know exactly who will be at his side when he gets there.

Jegs, Exley, Grimshaw, Chen, Elina, Manny, Priyessa—even Nayan, Sharlat, Isida, and Shio.... All of their voices are a quiet static in the back of my brain. I don't think they'll allow me to hold them back for too long. The Borders War is two hundred and fifty thousand words in five books, spanning over twenty years in Merq's life, and there's so still so much more I could tell you about this world.

For now, let's all channel Merq and take a collective, cleansing inhale and remember not to lose hope.

I'll see you on whatever flip side we end up on,

Sam xx

SANCTUARY

THE BORDERS WAR #5.5

Trademarks Acknowledgement

The author acknowledges the trademarked status and trademark owners of the following wordmarks mentioned in this work of fiction:

Olympics: United States Olympic Committee Corporation

Winchester: Olin Corporation

ABOUT SANCTUARY

Book five-point-five in The Borders War series

They were never meant to find peace.

It's been five years since Merq stood in front of Armise's rifle, facing the truth that their relationship would inevitably end this way. Five years since he woke up to darkness but immediately knew Armise was at his side. Both of them are heavily scarred and battling a past they will never be able to fully outrun.

But maybe, against all odds, they've finally found a measure of peace.

Reading Order

One Breath, One Bullet
Dominant Predator
Powerless

Falling, One by One
Strength of the Rising Sun
Sanctuary

To Ely

SANCTUARY

MERQ

October 20, 2565
Merq Grayson's 42nd year
Northern Territories—home

ARMISE BARELY MADE it inside the front door before I stripped him of his coat so I could drag him into the bedroom. Anger rippled along my skin—barely restrained fury that I hadn't felt in a very long time. He had to know I was upset because he followed me willingly, silently, his hand entwined with mine.

"Boots off now."

I reluctantly let him go, then shoved him onto the bed.

He thumped his boots to the floor without a word and I slid my hands over his shoulders and to the back of his neck, gritting my teeth. His hands gripped my hips and he dropped his forehead against my stomach, his breath coasting over my skin as he breathed deeply. My anger ebbed. Fractionally.

I tugged his shirt off, pushed him down and slid between his thighs, setting my palms on his chest and curling my fingertips into the warmth of his skin. I tugged gently on the hair there. Couldn't get any words past the tightness in my chest.

"Merq—"

"Just be quiet," I demanded.

We each needed our space—even the expansive, unpopulated Northern Territories felt too small to hold both of us somedays. But he'd been gone too long this time.

"Nine days," I rasped out, unable to hide my fear. "It shouldn't have taken you so long."

"I know."

I draped myself over him and breathed in the scent of his skin. Of the ozone tinged air of the Northern Territories. Of the Singaporean balms he'd learned how to make on his own here —in our home. I ran my hands over the unmarked skin of his synth, then the scars hidden underneath tattooed flames. I listened to the steady thrum of his heartbeat and pressed my lips to his neck so I could feel his pulse there too.

"I'm okay, Merq."

"I don't care," I bit out.

Armise's shoulders lifted with a silent laugh.

Asshole.

He gripped my biceps, the stone and wood of his bracelets clacking together with the movement. "I missed you."

Fuck. I couldn't hold onto any anger when he said things like that to me.

I inhaled deeply. "You ran into complications?"

"An early blizzard. I had to hole up in the refuge."

A natural complication, not man-made. For the last four days, as I'd counted the minutes slipping past the time when he should've been home, all I'd been able to think about was that we'd been found.

For four days I'd been thinking of the time—years in the past and continents away—when I'd desperately reached out for him, seeking his solidness and the warmth of life, after I'd washed Ahriman's blood from my hands.

Our lives had unraveled into chaos after that night, causing infinitely more pain than I'd ever thought either of us would have to bear. We'd survived, but only because we'd worked together.

For the last four days, I hadn't been able to shake the thought that he was out there alone.

I still couldn't shut down the barrage of memories that rolled through my head like a churning electrical storm, even with his massive frame under my fingertips. Thoughts always swirling back to Ahriman, a man I didn't want to think about at all.

Every crossroads I'd ever faced had intersected the same way —regardless of place or time—the instances stacking on top of each other instead of along a line. As if fate had the ability to circle back in interconnected loops—always returning me to a place where my body was broken and only my will existed to pull me through.

But these last five years had been different. Every moment with Armise was different.

I didn't want to live a life without him.

I lived with fear because I had him to lose.

I sighed.

Both of us refused to use comms, trackers, or the one transport chip we did have. When either or both of us set out, it was in true isolation. Although he was able to stray much farther from home territory, alone, than I.

"You're not going alone again," I insisted.

"I thought you didn't care."

I heard the smile on his damning lips.

I huffed. "Just tell me what Chen's letter says."

Armise shifted to the side, nudging my arm out of the way so he could dig into his pocket. When he settled again, I propped my chin on my hands, looking up at him even though I couldn't see him.

Armise languidly arched into me, pressing his palm into the small of my back. The piece of paper in his other hand crinkled.

"She is well," Armise answered, his rumbling voice rolling through me. "But I don't think Chen would tell us even if she wasn't."

I swallowed around the discomfort his statement raised, but I couldn't fault him for being as bluntly honest as he always was. Armise didn't lie to me.

"What else?"

"She sent new types of seeds we can try out, a few books, the usual supplies.... She also said she's sorry but she's going to miss the next shipment date. She's heading out on a mission."

"A mission," I repeated. I didn't bother to filter the worry from my voice.

"She's twenty-two, Merq, and nearly indestructible. Neveed and Manny can't keep her hidden away forever."

I paused before I asked my next question, even though Armise already knew it would be coming from my lips. "Any other news?"

The Revolution, rebuilding, the hybrids, Sarai Kersch.... I shouldn't have cared, I didn't need to anymore, and yet I wondered.

Armise's heart beat steadily under my hands as he shifted to set the letter aside. The hand that had been holding Chen's note dragged through my hair, urging me closer. "Nothing," he answered as he coaxed me up to his lips.

I lingered with my mouth against his, a chaste, slow kiss of reacquaintance. My anger—my worry—completely dissipated.

"Chen is still alive," he continued when I drew back. "As is everyone else."

"I suppose that's all that matters."

Sanctuary

"Neither for you, nor for me," he said. "But we made our choice."

We had. "No word from anyone else?"

I felt the shake of Armise's head as my fingertips traced his jaw, at his overgrown beard. "I can only assume she still hasn't verified we're alive."

I should've felt guilt for that, and I did to an extent, but not enough to risk the safety I'd died for. Not enough to risk our peace.

"She'll go to her grave carrying that secret."

"Whenever that is," Armise noted.

I hummed and sat up, straddling his waist. Neither of us knew how long her life would be extended by her hybrid transformation—or how long ours would be because of the same process. Armise was on the downslide to fifty years old now, but his body felt stronger underneath my fingertips than it had in his twenties.

I reached out, tangling my fingers in his hair. "How much of this is silver now?"

Armise swatted my hand away with a gruff grunt.

I had to laugh. "That much, huh?"

Armise set his hands on my hips and pushed me off him as he grumbled. "We should unpack the crate she sent."

The mattress dipped as Armise moved. His bare feet slapped against the stone floor. A protracted sigh escaped his lips as he stood.

Less than an hour after returning and he was already annoyed with me. I smiled even though he likely had his back to me. "I missed you too."

I didn't hear a hint of movement then I was being pinned to the bed, Armise's body covering mine, my hands trapped above my head, wrists caught in his iron grip. I didn't fight his hold on me.

"Fuck you," he growled in my ear. "For nine days I was surrounded by silence and all I wanted to hear was your voice."

"I thought you needed the silence." It was the reason he'd stated for traveling to the extraction point of Chen's deliveries alone this time.

"Apparently, I no longer know how to function without endless questions being tossed at me throughout the day."

I smirked. "Is that so?"

"Merq...."

The warning in his tone sent shivers up my spine.

"Yes, Darcan?"

His hold around my wrists tightened. He bit down on my earlobe—hard—and the searing pain brought my cock to full attention.

"Not one more question."

I couldn't see, and I'd never be stronger than him, but I had one distinct advantage that would always overpower him.

I craned my neck back to give him better access. Giving myself over to him. Giving him what he wanted. "None needed. You already admitted that you missed me."

He nipped at my neck, and released my wrists to drag his hands down my sides. "I lied."

I smiled.

His lips followed the path of his hands, his beard scratching at my stomach, and I arched into him, grabbing onto his biceps. His palms burned hot against my skin and his teeth sank in over and over again, marking me, even though, because of my modifications, those marks would be gone in minutes.

I bit at my lip piercing, holding back a smile. "Were you lying?"

Armise set his hands on my shoulders and ground down against my cock harshly, the pain stealing my breath.

"I warned you, Merq," he growled.

I slid my palm up his chest, over his neck, and gripped his beard, yanking his lips to mine. "Welcome home, Armise."

* * *

I CROUCHED and fed another log into the fire, using the crackling pops and the heat of the flame to guide my placement. The licking flames warmed my face and chest as I sat back on my haunches and ran my hand through my shower-damp hair.

"Next time, we should see if Chen can procure us new boots."

Armise's voice came from across the main living area where he was unpacking the crate Chen had sent, cataloging the contents before I stored them away in their designated spots. A duty I'd taken on years ago to ensure my path around our home always remained clear.

I stood and brushed my hands clean on my pants. "That would be good."

"And Chen sent arrows. Why arrows?"

I grinned. It hadn't been a guarantee that she'd be able to accommodate my request in time, but, as she always did when either of us had a specialized need, she'd found a way.

Because I asked her to, was the easy answer to Armise's question. Instead I crossed the room and uncovered the weapon I'd been working on for months—hidden away from Armise's prying eyes behind the volumes of journals lining one of the bookshelves.

I had notebooks full of thick paper dotted with the sensory script one of Chen's shipments had introduced us to. A language Armise had learned as well, but never read any of my entries unless I invited him. I spent quiet hours hunched over those notebooks, reconstructing the events of my life— our life—in ever growing detail. Unraveling timelines and previously hidden motivations. Piecing our pasts together in a new way.

I'd always been the one to ignore the passage of time, but time mattered. Each day, each second, held an immeasurable value I couldn't deny anymore.

When he'd set out for Chen's drop point on October eleventh, I'd been surprised. The trip to pick up our supplies took five days and he'd always separated himself from me, somehow, on October twentieth. I had pages worth of documentation verifying that pattern.

A decades old pattern he'd broken this year.

If not for a snowstorm, he would've been back on the sixteenth. Even with the blizzard, he could've waylaid, taking another day to return. But he'd returned to me today.

I didn't believe in the god Wensen Kersch had, but I believed in the power of Armise's and my unbreakable bond to each other. I believed that, even after twenty years together, it only grew stronger, despite the secrets we still clung to.

Secrets that were no longer a necessity and instead an ever-evolving game of wits between two former assassins.

I smiled and handed him the crossbow.

"This is for me?"

I heard the furrow in his brow. "Today is October twentieth, isn't it?"

"It is."

"Happy Birthday, Armise."

His silence was complete, then, "How did you know?"

A memory flashed into my consciousness. Armise and I sitting next to another vast ocean and speaking openly, honestly, about his older brother, Armise's choice to turn his back on the country that had created him, his choice for me, and hints of how he'd been able to track me across the globe for so many years.

He'd answered more of my questions that night than I'd ever thought he would, but in the end he'd still managed to evade answering me completely.

We had many more years to learn about each other. To continue a game neither of us would grow tired of, because we both won in the end.

I shrugged and answered him just as he'd answered me that night. "Leave some things to be unknown."

* * *

I INHALED DEEPLY as we stepped outside, breathing in the frosty air.

I didn't venture far from our home without Armise, and with the impending cold snap, I'd been even more reluctant to do so when he'd left. It had taken years to perfect, to attune my senses in a new way, but I could now move around our home, the land surrounding our home, and on the hunt with Armise without him having to watch my every step.

I couldn't see anymore, but that didn't mean I didn't remember. I remembered a sky filled with the thrumming lights of electrically charged particles dancing in ribbons with Wensen Kersch at my side. I remembered the depth of stars and galaxies above the *ger* Armise and I had shared, his body warm against mine as the fire faded with the night. Darkness didn't always mean the loss of hope.

I carried my rifle with me, the Winchester that had survived through hundreds of years of war and Chen had ensured was returned to me. I felt safer with its weight on my shoulder, but not nearly as safe as I did with Armise's silent presence at my back.

I had the distinct feeling of being watched, of someone else's eyes on me besides Armise's, then a cold nose pressed into my hand.

"Hello, Narantuyaa," I said as I scratched behind the wolf's ears.

She pressed against my side, and I had to widen my stance to keep from being toppled over.

"Did she travel with you?" I asked Armise.

"The entire way."

He hadn't been nearly as alone as I'd imagined.

"Then let's find something to reward our *khasar*."

Narantuyaa butted her nose against my arm, urging me forward, as if she knew I was praising her loyalty. After three years at Armise's and my side, maybe she did.

As we tracked farther away from our home, Armise took the lead and I followed his nearly silent footsteps. Every now and then Narantuyaa nudged against my leg, keeping me solidly on track and away from any rocks or felled branches that could set me off-kilter. The hairs on my arm stood on end, a response to the palpable electricity swirling in the sky above us, which, Armise and I had to come to learn, sent the predators into shelter while big game emerged to graze.

We would only need one elk to maintain our meat stores through the winter, and possibly beyond that. We hunted judiciously and with a respect for the precarious balance of life in the NT—taking only what we needed and working to leave as little behind as we could.

That drive could be partially attributed to masking our presence here completely, for safety, but was a direct product of Armise's connection to the land. A connection I had begun to share.

"I don't hear anything," I said, coming to a stop.

I should've been able to catch the hush of small animals

whisking through the trees and over the leaf-covered ground at the very least. But even those normal sounds were absent.

Armise's footsteps slowed, then he tracked back toward me. "I'm not seeing anything either. Maybe the snow I encountered is heading here next."

And all the animals had taken shelter, more aware than us of the minuscule shifts in the atmosphere that signaled oncoming fronts. "Maybe."

A low whine emanated from Narantuyaa's throat and I reached down to pet her flank, only to find the hair at the back of her neck bristled.

"Or maybe not," I whispered.

Armise fell completely silent then. I couldn't even hear his footsteps. But within seconds his fingertips were pressed against my forearm, using the hand signals we'd developed years ago to adjust my position. I lifted my rifle and braced it against my shoulder. The air shifted around me as Armise maneuvered silently behind him, sighting my rife. He tapped me into place, making minor adjustments to my aim, then his hand stilled. I breathed and waited.

With a sweep of his fingers I pulled the trigger and the bullet exploded out, kicking the rifle back into my shoulder.

"Great shot," Armise said as he passed around me.

But I already knew that from the bounding of Narantuyaa's feet across the leaves and her howl, splitting the silence of the forest almost as much as my shot had.

I slung my rifle over my shoulder again and headed toward the sound of Armise's murmurs, where he would be hunched over, offering a blessing he'd learned in his childhood from Vachir.

I waited to speak until I felt his eyes on me again and heard the scrape of his boots against the dirt as he stood. "Enough?"

"More than enough to get us and Narantuyaa into the summer."

"A good birthday then."

"One of the best."

I'd given him a new weapon to master and ensured our stomachs would be full for months to come. For fuck's sake. It had taken me *twenty years* to even discover that today was the day of his birth.

"One of?" I grumbled.

I felt the warmth of Armise's breath on my cheek before he spoke. "On my fifth birthday, my parents gifted me my first horse. I became a man that day."

"I don't know how I could top that," I admitted. "There aren't any horses here, but I suppose you could ride Narantuyaa."

Armise chuckled lowly, a rolling rumble like thunder in the distance, and I pulled him into me before the sound had passed, pressing his smiling lips to mine.

I meant to only hold him against me for a heartbeat, instead I snaked my arms around him and clutched my fingers into his jacket, tightening my grip on him as the fear I'd lived through the last four days spiked.

This was the measure of our days—a continual loop of sleep, food, sex, and humble survival, of which the vital piece would always be Armise.

Armise didn't comment on why I clung to him so tightly, he merely responded with his own enduring force. I could barely breathe, and I didn't care.

I sank into his arms and allowed him to hold me up.

I lived in darkness every day, and yet the darkness I'd carried onto the battlefield for so many years no longer resided inside me. I hadn't struggled to let it go since we'd arrived here either. In surrender to my former enemy, I'd finally found peace.

My darkness had never been complete because of Armise.

ARMISE

21 October 2565
Armise Darcan's 46th year
At Merq's side

I STARED out the window of our bedroom watching the sun rise on a new year in my life and tried to tamp down my worry.

There were nights when Merq slept perfectly still now, streaks of peace. But that peace never lasted.

We'd agreed years ago to never speak Ahriman Blanc's name out loud again, that it was a name that deserved to fall into silence forever, but my extended absence had dredged up emotions neither of us had dealt with in that ensuing time. I heard Ahriman's name in every breath Merq had taken since I'd come home.

After twenty years with Merq, that our blankets now laid on the floor was all the verification I needed that he was struggling.

I turned on my side, facing him, and slung my arm over his waist, regardless of the possibility that he'd awaken suddenly and take a shot at me. Instead of lashing out at me, he curled into my chest, tucking his leg between mine. Seeking me out. For comfort.

My heart tripped an unsteady beat and I drew him closer.

"Do you ever think about using it?" he mumbled against my skin.

I didn't have to ask him to clarify, not after I'd been gone days longer than anticipated.

"No," I answered honestly. As I always did now. "Do you?"

He shook his head. "Then why do we still have it? If we were never going to use it, we would've destroyed it years ago."

We would have one fewer exit plan if we destroyed the single transport chip we did have. But it wasn't escape from our home or escape from each other that we were safeguarding. Holding onto that chip was a metaphorical escape from a past we couldn't outrun. "Because neither of us can forget those four months with Ahriman."

He sighed. His fingernails dragged across my skin as he flopped onto his back, fully awake now. "How much do you remember?"

I stilled. It was the first time he'd ever asked me that question.

I chose my words carefully. "Enough to know that if I could erase that time from my memory, and yours, then I would."

Merq slid his teeth over his lip piercing, thinking. His silence stretched on for minutes, and I remained still, steadfastly pinned to my side of the bed, giving him the time and physical distance he needed when he was deep in thought. He scrubbed his hands through his hair and clenched his jaw. "I don't want to forget it."

I couldn't begin to discern how he'd come to that conclusion, especially since he appeared pained by the mere idea. "Explain."

"Ahriman did us a favor."

I scoffed.

"He did," Merq said with a shrug. "The fallout forced both of us into considering things neither one of us wanted to think about, let alone talk about. I had to learn not to be such a self-involved fuck and you had to reconcile if your love for me was really worth the steep price you paid over and over again."

It always had been, and it always would be. But I couldn't deny that in the aftermath of our captivity, I'd considered the ramifications of my relationship with Merq with a greater weight than I had at any other time in our fifteen years before that.

I would've been content to do that soul-searching with my original arm, though.

"Merq. Ahriman did us no favors. He stripped away your confidence and fractured my faith in you."

"But you moved past that in months." His brow creased and he flipped onto his side, turning to face me. "I still think about me killing your mentor and Vachir. About Nayan and Sharlat and that you'll never step foot inside your *ger* again." His hand slid down my synth, fingertips tracing where my matching flame tattoos had once been. "I'm not plagued by thoughts of Ahriman exactly.... I don't know what I'm thinking."

I'd forgiven him, in word and action, for Torga and my brother a long time ago. He knew that. The rest.... No forgiveness was needed, because he'd taken nothing away from me that I wasn't willing to give. He knew that too.

I huffed. "You think too much, Merq."

"I know I do," he said, his shoulders easing with my taunt. His lips tipped into a smirk. "But work with me here for a second."

"Go ahead."

"You told me Sims called those five years before the

Olympics the callous years because of how cruel I was to you. So what would these last five years be called?"

Realization washed through me, and the weight of his thought process—from the transport chip, to Ahriman, to regrets, then to the span of time when I'd questioned whether I really knew him at all—dropped onto me, stealing my breath. I exhaled slowly, hoping that I'd remain still enough that he wouldn't feel the movement.

He sought reassurance.

Reassurance of the surety of *us* that I thought I'd given him yesterday, but hadn't been nearly enough for how shaken he'd become by my unintentional and unavoidable delay.

I twisted the set of beads on his wrist, pulling the stone my father had carved with his own hands to the front. The same one my mother had blessed only months before her death.

"My earliest memories are of my mother hunched over a fire or grinding dried herbs in a stone bowl. She always smelled of smoke and her fingertips were stained purple from crushing berries into a thick syrup that seemed to heal all ills. The villagers called her a shaman, but I had little concept of what that meant besides that I, too, always smelled of smoke and I had to wash my clothes, and myself, twice as often because she left streaks everywhere she touched."

"That explains why I'm the one who always ends up washing our clothes," Merq mumbled.

It did. But I'd never give him the satisfaction of admitting that out loud.

I ignored his muttering and continued, "When I asked her what her job was, how she contributed to the village like the hunters, horsemen, and farmers I could identify easily, she told me she provided *ariun gazar*."

"*Gazar* I know, but *ariun*...?"

"In Continental English, the closest translation I can think of for the term is 'sanctuary.'"

Merq's brow furrowed. "As in a church?"

"In a way. It can be taken to mean a physical place, but it is just as much a feeling of safety and peace." I slid my thumb over the stone then entwined my fingers through his. "An intangible yet unbreakable connection."

Merq's shoulders lifted with a deep inhale and he sank into the bed, relieved. He kissed each of my knuckles and nodded. "Let's get up and eat. We need to prepare for winter."

* * *

I GLANCED at the black semi-circle device on the table, contemplating when I would tell Merq about it. Although neither Merq nor I had requested it, the arrows hadn't been the only gift Chen had sent, and this one.... I wouldn't hide its presence from Merq. There was nothing I held back from him anymore. But I didn't know how to approach this subject with him either.

While who Merq was at his core hadn't changed with the transformation, physically he had. It had taken two years before the sudden bouts of vertigo faded away, and his steps became sure again. Another year after that for the time span between crippling headaches to stretch into months instead of days. His body had only become stronger because of his modifications, and his wicked tongue hadn't been blunted at all, but his eyes....

I still couldn't state with surety whether or not he regretted losing his sight.

He maneuvered around the galley with little hesitation, dividing his attention between cleaning up the last of our breakfast dishes and tending to a pot of gras beans that simmered on the stove. Despite the heaviness he'd carried to bed with him last night, he was in a good mood. I picked up my cup and decided to leave the discussion of Chen's device for later.

"Stop staring at my ass," he called out without turning around.

I grinned.

Technically, my gaze was focused higher.

I sipped at the coffee Chen had sent in her last package and continued to appreciate the defined lines of his shoulders. His tattoo rippled as he stacked dishes away and the overly bright lights in the galley glinted off the hoop in his nipple when he rotated to lift the top off the pot.

Even though I didn't make a sound as I set down my cup and stalked toward the galley, Merq licked at his lips to hide a smirk. He always seemed to know exactly where I was.

Since I no longer had the element of surprise, I stepped up behind him, gripped his biceps, and kissed just above the knob at the top of his spine. The galley was overly warm from the steam spilling from the pot and the fire Merq had stoked to life this morning. Warm from the heat radiating off his body and sinking into my skin. A familiar, comforting warmth that had chased the chill from my bones years ago.

A fine sheen of sweat had started to bead on his skin, so I dialed down my internal temperature and dragged my lips over his shoulders. Merq released a ragged, wordless plea and planted his hands on the counter, shivering. I slid my hands up his arms then down his back, circling my arms around him and sucking his earlobe between my teeth. "How much longer until you're done?"

He flipped the stove off, and as he rotated on his heel he swiped my legs out from under me, sending me crashing to the floor with him between my thighs.

Right where I wanted him to be.

"I can be done now," he rasped. His hands slid up the inside of my thighs, his touch muted by the cloth barrier between us.

I licked my lips. "Then get your cock inside me."

Within seconds he had me stripped and spread out on the stone floor, my hand fisted in his hair as he swallowed me down. I pumped into his mouth, a moan building deep in my chest that rumbled out of me when Merq slipped his thumb into his mouth, slicking it, then pressing it against my hole. My heels slipped across the floor as I dug in trying to force him inside, but Merq dragged his lips over my cock slowly, teeth catching at the tip, and coasted his hand over my ass before drawing back.

I thunked my head against the floor. "Merq."

"You wanted my attention, Darcan. You have *all* of it now."

Fuck.

He swiped the cooking oil off the counter, then spread his knees wide and pushed his waistband to his thighs. Just far enough down that I could see his stomach contract, holding him in place as he drizzled the oil over his palm. Just far enough that I could watch him slick himself, his back arching and teeth dragging over his lip ring as his hand tightened around the tip of his dick.

He didn't prep me at all, and I had to grip the base of my cock to keep from coming simply from anticipating the slow torture that would come next.

Merq lowered himself over me, merely nudging his cock against my hole and bracing himself with one arm planted at my side. The fingertips of his other hand fluttered over my chest, leaving streaks of oil in their wake, and my skin prickled with need. "I haven't been inside you in weeks, Armise. How tight are you going to be?"

I carded my hands through his hair, through his beard, then over his neck. "You know I can take it."

His lips tipped into a smirk. He took my nipple into his mouth, rolling it between his teeth and flicking it with his tongue. My desire spiked, the absolute need to have him inside me thrumming through my veins. While I could get off just by him fucking me, focusing solely on the slide of his cock driving deep and the demanding grip of his hands, Merq lavished me with his full attention—his lips, tongue, teeth, and the weight of his body over mine, expertly pulling me apart.

With each minute that passed of his intense focus centered completely on me and his cock rocking against me but never pushing inside, I unraveled even more. He nipped at my neck and teased his fingers through the hair at my groin, featherlight touches that drove me mad and left me struggling for breath. I dug my nails into his tattoo and arched into him, that oil slicking the press of my chest to his. Merq groaned against my skin, gripped my hip in a bruising hold, his bracelets digging into my side, and thrust inside me.

The pain was immediate, as was the uncontrollable moan ripped from my throat. I gripped the back of Merq's neck and slammed my lips against his, fucking my tongue into his mouth in the same demanding rhythm that he fucked my ass. Merq's responding rumble of need rippled over my skin and kicked up my heartbeat until I could feel my heart thudding against my breastbone. He shoved at my thighs, opening me up completely to him, and drove in deeper.

Droplets of his sweat beaded on his forehead and slid down his nose, and I ratcheted up my temp to match the fire of my need, my absolute and unending passion, for him. Only him.

Merq cried out desperately. His arms shook and his nails bit painfully into my skin. "Fuck, Armise. I can't...."

I couldn't hold out any longer either. He was just as lost to me as I was to him. I crushed our mouths together as he groaned and thrust deep inside me, and I gave myself over to him completely, just as I would over and over again.

He sagged down onto the floor and flopped onto his side, trapping my arm beneath him. "Fucking hell. I was supposed to ruin you, not have you ruin me."

He'd done exactly that, but I didn't have to tell him—he already knew.

I coaxed him off his side and into my chest with the arm under him, curling my hand over his shoulder and holding him close. Then I buried my nose in his hair so every breath I inhaled as I came back down was all him. Always and only him.

I would've been content to lay on this cold stone floor for hours, tracing lines, scars, and divots on Merq's body, but Merq's fingers fluttered against my stomach and his brow creased with thought, drawn into his unrelenting mental churning.

"We should get cleaned up now. We have work to do."

Work, tracking, hunting, survival.... All those words meant something different here. And all of them would mean something entirely different if Merq could see again.

"We do," I replied, my tone heavier than I'd intended. "But first, there is something I need to show you."

I RESTED against the wall and flipped my knife into the air, catching it by the blade then sending it spinning again. It was the only thing I could do to excise the unease setting my teeth on edge.

It wasn't working.

"You're telling me this will give me the ability to see again?"

I swiped my knife out of the air by the handle, slid it back into the sheath hanging next to my coat, and looked at Merq.

He held Chen's invention in his hands, his brow furrowed deeply as he ran his fingers over the edges. I'd watched disbelief, sadness, relief, and anger war over his features for the last few minutes, and I'd stepped back to give him time to process. Time which hadn't seemed to help him at all.

Now he simply looked lost.

S.A. MCAULEY

I pushed off the wall and approached him. "That is what Chen says."

"How can it possibly do that?"

"The note she attached to it states that it utilizes cameras and the bridge implanted in your cortex."

The one implant neither of us had bothered to remove because it was passive unless tethered to a chip. Or, apparently, this device.

"But the bridge is for auditory purposes only."

"I do not know who told you that," I said carefully, "but that isn't accurate. Our bridges are tied into all our senses. The memory projector was connected to your bridge as well."

Merq grimaced and swore under breath.

I reached out for the device—bypassing the reality that five years later Merq was still uncovering just how much he'd been lied to for most of his life—and tugged on it gently. "Do you want to try it?"

Merq relinquished the device to my control and slumped against the table. He crossed his arms, cracked his neck, and exhaled slowly. "I don't know. I've spent the last five years—" He snapped his mouth closed and clenched his jaw.

He'd spent the last five years relearning nearly every aspect of his life. Besides trekking out into the rough terrain of the NT alone or reading printed text on a page, there wasn't anything I could do that he couldn't. Like him shooting a rifle, he'd needed to adapt his approach, but the end result was the same.

I didn't know what to say to him, or what he considered the right choice for himself.

Before I could decide how, or if, to respond he held out his hand. "Give it to me."

"I read Chen's instructions. I know where to place it and how to activate it."

252

Merq pushed off the table, determined, and nodded. "Go ahead."

Now that he was no longer hesitating, I didn't either. I brushed my fingers over his forehead pushing his hair away and noting the rapid flutter of his heartbeat in the hollow of his collarbone. The semi-circle fit over the back of his head, with the band widening at the front, holding the device tight against his temple. I switched it on, pressed the recessed lever to sync it to his bridge, and stepped back.

The fire crackled and water droplets dripped into the herb pots we'd moved into the main living area, but Merq was silent. Uncharacteristically still.

I inhaled sharply through my nose and reminded myself to breathe. "Is it working?"

"Yes."

His entire body had gone tense, hands extended from his side as if he were trying to find his balance. And the expression on his face…. I hadn't seen the detached mask that fell over Merq's features in years. Not since I'd watched him go into battle without me at his side—seeking vengeance against a madman because I'd asked him to, not because it had been what he wanted.

He winced. "It's…disorienting."

I reached up and switched off the device. Immediately Merq's shoulders relaxed.

He breathed in raggedly and slumped into me, resting his forehead on my shoulder. "You kept the bullet casing."

If he hadn't been pressed into me, I never would've heard his voice at all.

"I did." It hung from a rope near the front door. The casing of the bullet he'd used to assassinate the premiere. The bullet that, in many ways, had started this all. "It reminds me of the price we paid to get here."

Merq lifted his head and slipped the device off, tossing it onto the table with unerring accuracy. His shoulders rose with a deep inhale as he faced me again. "You aren't quite as gray as I'd imagined, probably because of the serum. But these...." Merq stepped up to me and traced the lines at the edges of my eyes, then my mouth. "These are deeper than I realized."

I smiled and those lines deepened even more.

"And your eyes...." Merq chuffed. "They are just as soul-stripping as I remember."

My breath caught.

Even now, after all we'd been through, it wasn't often that Merq gave voice to his thoughts of me.

That moment in the stadium when he'd told me he loved me was the only time I'd heard those words come from his lips. He didn't have to repeat them though. I heard it daily in his exasperation, I read it in the volumes of history he wrote, I felt it in the touch of his lips to mine.

"We can keep Chen's device," he continued, "just like the transport chip—as a fail-safe. But I don't need it."

"You are sure?"

Merq shrugged. "I don't need to see your eyes to feel them on me, Armise. I never have."

He kissed me with a soft brush of lips and pushed away, stalking across the room with easy confidence—as if he hadn't just plunged my heart into the fires of his own passion then lifted it out with care, only for it to emerge stronger.

I chuckled in wonderment. In awe. And in complete exasperation when he called out from the galley that it was beyond time for us to get to work.

This physical place was our home.

Our safety and peace hard-earned.

And Merq and me....

The love we had for each other was our sanctuary.

THOUGHTS ON SANCTUARY

When I finished writing Strength of the Rising Sun almost three years ago, I swore that Merq and Armise's story had come to an end.

Both Merq *and* Armise had a different idea.

Months later, I still couldn't get their voices out of my head. I've always felt more like a conduit than a puppet master when it comes to Merq and Armise, and Sanctuary was no exception. They had a story to tell, so I started to write it down....

Then I took a two year break from publishing.

However, as it is with Merq and Armise, once I started editing the series for the rereleases, they came at me full force.

Now that this story is done, they've gone silent. I've been cut off from them just as much as Simion and Neveed have. But that silence brings me a measure of peace I've never experienced as a writer. They don't regret their decision to remove themselves from their previous world, so I can't either.

If they ever have more to say, then I'll listen. But if I never hear from them again, I'll be content that they've found their peace. I hope you will too.

THE BORDERS WAR IMAGES
AND CHARACTER PROFILES

THE SYMBOL OF THE REVOLUTION

MERQ'S TATTOO

IS MERQ GRAYSON A LIAR?

(Below is a blog post I originally wrote in March 2014 for The Novel Approach Reviews before the release of Powerless. You can find the post here.)

YOU WOULD THINK we know just about everything there is to know about Merq Grayson since he's the one telling us his story. But, I'm going to let you into one of the harsh truths of The Borders War series. As it turns out, Merq...lies.

He is the most unreliable narrator I've worked with so far.

That's not to say Merq is the type of narrator who is actively trying to deceive his audience. Not consciously at least. His fallibility comes from the skewed perspective of a violent and solitary upbringing. His hesitancy towards anything personal is the product of unrealistic expectations that have been laid on him since before birth, yet he's determined to meet.

The secrets surrounding Merq are fascinating, and a puzzle to be unraveled as the series unfolds. But the core of who Merq is as a person is just as intriguing. Maybe more, for me.

I've read a couple thought-provoking discussions on Merq's

"voice" and whether or not it matches the man that physically dominates the pages of these stories. That Merq's narrative voice doesn't match who he appears to be at first glance—or who he should be based on his history and his job—is one of the most interesting aspects of his characterization.

His inner dialogue, his curiosity of world history, and his philosophical bent—the words that show a depth of reflection that his actions don't—those are hints to who Merq really is, and more importantly, who he wants to be. Because what kind of fun would it be if Merq was solely an unthinking soldier? What would be the point of us listening to anything he has to say?

And the one question that raises so many other considerations: would Armise Darcan be willing to forfeit so much for a man who was ordinary outside of his prowess on the battlefield?

You get hints of the real Merq in *One Breath, One Bullet*. We discover more of who he is at his core in *Dominant Predator*. As he awakens to the world inside him (and not just around him) in *Powerless*, you'll begin to see who Merq is, not just who he appears to be.

As with any author/character relationship, there is some of me that bleeds through to Merq. That's inevitable. But more often than not, what Merq says and does surprises me. He has a distinct voice in my head. He doesn't tolerate shit. He has a low patience threshold even though that trait should have been drummed out of him. He misses a lot of what happens around him because he's blind to the emotional nuances flowing around him.

Merq is still like a child emotionally. And for good reason. He never had parents that showered him with affection, or any affection at all. He was ripped away from his only stable home when he was five and began training to be a soldier. He was raised to view his interactions with other people with suspicion —to seek out hidden motivations and to be so detached that he has the ability to kill anyone at anytime. Even his own life is not given as much value (by himself or his superiors) as the mission.

His "romantic" relationships during his teenage years were based mostly on a mutual need for physical release. And now the one man he can't get out of his head is Armise Darcan—the only person on the planet who is Merq's equal and, by all rights, should be Merq's enemy.

It's no wonder Merq has major trust issues.

Trust. Yeah, right. I can hear Merq scoffing in my head. It's a word Merq throws around a lot yet has no concept of what it really means. Or rather, he hasn't so far.

The Merq Grayson that emerges from the pages of *Powerless* is...grown. By the time *Powerless* ends, it has been almost two years since Merq restarted the Borders War with his Winchester and that bullet. It's been more than fifteen years since Armise kissed Merq for the first time.

Merq has witnessed much more death than he has life. He has experienced much more frustration than hope. And yet, he wants to live and he wants to hope.

He is a liar, but that doesn't mean he's dishonest. We just may have to endure more deception before Merq is ready to admit what his ultimate truth really is.

WRITING A CHARACTER WHO DOESN'T
WANT TO SPEAK

(Below is a blog post I originally wrote in January 2016 for The Novel Approach Reviews before the release of Powerless. You can find the post here.)

Almost four years ago, I wrote a two-thousand word draft that exploded completely out of control and is now five books and over two-hundred-fifty-thousand words about the enemies become lovers Merq Grayson and Armise Darcan.

As the single point-of-view, Merq's side of the story is on every page of The Borders War series. We get to see his world through his eyes. We get to learn about who he is as a person. We get to know Armise through Merq, but that's only part of the story.

So let me share an insider's view of Armise.

He is a quiet man. Contemplative and thoughtful in his intentions. He doesn't think, he *knows*. He is violent and vengeful—especially when it comes to protecting his own—and he is human, with all of the failings and flaws that go along with that. While you can read all about Merq's penchant for deluding himself **here**, Armise doesn't share that quality with Merq. Armise is guarded and always on the defensive, but he is fully aware of who he is. Who he wants.

He just doesn't want *you* to know.

Finding a way to break through that barrier has been a fight for both Merq and me. I've never written a character that was so unwilling to give up his secrets. At the same time, hearing Armise's voice in my head was infinitely easier than working with Merq—because of Armise's surety in his path.

Armise is not a complicated man, but he is complex. He is one of the most mysterious characters in The Borders War series...despite being one of the main characters.

Until now, Merq and Armise's story has been told solely through Merq's point-of-view. But all of that changes with the re-issues of the first three books. With Armise's point-of-view scenes added to the end of the new editions of *One Breath, One Bullet, Dominant Predator* and *Powerless*, you'll get an inside look into what Armise is thinking.

In *Falling, One by One* much of who Armise is at his core—his history and his motivations—will finally be exposed. *Strength of the Rising Sun* ends their journey when the secret Armise has been protecting Merq from is revealed.

That revelation may just be the breaking point for Merq and Armise—unless they can stand together.

MERQ'S FIRST KILL

ABOUT NOT LOOKING BACK

At the age of twenty, Merq immortalized his first five kills with five hoops in his left ear—a decision unconsciously pinned to the beginning of his pursuit to kill Armise. However, it would take another sixteen years before Merq discovered the identity of his first kill....

From Falling, One by One:

I took a step outside the room and inhaled the damp, warm air into my Chemsense-damaged lungs. Armise stood with his back to me at the edge of stone steps that disappeared into the water. I came up behind him, laying my palm at the base of his neck, curling pointer finger and thumb into the swell of muscle there and grounding myself.

"We find ourselves on the edge of another ocean," I said to him as I moved to his side.

Armise murmured, "It's almost peaceful."

"Minus the torture and mind games."

Armise's tongue appeared at the corner of his lips as he

stared out at the water. Neither of us had had surge or any kind of medical treatment since the incursion on the hybrid camps. Both of our bodies were covered in nicks and scratches from that battle and my voice was still scratchy. Between the two of us there didn't seem to be any injury that was serious in nature, but each wound was yet another physical reminder of damage that could not be undone.

He swiped at the bead of blood that gathered at a cut on the edge of his mouth and cleaned the pad of his finger on his pants, breaking whatever reverie he had been in. "I know Tiam, but not by that name. When he spoke in Mongol today I realized it was him. He was one of the men who trained me after the DCR attacked Murun. He may be the reason you and I are here now. Together."

"What do you mean? That he manipulated us?"

Armise shook his head. "An accident. I don't think even he could have known what he was setting in motion."

I pulled my lip piercing between my teeth and tried to rein in the frustration that overtook me when he offered me yet another vague statement about something in the past I didn't know about—or didn't have all the pieces yet to know there was a connection at all. "There's a whole lot in motion here, Darcan. Narrow down the 'what' you're talking about."

Armise's gaze dragged away from the ocean to my face. "You and me."

"Us...."

"Yes, Merq," Armise replied, a familiar, gruff exhalation of frustration in his tone as he settled his hand on my hip. "Us."

My hand dropped from his neck. "How the fuck did we end up here? I can't decide anymore if it was an accident, fate, or a willing choice. Because in the beginning it was all you, not me. You've always been one step ahead of me—" My words cut off as my thoughts did, like the snapping of a circuit that rendered a sonicpistol useless. There was only Armise in front of me, not a battlefield full of strategic and tactical inputs, and this one man was too much for me to understand. Just as he'd always been.

He squeezed my hip then let go, as if he knew I needed space. "Are you asking me why I pursued you?"

"Maybe," I answered without thinking, then took a step back from him and searched his face. He was half-turned toward me, hands in his pockets. His features were lax and his eyes mimicked the color of the slow-rolling waves in front of us. He was calm—and not a stoic, forced calm. He was genuinely at ease next to me in yet another foreign country.

"Yeah. That's exactly what I'm asking. Why me?"

He hunched his shoulders forward, chin curling into his chest. His eyes were closed for just longer than a blink, then he was straightening, facing me. "You were the one who killed my older brother."

"Shit." I licked my lips, tasting salt, dirt, and blood. Always blood. "That wasn't—" I hung my head and took the seconds I needed to consider the implications of what he was telling me. "Are you sure it was me?"

"Yes."

I ran my hands through my hair and realized my legs were shaking. I sat down on the edge of the top stone step, setting my elbows on my knees and resting my head in my hands. "I've killed a lot of men, Armise. I couldn't tell you which one he was."

There was no sound, no indication of movement, but I knew Armise had sat down next to me. Armise sighed, and the defeated sound was where I expected it to come from.

Armise was always next to me, even when it was I who caused him pain.

"I know which one he was," he finally said.

Did that mean Armise knew which of my kills had been his brother? Or that he would never forget I had been the one to take his brother's life? Both considerations were awful and I couldn't discern what he meant from his emotionless lack of emphasis.

My throat burned as I tried to speak, but no longer from the Chemsense. "Armise—"

He shook his head, quieting me. "In the beginning I pursued you for vengeance. But I'd never met anyone who could be called my equal, let alone could live up to that expectation. What I said to you that night in Singapore at the warehouse—that you fascinated me—was true."

"And now?"

"You still fascinate me. And you're still the man who killed Vachir, yet I have no more need for vengeance."

"You tried to kill me multiple times after that night in the warehouse," I reminded him.

Armise laughed, a low rumble that was becoming more recognizable each time I heard it. "That is because you still frustrate me as well."

then....

From Strength of the Rising Sun:

Armise and I had experienced so much violence. Perpetrated so much violence on each other.... Then we had changed our fate. Sneered at the expectations everyone had of who we were, and become more.

We couldn't end like this.

"Are you ready for the next one? This memory...this one isn't you, but it involves you. Another person I took away from you, and yet another name it's difficult for me to say out loud. I don't know if you'll want to see it."

"Vachir."

That Armise had known Tiam and that PsychHAg was the one to order my first kill.... That he steadfastly ignored the first of the five hoops on my ear marking the first five people I had killed, as if he knew what they represented when he shouldn't have.... "Yeah. He was the first one, wasn't he?"

I heard Armise playing with the safety on his rifle. "Go ahead."

"You don't have to, I take it you know where he was without seeing—"

"Please."

So I showed him, however little there was to show. I hadn't spent much time with Vachir, hadn't known who he was or what his life, and the end of it, would mean to Armise and me years later. But I showed Armise what I'd taken away from him when I'd slashed Vachir's throat—my first kill—in exchange for time on Tiam's biocomp. I'd been a government-protected sixteen-year-old child, already steeped in the language of violence. Unable to comprehend the gravity of how each life I took would change me. Stain me. And inalterably change the lives of the people my victims left behind.

There was so much blood on my hands. That Vachir had been the first and Armise taking my own would be the last.... It was a balancing act I hadn't thought the universe to be capable of.

Armise was quiet for a long time. I closed my eyes, cutting that memory off, and listened to his breathing. There was nothing I could say to make right what he'd just seen.

"That was not as bad as I'd imagined."

"Does that make it worse or better?"

"Neither. Simply more real. I forgave you long ago...."

Now you get to see what Armise did that day.

January 2540
Merq Grayson's 16th year
Capital of the Continental States - PsychHAg headquarters

"Kill him, Merq."

There was a part of me that knew the first question out of my mouth shouldn't have been, "What do I get in return?"

But it was.

Not "why" or even "how." The man's death wasn't a question of worth versus worth—of the value of my life over his—or of safety and survival. There was nothing the bound Singaporean in front of me had done to threaten me. But I hesitated because I had to be clear on what privilege I would earn from Tiam for ending this man's existence as fast as I could.

"What do you want?" Tiam responded.

I already knew better than to directly answer that. "What are you offering?"

Tiam laughed, a dark and vicious sound. "You're getting better at deflection."

"Wonder why," I muttered under my breath. I circled the Singaporean, studying him but not really taking in any details. He was silent, head bowed, every detail of his features was there for me to catalog and memorize. If I wanted, his face would never leave my consciousness. But I didn't want that. I needed him to just be... another.

Even if he would be my first kill.

"You know what I want, PsychHAg Tiam."

"You have until sunrise," Tiam prompted me.

"I don't need that long."

I swept my blade out of the sheath on my wrist and sliced it across his neck. I felt the resistance of skin and bone against the titanalloy blade and increased the pressure until it dug into his throat, opening a gaping wound that had the man's head tilting at a skewed bend and sending a spurt of blood toward Tiam. Tiam casually stepped away from the pool gathering at his feet then opened the door.

"Follow me."

The Singaporean's body cracked onto the floor as the door slammed shut behind me.

* * *

I sat in a dark hidden room, flicking through a secret database on a biocomp that was so old it had a mass of wires snaking out from the physical screen.

I wasn't supposed to know this room—let alone this database—existed at all.

I'd wanted Tiam to answer my questions directly—not to push me off here—but after two months in his custody, even the PsychHAg had been worn down by my endless stream of inquiries.

Neither he nor I had been concerned with the life of the Singaporean man on the other end of my knife. Maybe I should've cared, but I craved the promise of information more.

I leapt from topic to topic on the database, following a capricious stream of subject jumps. I scanned through each page until I'd devoured the most interesting of the details, taking as much in as I could, knowing that this chance wouldn't return. Even though I was only sixteen and I'd have access to a biocomp permanently when my comm chip was implanted, this particular database would never be at my command again.

I couldn't piece together how they'd gathered this store of information in the first place. I had no way to verify its accuracy.

Who knew about this place? Who had inputted this data or cate-gorized it?

But more importantly, why were we still seeking out the infochip when something like this existed?

None of it made any sense, but I set aside all those consider-ations for the sake of consuming as much of the information as I could in the limited time I had before Tiam came to drag me out of here. He'd told me to lock up when I was done, but I wasn't going to leave this room willingly. I was sure Tiam already knew that. So I waited for him.

A slant of light came from the hallway hours later. Much longer than I'd anticipated he would give me.

By then my eyes were dry and scratchy from the harsh glint of the screen and the inability to ramp down the contrast to something visually manageable in the dark. My back was sore from bending over the table. My wrists were frozen in a curve from where I rested my fingers on the keyboard—unwilling to set my hands anywhere else for fear the information would just...disappear.

I tracked Tiam's movement by the sound of his uneven foot-steps, aggravated by knobbed knees and severely bowed legs.

"What did you land on?" he asked.

"I've spent the last hour reading about ancient mythology. Gods, warriors and battles between heaven, hell, and earth."

Tiam peered over my shoulder, setting a hand on my back to steady himself as he surveyed the screen. "Icarus," he mused. He pushed back from me. His physical form disappeared outside the halo of light from the biocomp and my hackles went up because I could feel him rather than see him. "It's a lesson on pride. Humility and knowing when to take risks. With whom to take those risks."

"I got that," I huffed in frustration.

My education wasn't standard, but it was more than most

kids had received over the last hundred and some years. At least I'd had the opportunity for formalized education of some kind, even if it was slanted to the Revolution and more about combat strategizing and tactics than well...what *I* considered interesting.

There was little that disturbed me more than the view that I was merely a soldier. I was learning to control my anger, to use it as a shield—because other people's perceptions of me mattered very little in the end, as long as they were afraid of me.

"Don't be prissy," he chastised me. I had no idea what the word meant but I could assume from his condescending tone that it wasn't a compliment. "You're different than any of the other trainees I've worked with. You're special, Merq, but that doesn't mean you're better."

And that was why I continued to engage with Tiam. Why I continued to listen to him. He was the only one who didn't try to tell me that I was destined to be the best.

Priyessa frightened me. I was learning how to control my fear response through her training.

But Tiam mentally challenged me.

It was too bad I wasn't attracted to him at all. I didn't know if there would ever be a place where I could live with a partner like the president did with Sarai. Like my father did with my mother. For now, intermittent physical release was enough. Who knew if I would live long enough to consider the steadiness of home or family.

But if I ever did, it would be with someone like Tiam.

Someone who made me think. Who encouraged me to be more than an ordinary soldier.

More than an ordinary man.

But that possibility was far off, if possible at all. I was only months into training with the PsychHAgs and already I felt a shift coming. The first few weeks had been confusing, disorienting. The last few had begun to be physically painful and mentally draining. I'd talked to enough Peacemakers to know the PsychHAgs wouldn't go easy on us. I'd seen enough body bags being dragged from the headquarters to know what was coming would be violent and brutal.

"Next time, earning a privilege such as this won't be as easy." Tiam reached an awkwardly bent arm over my shoulder and clicked off the screen, plunging the room into complete darkness.

I tamped down the urge to scream. To run.

I waited for what test Tiam would subject me to next. But it didn't matter how vicious it was. I would become stronger than him.

In the corner of the room, as my eyes adjusted to what appeared to be an impenetrable depth of black, I saw the hints of blue-gray against a metal, rectangular frame.

I had ended another man's life, but for me a new day was beginning.

The sun was beginning to rise.

THE STORY THAT STARTED IT ALL

ABOUT PRONE

As a writer, I'm used to messy first drafts with disconnected thoughts, inconsistencies, and truly awful grammar. I don't let many people see those first drafts, because my fragile writer soul curls into the fetal position, overcome by dread, at merely the thought of exposing my weaknesses.

And yet, here we are.

Prone is the very first draft of the story that became One Breath, One Bullet. The following two thousand words is completely unedited—in the same messy, incomplete form it was when I sent it out to betas almost six years ago.

It's in first person present tense—instead of the first person past tense I ended up with for the life of the series—and some minor details have changed, but Merq was pretty insistent about the direction of his story from the very beginning.

So was Armise.

Armise's eventual role in Merq's life was hinted at from the very first time Merq said his name. Merq, Jegs, and Simion were all names that just appeared out of thin air, but Armise.... His name comes from the word "armistice"—an agreement between warring parties to end fighting. A cessation of hostilities. A truce.

Yes, Merq's life was always destined to end in front of Armise's rifle. But not as a sacrifice—as one final promise.

Of crossing their respective battle lines and signing both their names to an unending armistice.

PRONE

One breath. Inhale. Hesitation is my enemy. Solitude my ally. Death the only real victory. Exhale.

The bed shifts next to me and I can't help but think that if the mantra is true then I've already lost.

"Shut down that maniacal brain, turn off the light, and go to sleep," Armise grumbles, his massive frame turning away from me, away from the overly bright light all the athlete rooms are issued with. "It's going to be too easy to beat you tomorrow."

Exactly my point, I want to say but he will understand too well what that means. Instead I flip the light off, put my back to Armise's, and repeat the mantra, begging for sleep. But I can't relax.

"You have to go," I say to him too loudly for how dark it is in my room.

"Shutup and go to sleep already. It's safe. I had Manny swipe my card at check in."

I flip the light back on, my vision washing out for the briefest of seconds but it's enough for my panic to take hold. "Either of our coaches could come looking for us at any time."

Armise reaches his arm back and grips my hip. "Or war could flare again." His voice then takes on my eastern seaboard cadence; a tone he saves for the moments designed to mock me. "It is the eve of history."

I jab him in the ribs but he doesn't move. I'm almost as solid as Armise but where I have grace, he has power. We would be safer if we could master both. "Don't poke at me," I protest. "You may not think so, but this is a big deal. Neither of our countries is going to be taking tomorrow lightly."

"It's only a bullet."

"A real one. Shot in public. For the first time--"

"In two hundred years. I got it. Now go to sleep."

"If we're discovered, even with the treaty, we will be considered traitors."

"Then shut the fuck up so they can't hear us."

"You can't stay."

"Fuck you. I'm comfy. The States get much better accommodations. I'm not going back to that rat hole."

"Leave."

"No."

Armise nearly crushes me as he swats off the blinding white light. He pulls me into his arms, forces my head into his shoulder, and kisses my forehead. The kiss is more frustrated than loving, but anything more with Armise would be unnatural. And then his body eases next to me, rapidly dropping into a deep sleep, and he pulls me in tighter to his side. My chest aches because the panic slips away too easily under his touch. I cannot afford to get this close. And yet I do not move.

"Sleep, Merq," he mumbles just before his head lolls to the side, nose buried in my sex-mussed brown hair, lips brushing the piercings lining the shell of my ear.

And I'm flooded with a feeling that couldn't be serenity, because Peacemakers are never meant to know peace.

* * *

I DREAM OF WAR. A war I fought in but never loaded or fired a real bullet. A war where hundreds of millions died but none felt the slice of metal into skin, the shattering of bone from the contact of copper and steel. I dream of sound waves that crash and kill. The unadulterated power of a musical tone altered, harnessed, and let loose to decimate. My dreams are violent and bloodless and I know from history that it wasn't always this way. But carnage is carnage, death still final, regardless of the amount, or lack, of blood spilled.

When I wake up he's gone. Which is good. It's much easier to remember he's my enemy when his hands aren't wrapped around my cock.

The knock on my door is simultaneous with Coach barreling into my room and I start even though I know Armise is long gone. "Ass out of bed, Grayson."

Coach refuses to call me by my first name as I refuse to call him anything but Coach. It's an odd stale-mate. Completely unnecessary as power plays go, but he and I have a personal history that dates back way before my time as a Peacekeeper. Perhaps it's our way of distancing each other or, more likely, an unsaid fuck-you every time we have to acknowledge the other exists. It doesn't matter either way. For all intents and purposes he owns my ass until the games are over.

He's rummaging through my drawers, flinging clothes haphazardly around the room, studying and discarding item after item, leaving only a select few on the top of the dresser. I'm not nearly awake enough to figure out what kind of training exercise this is. I scowl and slump back onto the bed, pulling a pillow over my face.

"Nu-uh. No going back to sleep. We have press waiting for you."

"Press? What the fuck do they want with me? Send them to Jegs or Simion."

"Neither Jegs nor Simion is a Peacemaker turned Olympian. Plus, they're profiling the front-runners for who's going to shoot the first bullet."

"When did I become a front-runner?"

"When the committee found out there was more to your name."

I don't have to ask what he means, I already know. But I'm surprised that he seems to know as well. "This isn't new to you."

"I figured it would probably come up."

I want to ask him how long he's known about my great-grandfather. Of the heritage my parents died to hide. The same heritage that is now buying me attention and favors.

Time distorts the reality of history. It's sadly poetic and yet I will take full advantage of it.

He throws a pile of clothes at me. It's not the traditional uniform for The States or what I will be wearing in competition today, but he's chosen colors that will reflect pride in my country, a style that will accentuate my size, and a quality that hints I am not rich. It's exactly the kind of quick calculation that the Coach is revered for.

As soon as we walk out the door, Coach flanking my right shoulder, the press descend.

"Did you know you're officially a front-runner for the inaugural shot today?"

"Coach just told me. I'm honored to be considered."

"You're a Peacemaker for The States. Do you think you are too controversial of a figure?"

"I'm proud to have served my country when they needed me. If the Committee has placed me as a front-runner then they obviously view my service with the same pride."

"Where does your name come from, Merq? It's so unusual."

"The real meaning was lost somewhere in the decades when paper records were purged."

"So you don't know if it comes from your family?"

"I don't," I lie.

"Your parents died when you were very young. We understand they were casualties in the attack on DC that led to the power shift."

"That's right. I was lucky. They are the reason I'm still alive today." That isn't true either. But I know the orphan story is going to give me more sympathy and therefore a greater chance of being the first to fire that bullet.

Coach pats me on the back in a pretend show of sympathy. I try not to flinch away.

"What would it mean to you to be chosen to take the shot?"

My eyes begin to mist over. I don't have to fake this emotion, but I do.

"This is the first gathering of the world since the treaties. To be on the ceremony stage representing all of humanity and the change we want to see in this world... It's overwhelming. Honored doesn't begin to scratch the surface of what it means to me."

We pass through the soundproofed metal doors into the building that houses the range I will be competing in later today. The press follows, continuing to ask questions, but I've already answered the ones that were the most important. So I respond, but only with part of my mind engaged in the back and forth. The other part is searching the range for Armise.

* * *

I SEE Armise as soon as I locate the rifle course. He's impossible to miss. He is wearing the black and tarnished silver of Singapore, his uniform tight across shoulders that should hinder his ability to shoot the competition Terfiner XMP. But his country has used all the allowable modifications and Armise's aim is one of the most reliable on the range.

He towers above the other shooters, in height and width. I feel that familiar churn of desire coil in my groin. It's a dangerous drive and one that is stamped out when I watch him turn to study me and all I see is contempt. In competition and in battle we are enemies. There is no middle ground.

I worry if my emotions have played too obviously as the press corp around me goes unnaturally quiet, but it is because the President has appeared in the stands.

Armise's words from weeks earlier echo back to me, They are too wrapped up in pomp and circumstance to notice us. We are a decoration, Merq. Nothing more.

Everyone in the artfully designed range waits, the silence spreading and dragging on for an uncomfortable amount of time. The President is not oblivious to it all, he can't be, but he doesn't react to the absolute stillness filling a building crammed with athletes, coaches, and press. He talks with a man at his side. His laughter ripping through the chemically cleaned air. The sharpness of the sound makes people jump, sets all our nerves on greater edge. None of us knows what to expect when he makes an appearance and this time, only hours away from the start of the first games in almost three centuries, we are even more unsure.

The President lifts his head, searches the packed room and smiles when he sees what or who he is looking for. "Armise Darcan!" He calls out over the silence and everyone stays frozen. Despite the smile leeching any last pretenses of his own humanity away, the President's tone is neutral. My stomach drops more from anticipation than dread. I can't deny that if

Armise disappears today my chances at a gold model are greatly increased.

I look at the Coach and he's grinning, obviously thinking the same thing.

Armise shoulders his rifle instead of leaving it with his Coach. It's a small act of defiance, but enough to make his point. This President is not his. He saunters toward the stands, his gait slow and unaffected. His eyes gives nothing away. But I can see the slight tick in his jaw, nearly hidden by his graying beard and I know he's nervous. It was that same tell that told me it was time to attack when we met last in battle and he ended up with one less finger.

The crowd doesn't clear for him. He has to maneuver around the slaw jaws and downcast eyes of those occupying the space between him and the President. The guard unlatches a door on the field lever allowing Armise to climb into the stands. He takes the time to nod to both of the guards as he passes by without handing over his weapon. It's exactly what I would have done were I in his place. And for the briefest of moments I feel a connection to Armise that is more than that gut-clenching need for release. I see the soldier in him and respect that. Even if he is indirectly threatening my President.

The President doesn't stand when Armise approaches. He beckons Armise with a waved hand, and Armise bends at the waist, putting his ear almost to the President's lips. From my vantage point I can no longer see the President's face, just the profile of Armise as he listens. The President gesticulates, but Armise stands stock still. After a long moment, every eye still transfixed to the conversation all of us are participating in through setting if not tone, Armise starts to laugh. A low, guttural chuckle. Genuine. I know because I've heard it only once before. And my gut clenches.

* * *

ARMISE and I met through the eye of a rifle scope. Sometimes I wonder if that's also where we'll end.

And other moments, like this one, I am sure of it.

INDEX

Timeline of the Borders War

- 2058 - Winchester rifle built that will be fired in the opening ceremony
- 2256 - Last Olympic Games held
- 2256 - Singapore takes over China after nuclear meltdown and the economy collapses
- 2258 - Borders War officially starts with Singapore's attempt to take over Australia and Russia
- 2268 - Merq Grayson (Merq's great-grandfather, six generations back) is born
- 2308 - Sonicbullet technology is invented by Merq Grayson and his name is officially classified
- 2348 - Last real bullet fired during the war
- 2352 - Paper records are purged and transferred to electronic format
- 2372 – Nationalist underground movement formed
- 2417 - Targeted electromagnetic pulses, unleashed by the Nationalists, destroy all records
- 2491 –Wensen Kersch born

- 2493 - Merq's dad, Lucien Grayson, born
- 2498 - The existence of one remaining infochip begins as a rumor
- 2502 – Opposition rises
- 2503 - Merq's mom, Tallitia Grayson, born
- 2511 – Ahriman Blanc born
- 2512 – Revolution formed
- 2518 – Neveed Niaz born
- 2519 - Armise Darcan born
- 2522 – Holly Jegs born
- 2523 - Merq Grayson born
- 2524 – Ricor Simion born
- 2528 - Merq's parents "die" in the attack on the capital that places President Kersch in power, Merq becomes a ward of the Continental States
- 2538 – Merq joins the Youth Peacemaker training program
- 2539 - Merq and Neveed start sleeping together
- 2540 - Neveed becomes Merq's handler
- 2541 - Merq meets Armise in Bogotá through the eye of the rifle scope
- 2542 - Merq learns from analysts who Armise is
- 2545 - Jegs is captured in Singapore, and during her rescue Armise kisses Merq for the first time
- 2546 – Armise slices Merq neck in the Outposts
- 2546 – Merq learns about his namesake's house in the Northern Territories
- 2546 - Armise begins working for the States, and the DCR standoff occurs where Merq acquires the infochip and takes Armise's finger in the process
- 2546 – Truce called in the Borders War, active combat doesn't stop for another two years
- 2548 - The Consign Treaty officially ending the

Borders War is signed in the United Union, Merq is recruited by Ahriman to be a part of the Opposition, Merq and Armise meet up in Bogotá

- 2549-2553 – Merq lives in Singapore with Ahriman Blanc as part of his protection detail
- 2553 - Planning and construction begins for holding the first Olympics in the capital city of the States
- 2558 - Merq reignites the Borders War when he assassinates the Premiere of Singapore, who is also the leader of the Opposition
- 2558 – Merq and Armise go on the hunt for members of the Olympic Committee
- 2559 – Nationalists attack the president's bunker in the capital
- 2560 – President Kersch assassinated by Armise
- 2560 – Merq and Armise held by Ahriman
- 2560 – Armise kills Merq to rid him of the reclamation virus, Armise uses the transformation serum on Merq, Merq and Armise disappear to the Northern Territories

Characters

- Merq Grayson – Peacemaker, colonel, for the Continental States
- Armise Darcan - Dark Ops officer for the People's Republic of Singapore
- Wensen Kersch (deceased) – Former President of the States and leader of the Revolution
- Neveed Niaz – Merq's former handler, former General for the States, Chen's caretaker
- Ahriman Blanc (deceased) – Former General for the States, former leader of the Opposition

- Elina – hybrid, affiliated with the Nationalists and the Council of Five, Athol's twin sister
- Dakra (deceased) – original second generation hybrid
- Nayan – Armise's aunt
- Sharlat – Armise's cousin and Nayan's daughter

Glossary

- Analyst - soldiers tasked with the study and interpretation of intelligence
- Anubis – scientific project that evolved into weaponized genetic modifications in human beings
- BC5 or biocomp – computer that is either hard-wired or carried with a user who has a comm chip (see also "comm chip")
- Blood tie lock – a lock that is preprogrammed to open only for someone with a certain DNA profile
- Borders War - a worldwide war that began in 2246 and continued until 2548 when the treaty was signed, over four hundred million people died in the three hundred years it was waged
- Chemsense - chemical weapon designed by Singapore, widely used in the Borders War despite being condemned and outlawed
- Comm chip - a communication and information transfer device that is either handheld or implanted in the body, often combined with a transport and tracker chip and implanted in a soldier's wrist (see also "transport chip" and "tracker")
- Council of Five – group consisting of the leadership of the five countries
- D3 – Peacemaker shorthand for "detail, ditch and decimate"

- Dark Ops - special forces for Singapore
- Dronebots - unmanned aircraft used for surveillance and attack
- Encryption chip – a microchip that unlocks the information contained on the infochip (see also "infochip")
- Genetmod – shorthand for genetic modifications of human beings and animals
- Infochip - a microchip rumored to be the only remaining depository of humanity's documented history (see also "encryption chip")
- Nationalists - people who want the five remaining countries to keep their superpower status to maintain order
- Opposition - a movement started by wealthy individuals who wanted to keep the balance of power in their favor, regardless of the formalized power structure of countries
- Peacemakers - soldiers for the States
- PsychHAgs - shorthand for Psychological Health Agents, a sector of the military with the responsibility of preparing soldiers for surviving the brutality of war with all of their secrets intact
- Reclamation virus – virus created by Sarai Kersch as a kill switch for the first generation test subjects of the Anubis project
- Revolution - a movement started with the ideal of bringing power back to the citizens and seeking to break up the five countries into districts that are representative of their citizenry
- Sleepsense – an intravenous drug used to incapacitate a person, also has hallucinogenic effects

- Sonicbullet - sound waves harnessed as ammunition that is able to explode internal organs on impact
- Sonicrifle, sonicpistol - weapons created to deliver sonicbullets
- Surge - medication that places targeted nanoparticles into the bloodstream to speed healing, also highly addictive
- Synth - synthetic limb
- Tracker - a chip that tracks the location of the person carrying it, either on or in their person (see also "comm chip" and "transport chip")
- Transport chip - a device that allows a person to use one of the sanctioned molecular transfer hubs scattered across the globe, transport is a painful process as the technology is still in its infancy, transport of any person can be harmful or potentially fatal so its use is limited (see also "comm chip" and "tracker")

Countries of the world in 2560

Continental States (the States)
Leader: President Ricor Simion
Color associated with the country: vermillion and yellow

People's Republic of Singapore (Singapore)
Leader: Premiere Shio Pearce
Color associated with the country: cobalt blue and silver

United Union (UU)
Leader: Prime Minister Franx Heseltine
Color associated with the country: royal purple and black

Index

American Federation (AmFed)
Leader: President Isida Agri
Color associated with the country: emerald green and peacock blue

Dark Continental Republic (DCR)
Leader: President Kariabba Tivy
Color associated with the country: gold amber, white, and earth brown

ABOUT SAM

Sam is a wandering LGBTQ author who sleeps little and reads a lot. Happiest in a foreign country. Twitchy when not mentally in motion. Her name is Sam, not Sammy, definitely not Samantha. She's a dark/cynical/jaded person, but hides that darkness well behind her obsession(s) with shiny objects.

Sign up for Sam's (infrequent) email newsletter and receive a free short story!

samcauley.com
authorsamcauley@gmail.com

ALSO BY S.A. MCAULEY

The Borders War

One Breath, One Bullet

Dominant Predator

Powerless

Falling, One by One

Strength of the Rising Sun

Sanctuary

Standalone Novels

An Immoveable Solitude

Where Wishes Go

Tread Marks & Trademarks

Damaged Package

Ruin Porn (co-written with SJD Peterson)

Novellas and Short Stories

Someday It Will Be

The Hotel Luz

Anomaly

Free Reads

Where the Land Goes on Forever

This is What a Cold Lake Looks Like

Flash Knockdown

Heavy Dipping into the Holiday Spirits

You can find links to all of Sam's books at samcauley.com